THE GOLDEN GUARDSMEN

By
S. J. BYRNE

ARMCHAIR FICTION
PO Box 4369, Medford, Oregon 97504

*For more information about Armchair Books and products, visit our
website at...*

www.armchairfiction.com

Or email us at...

armchairfiction@yahoo.com

THE FATE OF EARTH HUNG IN THE BALANCE

In the exciting sequel to "Prometheus II," Stephen Germain once again battles Emperor Nicholas; but this time there is more at stake than just Earth.

With the renewed enthusiasm of a wounded, but not yet beaten man, Nicholas staggers out of the Martian desert looking for his ultimate ally, an alien force unlike any that man had experienced before. Soon mankind would quake in fear, for Nicholas had unleashed the horror of Izdran of The Thousand Lives—and he was not human…

Join Stephen Germain and his devoted commrades as they contend with the evil nature of man—and alien—to secure the sovereignty of both Earth and Mars, while the people of two worlds stand aghast and marvel at the abilites of a super human pitted against something not human at all.

CAST OF CHARACTERS

STEPHEN GERMAIN
With his mutant brain and the God-like skills aquired from outside sources, would he be the man to save the world…again?

NICHOLAS THE FIRST
His quest for power was neverending, as was his ability to overcome outlandish perils and land on his feet.

TRINHA LLIH
A beautiful girl bound for slavery, her dreamy ideals left her with her life in danger and her back against the wall.

LILLIAN GERMAIN
Loyal and dutiful wife to "Mutant Head" she had a secret of her own—what menace lurked within her gentle soul…?

IZDRAN
The most feared and reviled alien nightmare ever to be unleashed upon the Human Race.

PAVLOVICH
This natural born bully got a second chance at getting his man, but would he fair any better than the last time?

GERHARDT EIDELMANN
Since Nicholas lost his last loathsome Doctor this lucky man was the next to be picked—from a Nazi prison camp no less!

CHAPTER ONE

TRINHA LLIH rubbed the crystal griddle with rouge cloth so fine that it polished it like a mirror. She used washing sand on her personal eating thorns and those of her father, Grlahn. Curiously, she tried his on over her slim, dark fingers to see how much bigger a man's hands were than a young woman's. The hollow thorn talons slipped on all the way to the place between her fingers where her hand began.

"I could never eat with those!" she said, half aloud. But of course she remembered that her father's fingers were chubby, like the rest of his grotesque little scuttling body.

It seemed to her that instead of using them for eating he should wear a *pair* of thorn talons when he took in bartered goods and sometimes silver in front of their trading booth, in exchange for *bhurra* liquor and *charnhr* cheese and her own seed cakes, moss jelly and spider eggs, or for water, the most precious commodity in the world outside of *ca'ta*, which was dream manna from the sky, brought to them only by Izdran.

"I think father only lives for trading and haggling and chewing *ca'ta*," she mused. The thought made her look at her reflection in the crystal she had polished. Femininely, she tucked away at her long, black hair and surveyed her large, black eyes and pale red skin and high cheekbones. "When he comes to sell me he'll kill himself haggling. He'll try to get enough to retire by a crystal ridge and set up water farming."

With a little sigh of resignation, she threw some supper scraps into the hawk-beetle's cage, and the giant, golden-winged insect tore at the morsels as though it were on an assigned mission, killing some meat bearing creature of the great desert for its master, Grlahn. She checked the green, rustling *charnhraa* in their heated cave behind the booth to see how the aphid-like creatures were for milk and if they had enough moss to eat.

"Oh I'll milk them early tomorrow," she said.

"Where are you going?" asked her chubby little father from his clinging net woven of the *krnar* spider's web.

"Just to get some air," she replied as she threw a web-woven shawl about her shoulders and slipped into crystal-soled sandals.

"Do not go far or I will look for you."

"No. Not far. Just a breath of air, father."

OUTSIDE the trading booth the whole camp lay sleeping under the brilliant starlight and the racing, silvery moons. The latter limned the crumbling pyramids of Druhdrui with silver, like an outline of reality given to ghosts after midnight. Most of the Gdjinhji tribesmen feared those ancient piles of mystery and took pains to erect their temporary huts well away from their sloping walls, but Trinha's father always scoffed at such superstition and dug right into the dunes at their bases to find greater protection from the cold, desert winds.

Trinha looked at the pyramids now, noting as she always had that they were in pairs, one large, one small. There were about ten pairs of the structures at Druhdrui, but she had seen as many as a hundred pairs at other trading camps along the equator—like at Zridhn Nor. She wished she were there now, where the five greatest crystal ridges converged, bringing much more water, by osmosis, through their shining cells, from the shallow polar seas. Wherever there was better water farming the camps were more settled. There were more people, and a girl had a chance of being sold to a decent master rather than to the first, grinning ridge comber that wandered down out of the North with enough goods to make a successful bid—and enough *bhurra* on his breath to make romance fly to the sky like a wobbling djurnur pod.

As she climbed the nearest pyramid, she saw several djurnur pods break loose out of the desert and rise heavenward on the wind. Her mother used to tell her they were food for the ancient moon gods, but since her mother's death her father had insisted on the facts. The pods had something to do with replenishing the planet's water supply—something to do with a magical mixing of air in the high places, a drifting of all of them north and south, and of consequent snowstorms in the polar regions. She could not comprehend such miracles, but she remembered seeing the sky actually clouded over at times with the rising pods, and she used to dream that she was tiny enough to ride on one—up, up, into the freedom of the boundless heavens.

An inescapable restlessness assailed Trinha, and she could not fathom it. Had she had her mother to confide in she might have been led to understand that this was the subtle chemistry of maturity. But she did not know this. Nor could she ask her father about it. He was a merchant—and she was of selling age.

So Trinha looked at the stars and wondered if they had something to do with it. The old storytellers claimed the ancients knew about the stars and their effect upon one's destiny.

Particularly Panh, that biggest one up there beyond the silvery moons—that blue-green eye of the night that always seemed to follow her wherever she went. Tonight she had Panh all to herself and she looked at it, wondering if it were made of fire, like the distant sun, or if—and this childish dream she concealed from everyone—if it were perhaps a world like her own, even a larger and better world, with oceans of water and green lands filled with shining cities and happy people.

Entranced by the magic of the moonlight and the sight of the silvery djurnur pods rising on the night wind above the desert, she recalled a beloved fairy tale that her mother had told her when she was a child. An ordinary girl such as herself was born to poor parents, but none realized that she was actually Korla Na, a fairy princess. Just as she had arrived at the age when all girls were sold to the highest bidder and a very ugly old man was about to purchase her, Mrahl Sahn, Prince of the Sky, appeared to her in a dream, telling her to eat of certain herbs, which were ordinarily considered to be poison. Risking death rather than be the slave wife of the Ugly One, she arose from her sleeping net and obtained some of the herbs that same night. When she ate them, she grew smaller and acquired her true identity. As Korla Na, the fairy princess, she was able to ride on a djurnur pod up into the sky, where she entered the Kingdom of the Moon Gods and married Mrahl Sahn. The latter took her to his own special kingdom, which was Panh, the blue-green jewel that was the Guardian Star of the Twin Moons.

Somehow the story had remained ineradicably on the surface of her subconscious mind, emerging into consciousness, as it did now, in times of agitation, as though it were an escape mechanism for her restless spirit. She had believed, as a child, that the story would all come true, that Mrahl Sahn, the Sky Prince, would rescue her from the hopelessness of ordinary life.

As she stood there pondering on this, she was obsessed by a presentiment that something extraordinary was about to happen. And then she remembered. She remembered the purpose of her people in being here at Druhdrui at this time. In a few days the sky city of the Nrlani would materialize, and Izdran would bring them the dream manna, *ca'ta*, in exchange for their usual supply of *grabdal*—the black, sticky stuff they extracted from the bubbling wells of Khandarna in the South. What *grabdal* really was, or why they used it, no one knew.

Nor did anyone dare to ask questions about the god-race. For Izdran of a Thousand Lives was omnipresent, omniscient and omnipotent. If too many questions were asked, the telepathic robots would come from below somewhere, out of the subterranean slave cities, and that would be the last anyone would ever see of the victim. What went on in those underground work camps no one ever lived to tell about...

SUDDENLY, Trinha saw something moving in the desert. Two human figures, approaching Druhdrui. Or *were* they human?

Her pulse began to race.

Could they be human if they were emerging from the desert? No one crossed the desert. Human travelers would follow the crystal ridges where water could be found. But these two had come directly out of the arid desert, braving its unknown terrors and its wild beasts of prey. The desert was the natural habitat of the deadly *krnar* spiders, larger than a man and capable of tearing him apart in a matter of minutes.

Only robots could—

With wildly beating heart, she wondered if her mind had asked too many questions. Had Izdran found her out? Were these his emissaries from the slave cities come to take her prisoner?

But no. These two were not robots. One of them, the larger one, was obviously ill. He constantly stumbled and fell, and the smaller, thinner one had to pick him up and help him along.

In the moonlight she could discern that they were not Gdjinhji. They were slightly taller and their skin was as white and pale as the moonlight. Their faces were thick with hair, and their ragged clothing was obviously strange in cut and texture. Moreover, the thin one carried some sort of weapon in his hand the like of which had never been seen before. It was tubular and metallic, glistening ominously in the moonlight.

Trinha gasped, as for a moment she had forgotten to breathe. The strangers were human, but they were not Gdjinhji. In her world there were only the Gdjinhji, the robots, and the Nrlani. No one had ever seen one of the Nrlani race, but surely the god-people who ruled them would not come stumbling out of the desert like this! They would materialize out of the sky, riding high within the towering walls of their majestic city.

Therefore, by a simple process of elimination, these two were from another world. And that world would be Panh, if any.

Trinha wanted to believe in this miracle. However, there was something strong and purposeful about that slender one that drew her to him. She remembered her fairy tale. Her prince had come, to take her to Panh, to the blue-green world in the sky that was filled with oceans and green-clad countryside and shining cities and happy people.

Rejecting thoughts of possible danger to herself, Trinha ran down the pyramid to greet the strangers…

THEY saw her coming toward them. The big man fell down and lay in the sand, mumbling as though in a fevered delirium. The other one stood there, straight and tall, with chin up and shoulders back and his strange weapon lying idly in the crook of his arm.

As she reached their immediate vicinity she saw that the thin one was somewhat older than she had imagined, but he was none the less attractive, despite the unruly growth of beard that covered the lower portion of his aquiline face. It was the strength of his personality that drew her to him. The males of her own race were dulled and weakened by the universal male habit of chewing *ca'ta*. This was the first time that she had ever looked into such an alert pair of eyes—ice-gray eyes that seemed to cut through her like a knife.

"Is this Druhdrui?" he asked her. She was amazed to hear him struggle with the words, as though speaking in a language that was foreign to him!

"Yes," was all she could answer, for staring at him. She also examined the other one more closely. He was fat but powerfully built, his face huge and round. His eyebrows were bushy, with a large wart between them. She had never seen a wart before and it frightened her. The robots had three eyes, the center one being telepathic-hypnotic. Could these be robots in disguise, after all?

She trembled, wondering at her own rashness.

"What do you want?" she asked the slender one. "You—you came across the desert."

"Is not Druhdrui the place where the Nrlani will soon appear?" he interrogated.

"The Nrlani!" Her hand went to her mouth and she drew back a step. "What would you with the Nrlani?"

"I seek them."

She stared at his firm, thin face, incredulously. He did not look insane.

"No one *seeks* the Nrlani," she gasped.

"But *I* do," insisted the stranger, with overwhelming self-assurance. "And you have not answered my question."

"They—they will come," she answered.

"When?" The question was hissed between his white teeth, his eyes flashing a command for her to answer, his face lined with the signs of struggle between burning hope and anxiety.

"In a day or so. But who—"

The slender one swayed and reached out his hand for support. He would have fallen had she not helped him to stand. A tingling thrill ran through her as she felt his hand on her arm. It was firm, and very warm.

"I have sought them for over a year," he said. "At last—the goal is at hand! Take us into your camp. We are weak with hunger and thirst."

"Tell me," she said, trying to meet his eyes with hers. "Are you Mrahl Sahn, Prince of the Sky? Have you come to take me back with you—to Panh?"

The stranger stiffened, regained his balance, and stared at her.

"What made you say that?"

"If you are not from Panh, then you are from the slave cities," she persisted.

"We have visited several of the slave cities," he replied. "But the robots let us go."

"Then—" Her eyes widened. "You *are* from Panh! None of our people have ever returned from the slave cities!"

The stranger hesitated, still watching her curiously. The big man on the ground emitted a groan. "*Sukin syn!*" he exclaimed, in a strange tongue. And he went on as though cursing and pleading for help at the same time.

"Run for help," said the thin one. "I can drag my companion no farther…"

THAT night, Druhdrui relighted its campfires and the whole market came to life, all because of the crazy strangers out of the desert. Much to Trinha's surprise, she had little difficulty in influencing her father to take them in. Soon, however, she saw that it was not the milk of human kindness that had asserted itself. What Grlahn immediately perceived was that his two guests stimulated business beyond his wildest hopes.

It did not matter who the pale-faced imbeciles were, he told Trinha. If he and she fed them and tended the sick one and kept them both warm, they would stay in his booth. And as long as they stayed, his fellow tribesmen would congregate under his improvised roof and he would the more quickly barter his wares and fill his leather cases with more barterable goods for the coming season at Zridhn Nor.

Everyone wanted to see the madmen and hear their strange speech and learn of their insane desire to contact the Nrlani, to hear the thin one's tales concerning the slave cities and to watch the fat one rave and cry in his sickness and cling to his companion as though he were his mother. The two were a very lucrative attraction.

It was Singh, especially, who laughed at them and said they were idiots and colorless freaks who would make a good sideshow. Singh was Grlahn's chief competitor at Druhdrui and he was jealous of all this midnight business concentrated in one trading booth. Much *bhurra* liquor and *charnhr* was being sold, and the crowd was beginning to get hungry and buy seed cakes and moss jelly.

Singh was a big, powerful, unprincipled cutthroat, and those who knew him were just as pleased to trade with Grlahn, who was lazy and fat and greedy, but not so dangerous. And he was reasonably honest, whereas Singh would cheat and challenge the victim to prove it. Realizing the general attitude of the camp, and secretly resenting the strangers, Singh had enlisted the support of three of his cronies, who carried five-pronged *baclai* hooks, with which a man's flesh could be torn from him. They were determined to make trouble.

What really set Singh off was the attitude of the lean, suspicious looking stranger with the ice-gray eyes and the mysterious weapon. Through all the shouting of insults he had sat calmly on one of Grlahn's leather cases and questioned various customers without paying the slightest attention to Singh. He acted, as Singh loudly pointed out, like the Overlord Chief of all the Gdjinhji.

"Who are you," he challenged, "to take on the airs of a great chieftain and question us? We are the ones who should be questioning you! Whence come you?"

Other tribesmen moved aside to give him room. They saw that he and his companions carried *baclai* hooks, and they tensed, waiting.

Grlahn rushed to the scene, his belly quivering with anxiety.

"Now Singh," he pleaded. "Let us be fair. Don't make trouble again like you did last year, just because I place my booth against the pyramid walls and you do not. I told you that's the best way to bring in trade, because it's a better protection from the wind."

"You speak words of sand," scoffed Singh. "You have business because you feed these strangers who do not belong here. You keep out of this, Grlahn. I speak in the interests of our people!"

With this, he walked directly over to the thin stranger and faced him. The onlookers did not envy the stranger, because they feared Singh. He was strong, quick to fight, quick to kill.

But the thin one from the desert only glared back at Singh without moving. And he answered, saying, "You claim we do not belong here. That is true. Nor is it our desire to be here. We have come to this place seeking the Nrlani, who may be the only ones who can help us to return whence we came."

Singh threw back his head and laughed, and his broken teeth, though stained blue by *ca'ta*, glimmered in the firelight. "How big this insect talks! Izdran would cook you for supper!"

At this there was a titter of sympathetic laughter in the crowd, and that was enough to set the stranger off. He stood up, not swiftly, but with cold dignity and practiced disdain.

"It is time I told you the facts," he said, gazing momentarily at Trinha, who watched him adoringly. "Look, all of you, at that great star that rides the sky between the inner and the outer

13

moon. You call it Panh, do you not?"

Heads swung about, including Singh's, and they all looked up at bright, blue-green Panh, shining in that portion of the clear night sky, which was visible from under Grlahn's improvised roof. Trinha's heart beat so hard now that she thought everybody would hear it.

"That is another world, a larger world than this, a world of continents and oceans and lofty mountains and forests and rivers, teeming with thousands of millions of inhabitants. There they live in tremendous cities and travel in ships that fly through the sky like the Nrlani. That is our world, which we call *Earth*. In fact, I was its ruler."

A HUNDRED widened eyes stared. Grlahn stopped waiting on customers. Trinha stopped serving *bhurra* liquor. Everybody stared at the thin one.

But then Singh laughed again. "The insane have large imaginations," he said. "You are a raving lunatic!"

In that moment, the thin one struck Singh in the face with the back of his hand, not challengingly, but contemptuously, as a slave-master might punish an unruly servant. The crowd gasped, drawing back to clear a space for battle, which was certain to ensue. Grlahn popped his more fragile wares miraculously out of sight.

Singh and his men did not wait for any more encouragement. They closed in on the stranger, brandishing their murderous *baclai* hooks.

Trinha screamed, "No, Singh! Don't do it!"

It was then, however, that they learned that the stranger was definitely not of their world, that he came from a greater one, with muscles equipped to react to greater forces of gravitation. With a quick sweep of the butt end of his weapon, he knocked Singh off his feet and broke his arm. With a kick of his booted foot he sent another of his attackers reeling. Trinha drew back into her father's trembling arms, simultaneously amazed, frightened and thrilled.

The remaining two attackers hesitated. Whereupon the stranger threatened them with the back of his hand, contemptuously. Then one of the attackers sprang upon him, determined to tear him down.

But the stranger seemed made of a different flesh than they. Fatigued as he was, he managed to lift his assailant into the air and throw him away.

The last attacker turned on his heels and ran shouting an alarm to the rest of the camp.

Writhing in pain on the ground, Singh cried out a warning. "They are robots in disguise!" he yelled. "They are made of metal! They are from the slave cities, come to trap us!"

But the thin one had been grazed by a *baclai* hook, and he was bleeding.

"Do robots bleed?" he asked. "I tell you I am from Panh, and I want to return to it. But there is more that I want from the Nrlani than that. I have come among you to warn you that Panh is now in the hands of one who would destroy you. He is perhaps even greater than Izdran of a Thousand Lives. Even now he is preparing thousands of men to come here and subjugate all of you to his rule. And it is him I would conquer. Once I ruled that world, and he took it from me, not because his forces were merely stronger, but because he was not of my kind, just as I am not of yours.

"You could not know the meaning of the word, 'mutant,' but that is what this ruler of Panh is, and as such he is to be feared. Just as the name of Izdran terrorizes you now, one day it could happen that the name of Stephen Germain will terrorize you more!"

"Germain!" shrieked the sick stranger on the ground. His eyes widened and his oily face became distorted with an expression of fear and hate. He sat up, panting with the effort. "Where is he? Don't let him find me like this! He'll kill us both on sight!"

Inasmuch as the sick one spoke in a language that had never been heard before they could understand nothing except the name, *Germain.*

"You see?" said the thin one. "I speak the name of Panh's present ruler and my companion cringes, just as all of you will unless you cooperate with me in my future plans to take Panh away from him and rule it again, in my own way."

CHAPTER TWO

TO Trinha, the impossible dream had come true. Panh was a greater world, full of oceans, cities and people. And the stranger was actually a prince—a ruler! Now she felt in her heart of hearts that the denouement of the dream could be taken for granted. He would buy her and take her to Panh.

"Trinha!" shouted Grlahn. "You are pouring *bhurra* all over Krahlarg's eggs!"

She stopped to look into the startled customer's face. Then she laughed. What did it matter? Her dream was coming true!

Many of the tribesmen were now impressed, but none of them knew that it was this same Nicholas the First of New Russia who had ruled the Earth with an iron hand, enjoying a greater might and power than Hitler or Napoleon or Genghis Khan. He had marched ruthlessly to an unprecedented pinnacle of fame and power across the broken bodies of millions of his victims, waving his hands magically and causing empires to tremble and fall, sealing the destinies of presidents and kings.

But he had met with defeat in the midst of victory, and fate had cast him adrift on an alien planet where he was certain no Earthman had walked before. He was alone, forgotten, his pride and glory and power buried up there in the heavens beyond his reach, with no one to recognize him for what he had been. No one, that is, except Pavlovich, an ex-major in one of his many armies. No one to share his frustration except Pavlovich. Pavlovich knew the whole, involved story. He needed Pavlovich.

But Pavlovich was in delirium half the time, and part of his mentality had been impaired by the fevers he had suffered.

Nicholas had grown lately to fear that he would end up with nothing but a madman to keep him company, and so his desperation to find a cure for the other had increased proportionately.

Then, too, there was something else, much more important. Their mutual bond—which was their equal hatred of Stephen Germain. Bitter it was for Nicholas to realize that it was he, himself, who enabled his greatest surgeon, Dr. Julius Borg, to use the captured American spy and former, Red-baiting journalist, as a guinea pig, which had resulted in his becoming a surgical mutant who rose up to defeat his greatest purpose on Earth. Germain was master of that planet now.

His purpose in creating Germain, the mutant, was to use his mind, to discover a means of overcoming gravitation. Germain, under an ever-waning hypnotic control by Borg, had no sooner presented him with the secret he sought than he forced Nicholas to make use of it in order to escape with his life. Even out in space he had been pursued, but he had managed to make a crash landing in an auxiliary flier, on Mars, after his main ship had been destroyed by remotely controlled atomic rockets. The fact that he had escaped with his life he was sure Germain did not know.

Germain did not know that he, Nicholas I, and his lesser enemy, Pavlovich, still lived, or that they had both sworn to return and wipe him out. At first, in the face of his hopeless isolation, Nicholas had felt it was futile to harbor such a dream. Yet Pavlovich's personal hatred of their common enemy had sustained him. He had begun to feel instinctively that he and his companion might yet find a way.

Nor was it all instinct. At first disillusioned by the primitive caliber of the human type Martian inhabitants, who looked exactly like a Western Hemisphere brand of Indians, he had become intrigued by his later discovery of the underground industrial slave cities and the telepathic robots.

These latter seemed to be the instruments of another kind of intelligent life on the planet. And as his knowledge of the

Martian tongue had increased, he had learned that there was, in fact, a concealed master race somewhere, to whom the natives, whether enslaved or free, referred to as gods. But Nicholas suspected from the first that these so-called gods were far from being supernatural. He was sure they were living, material entities.

The primitive Gdjinhji tribesmen referred to their feared and very mysterious overlords as the Nrlani, and there was much subdued talk of one entity in particular—Izdran of a Thousand Lives. No matter how many questions he had asked during his long sojourn on Mars, he had only been able to glean the repeated information that Izdran was indescribable, unapproachable, invincible, omnipotent, omniscient, omnipresent—that he was the undisputed lord of the planet and a creature or being of very great "magical" attainment.

Where could Izdran or at least some of the mysterious Nrlani be found? Once in a Martian year they showed up at a place called Druhdrui. That had been his goal, Druhdrui and a meeting with the dreaded Nrlani. If they were beings of a superior intelligence, which was strongly evidenced by their incredible robot policemen, then they were equipped with the tools of science and industry, and he had to find them. They might be his means of returning to Earth. Without that possibility to sustain him he knew he would die. So he lived for it, and he made Pavlovich live for it when he should have been dead.

JUST as Nicholas summoned Trinha to attend to Singh, something began to happen outside. Like the howling of a distant storm, voices began to rise in a single, fearful shout. There was a sound of hundreds of running feet. Panic had struck Druhdrui.

He stepped outside among the Gdjinhji. "What is it?" he asked of them.

Some of them joined the panic-stricken crowd that was running through the camp, while others fell on their knees and bowed their heads, trembling.

"*Izdran!*" came the cry of the mob. "Izdran is here! He walks alone!"

"Let me out of here!" shouted Singh, getting painfully to his feet. "I told you these strangers were instruments of the Nrlani! If Izdran walks alone, he comes for no good. We are trapped!"

Grlahn instinctively started to pack all his belongings. Trinha, however, came to Nicholas and clutched his arm.

"Save us!" she cried. "We have been kind to you, Prince! Do not let us be taken into the slave cities!"

Nicholas raised his rifle and fired a thunderous shot into the air. It stopped everyone dead in their tracks.

"Stay where you are!" he shouted. "If Izdran is here, he has come to see *me!* Where is he?"

The tribesmen cowered, not knowing which fear to obey. But one of them offered an explanation. He came to Nicholas, kneeling, and pointed to the adjacent pyramid.

"He is there!" he said. "He has emerged from the pyramid! There he is now! In truth, he seeks you out! Save us!"

Nicholas looked—and received a shock of surprise.

Pavlovich struggled to his feet and screamed. "It's Germain! Shoot him! Shoot him!"

"Shut up, idiot," Nicholas snapped at him. "It's nothing but a Martian *krnar*." He pointed his rifle at it as it approached him.

The eight-foot, semi-translucent spider was a murderous killer, a dreaded denizen of the desert. It raced directly toward him. He stood his ground, knowing that a single shot could bring it down. But he only had twelve precious rounds left. He hoped that the mere threat of the weapon would bring it to a halt in time.

"I don't understand," he said to the girl at his elbow. "Why do they think this is Izdran?"

"Izdran is everywhere," she said, trembling visibly, "and he lives in a thousand forms! He has been known to visit us before in this form, always with dire consequences for someone. An ordinary *krnar* would shun this camp. No, my Prince, it is

19

Izdran, himself, who seeks you this night! Beware!" She made a peculiar sign on her forehead, tracing the outlines of a pyramid with her thumb, then a square, representing the base of a pyramid. And she looked at him guiltily, because by modern Martian standards she was indulging in paganism, equivalent to black magic. He realized it must have been abject fear that led her to revert to the signs of the ancient Moon Worshippers who had built the pyramids.

"This is superstitious nonsense," he snorted. "That's just a lost and bewildered *krnar*, or else it's insane with hunger."

The spider beast came to a stop in front of him, with obvious deliberation. Those tribesmen who remained in camp stood still, watching breathlessly. They watched the stranger from Panh with his frightening weapon, and they watched the terrible materialization of their dictator god, and the only sound in all Druhdrui was that of the wind howling among the ghostly pyramids.

"Why doesn't it do something?" Pavlovich whispered hoarsely between clenched teeth and white, parched lips.

"Maybe it will go away," muttered Nicholas, glowering along his sights.

"Who are you?" came a strange, distant sounding voice. *"You are obviously not of this world,"* it commented coldly.

Pavlovich panted audibly. Beads of perspiration made his forehead glisten in the sickly light of the campfire. He said nothing because he reasoned this was just another case of the D.T.'s, in which Nicholas would not be interested just now. He made a desperate attempt to hold onto himself, to convince himself that the *krnar* had not spoken. Then, to his great surprise, Nicholas answered the spider beast's question.

"We are men of Panh," he said, testily, still holding his rifle well aimed. "The question is, who are you? I'll tell you right now, you're no *krnar*. Please understand you are not dealing with a superstitious Martian native. I am aware of the possibility of transmitted sensory impression and inducted illusion. You are using the beast as a disguise, and only the Nrlani could do that. Come out of hiding or I'll shoot!"

"I *am* Izdran," came the answer. "You are not at all superstitious. In fact, you give promise of even being intelligent. What do you want?"

Nicholas thought swiftly. He was aware now that he was dealing with a superior intelligence, and with such it was practical to avoid sophistries and come to the point. "I need your help," he said, frankly. "To purchase your aid, I offer a proposition. I want to bargain with you. But first, come out of hiding."

The *krnar* stood there motionlessly, glistening eerily in the light of the two small moons spinning on high.

"I stand before you," said Izdran.

"You do not!" retorted Nicholas, swiftly. "This proves you lie!" Whereupon, he shot the *krnar* and it fell dead.

Pavlovich yelled above the shouting and screaming of the Gdjinhji. "There's another one!"

"I am Izdran," said the second beast, which had just emerged out of the surrounding darkness. "With what would you bargain? You seem to have nothing to offer."

"I offer you half a world," said Nicholas, "if you will assist me."

"Half of what world—Panh?"

"Yes."

"And the other half?"

"Is mine."

"You speak in the present tense. Either you mean *was* or *shall be.*"

"Both," replied Nicholas.

"You were once one of the rulers of Panh?"

"I was its supreme ruler."

"Until what forces dethroned you?"

"Forces which you can help me to overcome."

"How do you know I can help you?"

"You obviously possess the knowledge and the tools of an advanced science. That's all I need, plus a little cooperation and

21

strategy."

"But Panh is highly populated. How do you know I could supply a sufficient army? Furthermore, what makes you think I would covet that world?"

"The answer to your first question is this. On Panh are untold millions who would still serve me. They can be recontacted and reorganized. The answer to your second question is that you live on a dying planet, which offers you nothing. If you are equipped with an advanced science and have not coveted Panh you are less intelligent than I have surmised."

There followed a lull in the conversation during which Nicholas thought he detected an echo of amused laughter. Then the spider beast said, "Who is your companion?"

"He is my aide. He is stricken with the desert fever and I need help. I want to make him well."

"Why?"

"He can be of great assistance to both of us, but I'm not going to go into the details of that under these circumstances," snapped Nicholas, impatiently. "Now come out of your disguise and take us to where you *really* are. We're exhausted. I've spent months groping through Hell to find you, so let's have an end to this nonsense!" He had to use his own language to express the word, "Hell," as there was no word for it in the Gdjinhji vocabulary, but his questioner appeared to understand perfectly well what he meant.

"What of the means of transportation back to Panh?" persisted Izdran. "Have you a space ship? I don't see how you could, since a hundred of your years ago your kind was merely playing around with the idea of a horseless carriage."

Nicholas was secretly exultant. Then these Nrlani did actually have intimate knowledge of Earth! "Only a wrecked commuter vessel," he replied to the other's question. "It could be repaired. My main ship was destroyed out in the asteroid belt."

"Destroyed? By what?"

"By remotely controlled atomic bombs."

"Whose atomic bombs? Who destroyed you?" There was a rising note of concern in the other's voice. "Surely your world could not have achieved nuclear fission so soon, and if the bombs were not from your world, then—"

"You ask too many questions!" shouted Nicholas. "Get that stinking *krnar* out of my sight and let's get together or I won't talk any further!"

"You are not giving the orders here!" came the other's voice pre-emptorily. "You are fortunate to be alive at all! Why do you suppose the robots permitted you to keep that absurd weapon of yours at all this time? Because I knew you'd need it to survive!"

For answer, Nicholas fired his rifle and killed the second *krnar*. Then he got to his feet and shouted into the night. "I said come out from hiding, damn you!"

But there was only silence, save for the wind among the pyramids. The stars and Panh looked apathetically down as if nothing had ever happened.

Pavlovich grasped Nicholas wildly by the throat. "You had a chance to get us out of this!" he shouted, in Russian. "You spoiled it for us! Now the voice won't come back!"

Nicholas brought the butt end of his rifle up sharply under his companion's chin, and the latter slumped to the ground. He stared resolutely above the heads of the Gdjinhji, into the Martian night. He knew that Izdran was not dead—not Izdran of a Thousand Lives. He knew he would return, for he had succeeded in tossing him the bait.

CHAPTER THREE

GRADUALLY, the Gdjinhji were coming back into camp. Grlahn, who had not been able to flee because he could not lift the bundle of valuables he had scraped together, returned mercurially to the business of waiting on trade. He was incapable of expressing his gratitude to Nicholas for having rescued them all from a fate worse than death. Moreover, he was honored, and his little ego was intensely inflated with his good luck. He was host to a mighty chieftain, after all. His guest had been and perhaps would be again someday, chieftain of all Panh!

As Grlahn watched Nicholas and saw that his sharp eyes rested not infrequently on Trinha, he had a sudden inspiration. It would be infinitely profitable for him to befriend such a man.

"You are deserving of the greatest gift I am capable of giving you, Sire!" he exclaimed in a loud voice that was recognized by his customers as a public announcement.

Nicholas turned to him, as did Trinha, her face flushed with pride and excitement.

"I give you—my daughter, Trinha Llih—gratis, as an expression of my enduring friendship!"

The crowd roared instant approval and congratulations. Trinha's eyes widened with surprise, incredulity—and embarrassment, because she knew her secret exultation was making her blush crimson. She looked at Nicholas' inscrutable face, then shrank away to hide from the leering, shouting crowd of Gdjinhji. Yet every fibre of her being was a little super-sensitive ear that listened for the words of acceptance she knew her Prince would say. She knew he would accept, because it was a predetermined part of her life's dream.

Nicholas turned to look at her again. She was seated on a mat beside one of Grlahn's bales of merchandise, hiding her face in her arms, her raven black hair glistening down her back. Without her web-shawl she was a healthy vision of young fem-ininity, and Nicholas reflected that her soft, freshly matured figure might have competed with that of any woman he had ever known. She was, by Earth standards, sixteen years old, more or less. Her complexion was light, only slightly tinged with the reddish hue of her kind, her teeth were strong and white, her brown eyes large and innocent, and her raven black hair—

That hair! For one fleeting moment it brought to his mind the vision of another woman with hair like that, but her skin was white and her eyes were blue. She lived up there in the sky, on

Earth. She had been his prisoner once, back there in the old victorious' days of expansion. There would never be another woman like her, and his dreams of conquest would be without basis for evaluation unless he could possess her. The only trouble was—her name was Lillian Germain. She was the wife of his deadly enemy, Stephen Germain, mutant master of a world that had once been his.

As Grlahn cleared his throat, expectantly, and as Trinha raised her head to look at him, he managed to smile, but his eyes narrowed.

"You are very generous," he said, non-committally. He was aware of the rigid social laws of the Gdjinhji, and he understood that when a man offered his own daughter in exchange for actual or imagined favors it would be an insult to refuse.

Taking his reply as an acceptance, the assembled Gdjinhji tribesmen followed native custom. As Grlahn had already filled their cups, they raised them in silent toast. Then they left, taking Grlahn with them.

Pavlovich, who had regained consciousness, rubbed his bruised jaw and belched.

Knowing what was expected of him, Nicholas approached Trinha and grasped her hair. The quick motion drew her head back and she looked up at him adoringly. She was not unattractive to him. Her lips were full, waiting for his own. Deliberately, she made a curious hunching motion that dropped her cloak-like garment to her waist. Her deep, young breasts rose and fell visibly with her agitated breathing.

He pulled her roughly to her feet, as was expected, crushed her to him in swift response. But he did not kiss her. Instead, he looked penetratingly into her eyes.

"If you would serve me," he said, "you will do as I command."

With half-closed eyes, Trinha was ecstatically obedient. "Tell me, Sire!" she exclaimed.

"You understand the nature of the desert fever, do you not?"

Her eyes opened and he felt her tense as she stared at him.

"Yes," she answered. "But—"

"Then you know one of the methods of breaking it," he persisted.

As she followed his gaze to Pavlovich, who lay on a floor mat watching them in a dull stupor, she recoiled.

"But Prince! I—you can't mean—!"

His ice-gray eyes blazed in command. "You will serve me!" he said. "For reasons which I cannot explain, you cannot be mine. But you *can* be his!"

For answer, Trinha collapsed to the ground, sobbing audibly. Nicholas watched her for a moment, then poured himself a cup of *bhurra* liquor. Pavlovich began to focus his fever-reddened eyes on Trinha.

It would have fanned Nicholas' ego to be the first Earthman to take a Martian woman, but there was one woman alone, among literally thousands he had known as First Czar of New Russia, who could ever mean anything to him, and she was on Earth. His abstinence in preference to her was a better pabulum for his ego, not because of idealism, of which he had none, but because of this demonstration of his superior will. When he could throw ripe plums like Trinha before his underlings, he was superior and deserving of the cream of the crop. Then, too, recapturing Lillian Germain would be the sweeter revenge.

IT was a long night for Nicholas. Fatigued as he was, the tremendous possibilities connected with his contact with Izdran kept him awake. The food and drink he had taken in gave him energy, and his keen mind denied the demands of his body for sleep. It was like the old campaign days when he was expanding his power over the Earth. His heart beat now in cadence with the distant drums of conquest.

He had striven long and mightily for a meeting with the mysterious Nrlani race, and now he felt that his goal was imminent. He tried to sleep but could not. Nor was he envious of Pavlovich's deep, guttural snores, nor of the slender shape that lay beside him. His thoughts were many, varied, and cunning. They had to be. He knew he was going to have to match wits with superior beings, and he was comforted only by the thought that the jackal had sometimes been known to outwit the lion.

He left the camp sometime in the dark hours preceding the dawn and climbed the nearest pyramid. He wanted to be on the top at sunrise and look out over the flat Martian landscape as far as he could.

Beneath the hard surface of his conscious deliberations a vague curiosity assailed him about these pyramids. Strange that there should have been pyramid builders in ancient times both on Earth and on Mars. The only difference here was that a large pyramid was always accompanied by a smaller one. What the significance of it was he could not guess, unless he could allow himself to infer that the ancient moon-worshippers who had built them were cognizant of the relative sizes of the two Martian moons and had represented the difference accordingly in their pyramids. But there were more important things on his mind just now. Later he might permit archaeologists to come here and figure it out. The living present was mystery enough. Yesterday could wait in its dust of ages for yet a little time.

He reached the top while it was still dark. Both moons had gone below the horizon, and only starlight and faint Earthlight limned a million tube-bark and djurnur bushes out on the desert with a ghostly fluorescence. Stars so numerous that they coalesced into celestial lakes of fire formed a mighty wall, as though protecting him from an intolerable nothingness that might otherwise have sucked his flesh dry of entity.

As if to form one of the poles of this far-flung Infinity, the green eye of Earth gazed at him from a point slightly above the horizon, and its light was reflected in his gray eyes like the reviving embers of the negative greatness that had once flamed there—mercilessly.

Suddenly, as he stood there with the cold night winds of the Martian equator chilling his body and the faint, musty odor of the tube-bark blossoms in his nostrils, he thought he was having hallucinations. It seemed to him that a half dozen djurnur pods had gone into formation and were power-diving in his direction. Six silvery globes descended swiftly in his direction, out of the glittering heavens.

He tensed with indefinable alarm as he noted the deliberation with which they approached him. What were they? Space ships of the Nrlani?

When they swooped past him so closely that he could hear the whistling of the air due to their passage, he knew that they were not globular space vessels, nor were they djurnur pods. They were approximately three feet in diameter, and as they passed him they turned on their edges and revealed disc-like silhouettes.

Then, as they turned upward into the sky again, they grew miraculously in size even as they receded from him. And as they grew they became transparent, suddenly attenuating into invisibility!

He knew what they were. He had heard often of their appearance in terrestrial skies. He had observed them in interplanetary space. They were "flying saucers." But the terrestrial name was inadequate. They were much more than that. Flying effortlessly in an atmosphere or in outer space, defying the laws of gravity and inertia alike, attenuating or densifying at will, they were to Nicholas a consuming mystery and a challenge to science.

Because they were *not* ships. *They were living creatures.* Denizens of the void. Even as these passed him he had observed the pulsating, slightly luminous nerve centers in the middle of each. How they lived, whence they came, or what the purpose of their existence was he could not begin to conjecture. Yet he knew these six were aware of him—that they would probably appear again.

He did not have long to wait. This time they were more densified than before. They were only one foot in diameter. But they hovered directly over his head now.

And suddenly a voice came to life inside his mind, just as it had once when Stephen Germain had spoken to him telepathically. He knew, in that moment, that these particular discs had become the instrument of Izdran of a Thousand Lives, for it was he who spoke to him.

You never ruled Earth, the nearest disc seemed to say.

"I did!" shouted Nicholas. "I was its conqueror!"

A second disc moved into nearest position above him.

What of the King of the World—and Agarthi?

This question silenced Nicholas momentarily because it shocked him. It proved conclusively that Izdran knew all about Earth, that he had either a means of visiting other planets or at least of spying on them in a very thorough manner. Even though this realization gave rise to new hopes, at the same time the mention of the King of the World and the mystic city of Agarthi filled him with misgivings. Agarthi's plan and purpose, now supported by Stephen Germain, had always opposed the world that Nicholas had sought to establish.

What of Agarthi?—came the repeated question.

"There were greater powers still," replied Nicholas. "My secret allies—possessed of interstellar science."

Gone!—retorted the mental voice of Izdran, as the discs still hovered above. *Vanquished by even greater powers! Your enlisting the aid of the malignant interstellar powers, which have held Earth in bondage for twenty millenniums led to failure, since their emergence brought upon your forces and theirs the far superior strength and power of the Elder Race—that same race, which destroyed my own world of Nrlan, whose fragments you now refer to as the asteroids. The Elder Race has declared our form of life to be outlawed and inimical to all civilizations in the universe, so the last survivors of the Nrlani have had to conceal themselves for millennia of time in a place, which seems to have remained even beyond the reach of the Elders, fortunately for us. For thousands of years I have been preparing to take the Earth and the solar system, to destroy the renegade interstellars who ruled your planet in secret, and to defy the Elder Race who forced this long exile upon us. Now your interstellar overlords are extinct, it is true, but your idiotic ambitions have again focussed the attention of the so-called benevolent Elders on Sol and its planets. It does not matter that they have already returned to their own distant part of the universe, and that with them has gone their Star Warden, whom you refer to as the King of the World. Still, Agarthi exists, and the elders are behind it. The Elders aided Agarthi in destroying your secret allies and they destroyed your ship in which you sought to escape to Mars. This I have learned by means that are unknown to you. If they should discover now that you and your companion did actually effect an escape to this planet they might follow and destroy you. If you attempted to attack the Earth, with our help, they might try to destroy us all. What have you to say to that?*

Without hesitation, Nicholas answered, "With the interstellar foes of Agarthi destroyed and the Elder Race and the Star Warden gone, that leaves only Agarthi alone, and the Elder's sole terrestrial deputy, Stephen Germain. Germain stands between us and the conquest of the solar system. If you attack swiftly and in force you have a chance of facing the Elders when or if they return. If you do not attack him, he will attack *you.* Do you want to sit and wait for it? Now cut out this childish witchcraft and let's talk business! Unless I see you personally I'll not commune with any of your disguises. Where are you?"

For several agonizing minutes there was no reply. The discs above Nicholas milled about restlessly. Then he heard again the same distant laughter he had heard before when Izdran had spoken to him through the *krnar* spiders down in the camp.

You have possibilities, came Izdran's mental voice. *We shall meet and discuss a few details concerning them.*

"When?" shouted Nicholas.

At dawn—came the reply.

In that instant, the six discs shot into the sky so fast that it was equivalent almost to instantaneous disappearance. Only the starlit desert remained, and the cold winds with their nostalgic whisperings of forgotten events beyond recorded time.

The broad firmament of the Unknown stretched before Nicholas' mind as immeasurable and unreachable as all the physical infinities of space, and for a moment he despaired of ever scratching its surface—there were so many mysteries, there was yet so much to learn.

But then, humanly, he sought to cover the nakedness of humility with a cloak of egotism. He caught again his old dream of conquest, his visions of triumph and glory. Once more he saw himself as Nicholas the First, Emperor of all Men. He walked again through the marble halls of his palaces in the major cities of Eurasia, his shining boots heralding his approach to the subservient multitudes who served him. But this time those boots would ring in the sacred corridors of a certain building at Lake Success. He would change the once-shattered and rebuilt United Nations into a United Empire! And he would rule from the caverned Paradise of Agarthi itself. As far as the Nrlani were concerned, they could go to the devil. He'd find a way to trick them out of their share once they had served him—regardless of who or what they were...

Having reached a point of decision, his will relaxed its intensity and he found no further armament against fatigue. He retired to the camp and Grlahn's trading booth. But before he surrendered himself to sleep his active mind unearthed several unsettled questions.

The Nrlani were unquestionably a superior race. The only defense against them would be to fight fire with fire, just as he had done before. When the hidden interstellar allies he had used to help him conquer Earth threatened Nicholas, Dr. Borg had created the surgical mutant, Stephen Germain, who had served, for a while at least, to hold them at bay before he, too, got out of hand and decided to join forces with Agarthi.

Now then, if after helping him to make a return conquest the Nrlani should play an ace card against him, what would be his defense? Dr. Borg? In the latter days of his defeat, Nicholas had lost Borg. The brilliant scientist might even have followed his own creation, Stephen Germain, over to the Agarthian side, for all he knew. He had always sensed in Borg that weakness that endangers all serviceable intellectuals—*Wisdom*, whose logic turns its victim inevitably from the practical contemplation of self into the stifling void of altruism. You could bargain with a man who wanted something for his own sake, but never with one who was contaminated with the incurable fungus of *Weltschmerz*—world pain, concern for humanity. In Nicholas' personal credo, humanity was a case of every man for himself. Anything else was weakness, fundamental immorality, idiocy. And so, perhaps, Borg would no longer be useful to him.

There was, however, another scientist of great stature in Europe, a German attached to the last remnants of the old Nazi underground movement. It was he who actually perfected the death ray and contributed directly to the development of nuclear energy from hydrogen and thus from seawater. A brilliant fanatic. When he returned to Earth, he would have to send out tracers for him.

What was his name? Eidelmann. That was it! Gerhardt Eidelmann! Nicholas dozed off, dreaming that bald, myopic Eidelmann was laughing derisively at Izdran. But his dreams could not envision Izdran of a Thousand Lives. In his place was only a terrifying shadow...

CHAPTER FOUR

HE was awakened by Pavlovich. He and Pavlovich were alone in the booth and the gray light of dawn was upon them. Trinha Llih was gone.

Pavlovich, bearded, pale, disheveled, kneeled over him and shook him. His brown eyes were wide with excitement, but they were clear.

"Better get up," he said. "Something's going on."

"You are well," said Nicholas. "The fever is gone. It's good to have you back, Sergeyev. From here on I'm going to need you."

"Listen," exclaimed Pavlovich, rising to his feet. "Can't you hear them all running away? They're leaving camp in a hurry, but they're not letting a peep out of them."

Nicholas heard the distant, scurrying sounds, but it was another, more distant sound that caused him to sit up, then spring to his feet.

"That's thunder!" he exclaimed. "There are no thunder storms on Mars…"

"Look! It's getting darker! There's a big storm brewing."

"But I hear no wind. Let's go outside."

Outside, the camp was already deserted. Trading booths were left intact with all merchandise and personal belongings. Not even Grlahn had appeared to scrabble up his most precious wares. The entire populace of Druhdrui had left as though threatened with plague.

"Look at the sky," cried Pavlovich.

Nicholas was already looking. It was black with towering clouds—and yet they were not clouds. They were incalculably high and were billowing wildly, like dense smoke in a violent fire. And from them in all directions shot long streamers of lightning, accompanied by reverberating thunder.

"*Proklaty!*" exclaimed Pavlovich. "What the devil is it? I don't like it. That thing's headed right for us. Let's get out of here!"

Incongruously, Nicholas started to laugh. "Do they take us for ignorant savages?" he asked. "It's an illusion, or camouflage. And it's all for the Gdjinhji, not for us."

"But what is it?" shouted Pavlovich, above the rolling roar of the thunder.

"It's the Nrlani," he answered. "They're staging an appearance. Just keep your eyes open and watch. In a little while you should see a city floating up there in the sky."

"A city? Are you crazy?"

Nicholas turned to fix him with one of his famous stares. "No," he answered. "But *you* have been out of your head for months. Now take my word for it and do as I say. The Nrlani are the only ones who can get us back to Earth. They are the only ones—"

The ground shook with the thunderings of the gigantic clouds thickening close above their heads and lightning tendrils licked at the tops of the pyramids.

Pavlovich winced, as he clutched Nicholas' arm in frenzied

desperation.

"Back to Earth?" he shouted. "Don't play with me! Tell me the truth!"

"It *is* the truth. I tell you I've already made an alliance. They will help us retake the Earth—and smash Germain. You want that, don't you?"

Pavlovich straightened. A cold gleam came into his eyes. His bearded chin jutted out and he swelled out his big chest and clenched his fat, muscular fists.

Smash Germain. Nothing in life would be more worth while. No man had contributed so much to his personal degradation and misery as had Germain. He hated Germain with a passion that seemed to eliminate any other reasons for living.

So here at last was a chance to get back. Pavlovich winced no longer at the lightning and the thunder. Like Nicholas, he waited, with an amused grin on his face and an icy gleam, in his eyes.

The Nrlani, mysterious survivors of the Fifth Planet, were emerging from *God knew where...*

SUDDENLY, the nature of the spectacle above them changed. The lightnings and the thunderings ceased. The wild billowings of the black clouds ceased, and from the depths of the induced darkness began to emerge an ethereal glow that rivaled the dawnlight.

Simultaneously, the clouds themselves began to attenuate, and their ears were assailed by a clash of celestial cymbals, initiating a roll of drums and a blast of invisible trumpets.

"No wonder the natives call the Nrlani gods," Nicholas remarked. "Such a spectacle could convert seventy percent of Earth's population to any faith overnight."

"Could gods do it any better?" put in Pavlovich. "They might as well be gods."

As an indescribably beautiful symphony hurled unearthly music at them from the sky and light emerged from above like a dozen sunrises, Nicholas' nostrils flared and his eyes narrowed.

"There is no sphere of supernatural phenomena," he insisted. "All is physical reality—even Heaven, itself, if it exists—as tangible as any concubine! Remember that, Sergeyev, in all that may soon transpire! For here is much of the Unknown—yet one thing we know about it. It cannot violate the physical fundamental of Cause and Effect. And as such it may be understood—and conquered!"

Pavlovich did not express the thought that perhaps his master was afflicted with insanity, after all. He was not illiterate, Pavlovich. There was a word for Nicholas' affliction. It was called megalomania.

But once before this megalomania had subjugated thirty nations of the Earth to his rule. What would happen now, with the Nrlani behind him? Mentally, Pavlovich shrugged. Why should he complain if it meant that the crumbs he would gather from Nicholas' banquet table of conquest would be as *empire* to others?

"Look," shouted Nicholas. "There it is..."

There it was, indeed. A city. A floating city, high in the sky but lowering rapidly toward them. A glowing city of vast splendour and beautiful simplicity, translucent, seemingly composed of a single crystalline substance. Actually, as they were to learn, it was made of a wonder substance, simultaneously metallic and plastic, transparent or opaque, as it pleased its inhabitants, densified or attenuated into invisibility, as occasion required—including the inhabitants, themselves.

"You say you have an alliance with these people," said Pavlovich. "When did you make it? Do they know we are here?"

"Their leader, Izdran, has stipulated he would meet me at dawn. Look. The sun is rising. I have an idea Izdran is very specific. He *means* at dawn. The time is now. Come on."

Beyond the pyramids, in the desert, the stupendous city was coming to rest. It towered well above the tallest pyramids, and it sprawled for miles.

Nicholas had brought his rifle. Now, with the dubious weapon clutched in his hands, he started running, which was an easy feat on Mars, even for the Martians, much less difficult for an Earthman. Pavlovich followed.

Beyond the pyramids they came to a halt, just once, to take in the situation. Before them, half a kilometer away, was the great sky city, resting silently and enigmatically on the desert, waiting. The thunders and lightnings and blinding light and celestial music and fanfare were all gone now. There reigned a silence, which seemed grimly purposeful.

Close at hand, the two Earthmen observed for the first time a row of man-sized jars, which the Gdjinhji had set out for the Nrlani. They were filled with *grabeal*, the black substance from Khandarna in the South. Across the desert marched an equal number of telepathic robots carrying bales of *ca'ta*, dream manna from the sky.

"Come on," said Nicholas. "Let's get going."

"*Wait!*"

It was Trinha's voice, behind them. They turned and observed her girlish figure emerging from between the outermost pyramids of Druhdrui. She was without her *krnar* shawl, but the cloak garment concealed her breasts. Her black hair danced behind her as she ran—desperately.

"She is a hindrance," growled Nicholas.

"She's terrific," said Pavlovich.

"We must get rid of her." Nicholas fingered his rifle, purposefully.

"No!" exclaimed Pavlovich. "Wait."

"With the fate of worlds at stake? Come to your senses. Better to shoot her now than be encumbered with a brainless female—"

Trinha heard this latter remark as she came up to them. Her eyes flashed as did her white teeth, and her nostrils flared. She spoke to them in the higher language of Mars. There were two languages, an ordinary one, and a higher form of the same language, with more colorful inflexions and shades of meaning, which both men also understood. I t was called *Dlanat'la*.

"Think you that I am a senseless clod of clay?" she fired at them. "My people are conditioned to flee in terror from the sky lords whenever they appear, but my star-longing has vanquished my instinctive fears. I am here—and I claim a place among you. Take me as you will—as mistress or partner—but take me! I would enter the sky city and go with you to the ends of Creation if it lead me one day to Panh, planet of seas and mountains and teeming cities. Only death alone could stay my will."

As Nicholas turned the muzzle of his rifle at her she clutched it to her breast and glared at him. "Either take me with you or kill me," she said.

It rang a bell in Nicholas. Either he would conquer the Earth or he would destroy it, himself included, if need be. Hers was the same principle—the end justifying the means.

"Let her come as far as the Nrlani will permit it," said Pavlovich. "They'll decide for her."

"Come on, then," said Nicholas.

The three of them ran as fast as they could toward the Nrlani city...

THEY passed by the robots without incident. Either the three-eyed automatons were under control to accomplish one purpose, or the Nrlani were deliberately lowering all barriers to receive their three guests.

As they approached the base of the sky city an opening appeared. A circular, translucent section ten feet wide suddenly attenuated, exposing a lavender light behind it. Here was no door or sliding hatch—just a space where the wall had been.

Wordlessly, they entered a square, empty chamber, and as they did so the wall densified behind them.

"We're trapped," shouted Pavlovich.

"Shut up," said Nicholas. "The more you show fear in this place the more it's going to cost us."

Trinha said nothing, but her face was flushed and her lips were nearly white with terror, but her eyes stared at Nicholas with strange determination. A light film of perspiration lay on her forehead and upper lip.

"Do you notice they've given us Earth atmosphere and temperature?" Nicholas remarked. "I'd say it's an even sixty-eight degrees at fourteen point seven pounds and about twenty percent oxygen, plus about sixty percent relative humidity. Not bad."

As Trinha sank to her knees, Pavlovich made a further discovery. "And this is Earth gravity... How do they do it?"

"Have you noticed the scent? It's an odor, a familiar one—yet not experienced in years."

"Yeah. It's familiar and I like it, but what is it?"

Nicholas grasped his companion's arm. "Sergeyev, do you remember the Black Sea—Sochi, Alupka? My summer villa at Alupka... *That's* the kind of air they're giving us. I could not have imagined such perfect synthesis. It's marvelous!"

"I'm glad you think so. It scares hell out of me. *Sukin syn!* My hair must be standing on end!"

Suddenly, the translucence of the inner walls resolved into transparency. Through them they could see an endless succession of rooms similar to theirs, as though the whole structure of the sky city's foundation were a glass bee-hive with square cells. The transparency tapered off with distance, as though they were in the depths of a tropical sea gazing upon an endless jungle of crystalline coral. Here and there were denser shapes suggesting compact machines. By their very compactness they demonstrated to Pavlovich and Nicholas a power and efficiency that lay centuries beyond their own age.

"Ye gods, look," cried Pavlovich.

Trinha gasped, stifling a scream.

Approaching them, *through* the walls, came a telepathic robot. Attenuation occurred before it in each wall as it advanced. Thus the two Russians perceived that corridors were not necessary in this place.

"I want to get out of here," yelled Pavlovich. "To hell with it."

Nicholas gripped his arm fiercely. "Get hold of yourself or I'll blast your brains out." He still held his rifle.

Pavlovich's eyes were wide, staring at Nicholas, the rifle and the approaching robot, like an animal at bay.

Swiftly, Nicholas added, "What transpires in the next few hours and how we react to it will affect our entire future and that of the Earth, as well—perhaps of the entire solar system. Now straighten up that goddam backbone of yours and act like a man."

There was nothing more to say, inasmuch as the robot came through an attenuated wall-section and stood before them. Trinha, perspiring and terrified, crowded into the farthest corner of the room.

Nicholas took the initiative. "Take us to Izdran," he commanded the robot.

Expressionlessly, the tall robot, towering a head above Nicholas, focussed its central "eye" upon him, and all three humans in the room *sensed* its telepathic reply.

They were welcome. They would see Izdran. But first—they were to be reconditioned...

CHAPTER FIVE

FROM that moment on and over the space of twenty-four hours they had little sense of the passage of time. They could only look back on the episode as a peaceful dream—a dream of resuscitation. Chemical baths and radiant treatments plus special injections and perfectly prepared meals and induced sleep completely rejuvenated the two Earthmen after their year-long exposure to the Martian environment. An extra treatment was given to Trinha, which enabled her respiratory organs to make a more comfortable adaptation to Earth's atmospheric conditions. Furthermore, synthetic clothing was supplied with meticulous thoroughness, each of the two men being dressed in the best taste according to their native world. They were even dressed to suit their individual temperaments, Pavlovich in a pin-striped double-breasted suit with a loud tie and a simulated diamond stickpin, and Nicholas in formal evening dress. Either out of meticulous forethought or premeditated irony, his old medal was back on his shirt-front where he had worn it on state occasions—the ruby and diamond studded Star of Honor, symbol of his erstwhile imperial power over all Eurasia, not to mention the lower half of South America.

Trinha was garbed in a gorgeous black taffeta evening gown creation with low neckline and broad, off-the-shoulder straps supporting transparent kimona sleeves. Her make-up and pageboy coiffure were perfect. Thus transformed in appearance to Earth standards she came near to surpassing them.

She could say nothing, but her sudden delight and wonderment enabled her to stand, in spite of her unaccustomed high heels. Pavlovich was torn between fear of the miraculous Nrlani and desire for Trinha. He took hold of her arm to give her support.

But Nicholas fumed. "What do they think we are—children? Are they trying to make fun of us or just waste time?" He shouted at the walls, since their robot had disappeared. "Let's get on with it, Izdran! There's work to be done!" In his hands, incongruously, he still held his rifle.

The walls, which had become translucent again, suddenly became transparent—and Trinha screamed. Beneath their feet was a great glowing globe suspended in space. It was Mars. The sky city had retreated into the void.

"You have but to approach me," said Izdran. His voice seemed to emanate from nowhere and from everywhere. *"Just follow the disc."*

In the center of the room a small disc creature appeared, such as Nicholas had seen atop the pyramid. It moved away from them toward one of the walls, and as it did so the wall attenuated.

"Come on," said Nicholas. "Believe only half of what you see and forget about the rest. I'm going to Izdran." Whereupon, he stepped into the next chamber, following the disc.

"Come on," echoed Pavlovich, tugging at Trinha's arm.

"I—I can't," she exclaimed. "I can't face—Izdran…"

It was a good excuse for Pavlovich. He picked her up in his arms and followed Nicholas and the disc through the walls…

BEFORE long, they were on the main level of the city proper. Streets were mere channels for moving ramps, which carried the omnipresent robots to their destinations. The buildings were neither dwellings nor places of business. They were windowless, vaguely transparent, apparently housing endless batteries of power generators. Some were factories. In others they heard multitudinous clicking noises like those of gigantic cybernetic brains making ceaseless computations. There was also great evidence, as Nicholas pointed out, of an abnormal amount of ultra high frequency reception and transmission, because there were transmission towers everywhere. There were no clumsy antenna wires for multiple meter wavelengths, but mysterious globes, which seemed to house tiny condenser apparatus for the reception of wavelengths less than a centimeter in length. And there was much that was beyond their comprehension. But it soon became evident to them, and to Trinha, as they were carried along the ramps, that this was no city designed for living. It was a superman's fortress buzzing with a fixed design and purpose.

But where were the overlords of Mars? Where were the Nrlani—and where was Izdran of a Thousand Lives?

Abruptly, as though their flying disc guide had read their minds, they were led off the ramp into a building that towered ten stories high in the approximate center of the city, beneath the transparent dome that protected them from the empty cold of space. Here, for the first time, were signs of another type of life. At least robots would not have appreciated the rich, colorful carpeting, the scenic murals of an alien planet—now long dead—or the jewel encrusted pillars and sweeping staircases.

"At least they must be human," remarked Pavlovich, still holding Trinha in his arms.

"Don't be deceived," said Nicholas. "The very lack of necessity for such things as these reveals that it is all illusion—or camouflage—for our benefit. Remember how easily they produced our present clothing. Be on your toes, Sergeyev. Let me do the talking. And even watch your thoughts. Think as little as possible. This is our big chance, but one slip can cost us the Earth, itself."

An elevator bounced them to the tenth floor, where Izdran awaited them.

The room occupied practically the whole top of the building. It had neither walls nor ceiling. Just a transparent dome, which was a miniature replica of the titanic dome that covered the city. Around the sides of the room were banks of controls, visiscreens, uncountable instruments, flickering signal lights. In the center of the room, on a large raised dais, was a horseshoe shaped master control bank.

In the center of the horseshoe was a ban of light...

"I shall reveal myself to you," said Izdran in the Martian tongue, "at your own risk. I must warn you that not only am I not human; I am anathema to human life. When you see what I really am you will realize why the Elder Race destroyed Nrlan, the planet on which we evolved. To behold me in reality is to require no further explanation. But perhaps we have something in common, after all. Tell me this. Suppose I were to place in your hands the means of conquering Earth. What is there to prevent you from trying to take over my share of the spoils as well as your own? Or I'll put it this way. Is there room enough for both of us on your planet?"

"You have asked me a double question," replied Nicholas, quickly, "so I will give you a double answer. There *is* no room for both of us—naturally. In regard to your first question, what is there to prevent you from blotting me out after I have served your purpose? We both know the answer to that. So it seems we have two problems. The first is to conquer Earth and entrench ourselves against the return of the Elder Race. That we must do together. The second problem is that of conquering each other. That is an individual problem, and I'm prepared to gamble on its outcome when we get to it."

The globe of light flashed with iridescent colors. But this was not a sign of anger. It turned out to be enthusiasm.

"I had feared this was going to be boring," said Izdran, suddenly expressing himself in Russian. "But I see you are mental rather than neuro-endocrine reactive, like your companions. We can talk…"

PAVLOVICH lowered Trinha to the floor. She instinctively kneeled and bowed her head in fear and reverence. Pavlovich extracted a loud handkerchief to wipe cold perspiration from his face.

"Give me first," said Izdran, "the answer to this question. Why do you wish to conquer Earth or the solar system?"

Nicholas hardly hesitated before answering. "Because Earth is run by fools. It is in need of true leadership."

"Do you consider yourself to be worthy of that leadership?"

Nicholas sneered. "It is not a question of worthiness in the moral sense. The fittest shall survive, and the fittest shall lead. I shall take the Earth or its fate will become immaterial to me."

"But why?" persisted Izdran. "What is the basis of your desire to conquer and be the leader? Is it merely a function of your glands?"

"No, it is a function of the mind, just as it is with you. I seek reality, and the only reality is *Power*. I had it once. I shall have it again."

"But you are willing to take grave risks?"

"Naturally."

"There is one risk you have not dwelled on sufficiently."

"What is that?"

"The risk of helping me and my kind to emerge into Tropospheria once more."

"Tropospheria?"

"Yes—the plane of existence that you regard as the Universe, in your own physical sense of the word."

"We have gone over that," said Nicholas. "We are allies. I take it you need me and my organization on Earth to cover up your own identity until the necessary groundwork has been laid for you to stage an appearance. After that it may be too late for the Elder Race to interfere."

"Precisely. But by the same token it may be too late for the human race. *Look!*"

Abruptly, the globe of light collapsed, and Izdran was revealed plainly to them.

Trinha screamed, then fainted.

Pavlovich and Nicholas both staggered back, mouths agape.

"Mother of God!" yelled Pavlovich, forgetting the atheism that had been a part of Nicholas' New Russia.

Nicholas' face was a marble mask as he aimed his rifle and fired at Izdran, point blank. But the bullet attenuated into nothingness and the rifle turned into a snake. Nicholas dropped it.

Izdran roared with laughter. "You *are* the servant of your glands," he said to Nicholas. "Now you can understand why humans can never be as adaptable to their environment as we. We combine the strengths of both human and machine, yet we have eliminated the shortcomings of both. As such we can rule as we please and where we please—except where the accursed Elder Race is concerned. Were it not for them—"

Nicholas scowled. Deliberately, he stooped to pick up the snake he had dropped. As he did so, it became a rifle again. He pointed it at Izdran, or rather, at one of his triple hearts beating behind the walls of transparent metal cells.

"Now that I have had time for adjustment," he said, "I won't be fooled again."

Pavlovich grasped his arm. "Shoot him!" he screamed. "Kill him! Nothing like that should live."

Nicholas jerked his arm away and continued to address Izdran, while Pavlovich struggled to quell a violent surge of nausea. "You speak of the Elder Race as being your only barrier. Have you not heard of the present ruler of Earth?"

"Stephen Germain? Yes," replied Izdran. "But you do not know that he has given the government of the planet back into the hands of the people."

"I told you they are all fools," exclaimed Nicholas. "Germain included. But ordinary terrestrials are worse fools. So Germain has taken a back seat and retired benevolently to Agarthi."

"On the contrary," said Izdran. "He now represents himself as the Star Warden. He has assumed responsibility for the entire Solar System and even plans an early military excursion to Mars."

Nicholas blanched slightly. "What are his plans?" he asked.

"An interesting question. I'd like to know, myself."

"But you have readily acquired all this other information overnight—"

"True, but your Germain is an interesting mutant. He possesses a highly developed ESP. My normal method of investigation would enable him to discover that I am eavesdropping. So far, my—ah—*investigators* have not been able to get to Germain directly. Of course, if I wished to make a *personal* investigation I could find out what I wish to know, but I think Germain is not particularly worthy of much concern on our part. Of course he will have to be eliminated, but the main question is—now that you have seen me—do you wish to continue in alliance with the Nrlani?"

"No!" shouted Pavlovich.

Nicholas struck him again with the butt of his rifle and he slumped to the floor with a nasty trail of blood coming from his mouth. Then he turned to Izdran with an icy calmness. "I have seen your work cities on Mars," he said. "Your robots have been building something there for a long time. From what little I saw, I'd say you had a fleet of space warships."

"That is simple deduction. I have several hundred such ships, any *one* of which could wipe out all the orthodox armies, navies and airforces of Earth in forty-eight hours! They are all robot controlled. Moreover, in regard to Germain's intended visit to Mars, should he or some of his underlings achieve this before we strike at Earth, you may have noticed that the Martian natives in those work cities were not so much slaves as trained soldiery. They are equivalent to a military cadre, and they can be released at any moment to organize all the so-called free natives into a planet-wide army, manning defenses, which can be provided by robot teams, within a period of a few days."

Nicholas did not mention that he had also noticed the work-city populaces were permanently hypnotized, devoid of self-determination. A machine-perfect dictatorship worked here, and he envied it. "Give me *one* of your warships only," he said. "I will go in secret to the Earth and set up the machinery for expanding my contacts and controls in all the nations. It is one thing to conquer by means of superior force. It is another to make good the conquest by installing an efficient governing machine. Once my former agents have lined up their men in each country, we can strike in force. But before I can even operate in secret Stephen Germain must be eliminated. Even when we strike after he is defeated, ninety percent of your fleet may have to concentrate on Agarthi."

"Your companion may serve us in regard to Germain," said Izdran. "He despises Germain worse than he fears the Nrlani. I could give him a specially equipped vessel—"

"Pavlovich?"

"Yes. A suicide vessel. That is, let us call it an expendable vessel, together with the robots I shall place under his control."

"But if Agarthi should even detect his presence—"

"It is an invisible vessel—invisible even to radar. As a matter of fact, no *primary* order of energy could touch it."

"But Germain—"

"Germain and his ESP are elsewhere engaged just now. He is soon to put in an appearance at Lake Success before the Supreme Council of the newly established Terrestrial Government. Lake Success, I understand, is far removed from

Agarthi and Agarthian protection. Of course, Germain's ESP is actually second order energy, which could detect the death ship Pavlovich will pilot, but he would have to detect it far out in space or it would be too late. Even if the vessel remained out of range of his ESP it could still operate against him. Moreover, I presume that the affairs at the Council will require sufficient concentration on his part to enable Pavlovich to surprise him."

The old gleam of triumph crept into Nicholas' gray eyes. "And while Germain is in New York, exposed to Pavlovich, I can start work in Russia."

"Precisely. I will give you a first line warship, and at your command in outer space will be a hundred more."

Just then Trinha regained consciousness. Simultaneously, Izdran surrounded himself with the globe of light. She drew in her breath sharply and looked at Pavlovich's prostrate form.

"What of this girl?" asked Nicholas.

Mentally, he was aware again of distant laughter; but audibly Izdran's voice said, "There's something in her that can be useful. For the time being, I suggest that you keep her with you."

"But I can't be encumbered—"

"It is a condition of the alliance. Where you go, she goes also."

"But why?"

"I said—she would be useful..."

But Izdran avoided mentioning to *whom* Trinha would be useful. Easily, he saw in the Martian girl her new motivation. Earth was no longer her primary goal. Her dream of childhood, her hopes of virgin womanhood, her honor, and the codes of her people—all had been mercilessly shattered and violated by this gray-eyed Earthman whom she thought she had loved. Now he was her first hate. She did not merely wish to destroy him. She wanted to destroy his dreams as he had destroyed hers—then leave him to live with the mangled remains of an existence totally bereft of all meaning and purpose.

Just how she was going to achieve all this she had left to fate alone. But now Izdran was determined to give her assistance...

CHAPTER SIX

AFTER Nicholas and Pavlovich had taken over their respective commissions, Izdran had a short conference with his chief aide, Prahl.

"It is to be hoped," said Prahl, "that your game of spider and fly does not trap the spider." Prahl was viewing Nicholas' distant fleet in a second order televiewer, because to primary sources of energy it was invisible.

"Nicholas is a clever planetary, but only that," replied Izdran. "He is only a convenient tool, a thousand years removed from interstellar intelligence."

"But what if the equipment you are placing at his disposal makes it possible for him to take over and use it against us? You know he's planning just that."

Izdran's multi-faceted eye regarded his aide curiously. "Is it possible," he said, "that you are deteriorating? If you were human, I'd say senility was creeping in. Do you forget our secret abilities? And have you forgotten Central Control and its powers? Have you lost confidence in our *greatest* secret of all?"

"All right," retorted Prahl, calmly enough. "What if Nicholas, Pavlovich, or this infant mutant, Germain, should stumble upon *that?*"

"What could they do even if they did? Could any of them get *in* to Central? You know what would happen to any Earthman who tried it. No, Prahl, this is our time. True, our seventh sense warns us of danger ahead, and this is the deepest bond between us. The picture is almost impossible to grasp, a kaleidoscopic tapestry of inevitabilities mixed indefinably into vague probability patterns. In those patterns are the shapes of space armadas engaged in mortal combat, of worlds afire, and of mentalities locked in a struggle that will affect the destinies even of interstellar races. But this very danger calls us into action. The time is ripe for emerging from this accursed secret hiding. The Nrlanian race can no longer continue as the abhorred species of the Universe. We must rebuild ourselves, even to in-

She threw in more switches, and a prismatic display of colors began to dance in the room to the tune of harmonic effects in the atmosphere, which seemed to be akin to the very music of the spheres...

IN the meantime, Germain's perception raced elsewhere, afar into space, following the lead given him by Lillian's finder before it went dead. He detected a fleeing ship by virtue of its secondary screen, which he could not penetrate, and beyond it lay a gigantic screen, miles in diameter. There was something there of tremendous import, and he was determined to investigate it in the flesh.

Minutes later there arose from the remains of Amnyi Machen's peak a titanic vessel on the prow of which was engraved one word: *Nova*. Inside, in addition to a picked Agarthian crew, were Germain, David and Ingaborg.

And soon in its wake followed another special ship engaged in a separate mission, bearing Borg, Grange and a laboratory of equipment, including their new flying saucer trap.

Beyond them lay the unknown enemy, and out there in the great darkness were the Golden Guardsmen, the Lunar Interstellars, the Agarthians, and the inexperienced Terrestrial fleet. Behind lay Agarthi, commanded now by Mandir. And there was the whole world, waiting for new triumph and a further step toward the Infinite, or for defeat and slavery.

The battle was on...

CHAPTER ELEVEN

SAMMY, you sell newspapers. You ought to have an idea about what's goin' on. What d'ya think?"

High-powered traffic thrummed along Main Street where the car tracks used to be. There were no more streetcars. There were helicopter commuters.

Sammy thought: Thank God there's still hot dogs. I can understand hot dogs. And coffee. They can raise our taxes and

PAVLOVICH'S bushy brows drew together over the hairy wart between them, and his brown eyes narrowed in concentration as he watched Earth grow in his telescreen. From the very latest information given to him by Nicholas, who had gotten it from Izdran, Stephen Germain was in New York, more than twelve thousand miles removed from the Himalayas and hidden Agarthi. Just how long he would be there no one knew, but it was assumed he would be detained at Lake Success for at least a week.

Pavlovich's thick lips spread in a mirthless grin, showing large, uneven teeth. It would only take this space-buggy another twenty-four hours to get within striking range.

Before, he had feared Germain's mutant brain, but now he was heavily equipped with defensive and offensive armament that could give Agarthi, itself, a bad time. And he was not alone.

Each of the ten robots in his crew was the equivalent of a whole squad of geniuses. And they were response-conditioned to answer only to him.

He turned in triumph to look at them. They stood around the walls of the control room, towering above him, watching, waiting—mechanically, electronically, chemically, and *mentally* alive—superman machines of a future age.

"What are you thinking about?" he shouted at them.

In perfect unison, their quiet thoughts returned to him: *Stephen Germain must die, Sir.*

"Good," shouted Pavlovich. He rose to his feet and rubbed his hands. It reminded him of the old days in the training camps during World War Three. These were his new captains. He had always despised lieutenants because a certain second lieutenant had once made life miserable for him when he was a sergeant, so it had doubly fanned his ego to be in a position to berate their superior officers. He liked to think of the robots as captains, since his last commission had been that of a major. Now he paced the deck back and forth in front of them.

"What else did I tell you?" he barked at them.

To call you Sir.

"No. No. I mean—yes, that's right. But what happens after the death of Stephen Germain?" He stopped his pacing and tensed, watching them fiercely, as though he carried a whip in his hand.

We are to help you to overcome Nicholas, Sir.

The Russian's eyes glistened and his heavy brows arched, uncovering the wart. "Why?" he shouted.

Nicholas is no damn good. He's no friend of yours. He's going to pay for his past treatment of you, Sir, and his goddam arrogance.

"And what else?"

Trinha Llih, that little Martian bitch, will be captured, because she's yours and no one else's. Nicholas has no right to her. He just wants you to do the dirty work, Sir. He wants all the gravy, Sir. And you can go to hell, Sir. We are to help you see to it that the only gravy he gets will be the stains, Sir.

It was parrot repetition, but Pavlovich was content. These robots were worth all the generals in the world.

"Take the controls, Number One," he said to one of the robots. "I'm going to get some sleep."

Yes, Sir, replied Number One. Effortlessly, the robot moved into the pilot's seat and scanned the control panels, its synthetic brain absorbing all the factors of flight and its metal fingers making all necessary corrective adjustments in one one hundredth of the time it would have taken the Russian.

Pavlovich did not dare to condition the robots against their original masters, the Nrlani, for fear he would trip over a built-in defense mechanism and get himself betrayed to Izdran before he had even started to carry out his secret plans against them. Germain and Nicholas were merely in his way, and he sought his own kind of revenge with each. But the Nrlani were impossible. They *had* to be destroyed somehow.

He did not know whether or not the telepathic robots had read this intention in his mind and already relayed it to Izdran. If they had, he presumed that Izdran would be too derisive to do anything about it unless he took positive action against the

Nrlani. Out of their own egotism, the Nrlani would give him time, like cats playing with a very small mouse, or perhaps they regarded him as a flea.

Pavlovich bared his teeth and glared at his robots. "I'll show the sonsofbitches," he growled.

Thus Pavlovich and his invisible ship, equipped with weapons, which were new even to age-old Agarthi, ancient colony of the Elder Race. A little megalomaniac on a rampage. A chimpanzee on a holiday—in an atom bomb arsenal. Below him lay the naked Earth...

* * *

AT Lake Success, the newly reinstated United Nations, operating under their popularized but unofficial name of Terrestrial Government, were engaged in the formal business of establishing the Terrestrial Government officially. But first there was the dubious matter of the "World Charter," which Agarthi had proposed. Russian delegate Gormski, soon to be Soviet Councilman for T.G., concluded his two-hour filibuster with unbridled accusations.

"Mr. Germain, who represents a supposed sovereign state called Agarthi, has not even any legal right to sit with us in council inasmuch as Agarthi has never been formally recognized by the established governments of the world. Yet he has the temerity, nay, the affrontery, to assume the position of benevolent overlord, and he seeks to cram down our throats a document, which he calmly asserts *must* be the charter and constitution of our Terrestrial Government."

Applause, at this point, from twenty-seven Eurasian delegates. The Western Hemisphere bloc of delegates either looked at each other in dismay or compared notes. Triumphantly, Gormski continued.

"He and his Agarthian accomplices in this insane and preposterous hoax are very kind to us—in that they have established in the main body of this document a truly democratic and self-determined system of world government—of the people, by the people, and for the people. But the Emergency Clause, gentlemen... I ask you to examine *that*. Are we to be besieged by the lunatic ravings of a hoaxter, or are we to engage in the sober activity of rehabilitating a world whose shambles are the direct *result* of meddling by these charlatans and turbaned stargazers of Agarthi?"

Fifteen Eastern bloc delegates got to their feet and cheered, while the Council's Australian chairman banged his gavel for order. Gormski dramatically poured himself a drink of water and made a Hitlerian gesture with his hand, for silence.

"The Emergency Clause of this idiotic document states, and I quote: 'In the event of further extra-terrestrial aggression, a state of Universal Emergency will be recognized. In this case, Agarthi will acquire all emergency powers of government, which are delineated under Section II-b of this Emergency Clause.'

"Those emergency powers, gentlemen, constitute sheer dictatorship. We are to manufacture munitions and armaments to Agarthian specifications, provide the Agarthians with all the manpower, industrial facilities and economic assistance that may be required, in their own vaunted opinion, to be necessary."

Former U.S. Senator Balfour, now a U.N. delegate, could not resist breaking the rules of order. "The Soviet delegate is begging many questions," he said to his microphone, in Esperanto, which was now the official U.N. language. "Agarthi has given us a gift of freedom from extra-terrestrial aggression. We are receiving the unquestionable benefits of interstellar science, we are beginning even to adapt the titanic forces of Universal Power to our needs, and we are even now being assisted in building this planet's first space armada. Surely the very spectacular and impressive events of the past five years—"

"I have not finished," shouted Gormski, appealing to the chairman, who regretfully informed Mr. Balfour that he was out of order. And Gormski continued, "Many of you wish to adhere to blind faith in relation to the events of the past five years. But this is *too* blind. It is not faith, but gullibility built upon a false premise. We are told that we have been saved from slavery at the hands of long hidden alien intelligences from the stars. We have seen cities vanish in the supposed struggle, which went on mainly above our heads. We have seen the Agarthian space ships, and we are building space ships of our own with the help of Agarthian technicians. All that this means is that the Agarthians are smart people and that Mr. Germain is, as proved further by reputable physicians and psychologists, a surgical mutant and therefore a super-genius. But it does *not* prove that he has not perpetrated on us a colossal hoax in order to deceive us and cause our more gullible associates to believe that it would be favorable to accept his terms. Then, to exert his emergency powers over us, he would have only to repeat his brutal and destructive hoax at the expense of a few more defenseless cities, and the Emergency Clause would be invoked.

"No, gentlemen, my government, for one, refuses to accept this charter. If Mr. Germain wishes to offer us his services, that is well and good. But we reject his right to dominate us. This is supposed to be a sovereign world now, so we reserve the right to govern ourselves, *even* in the emergencies. Is that simple enough for you, Mr. Balfour?"

The U.S. delegate glanced at Stephen Germain. "I prefer to give the floor to the 'defendant,'" he said, with unruffled sarcasm directed at Gormski. And again the chairman banged for order, while he nodded to Germain...

STEPHEN Germain's Indian physiognomy remained as inscrutable as ever as all eyes turned upon him. Under dark, forward-jutting brows, his shiny black eyes gazed penetratingly at Gormski. Although he was of American Indian extraction, the turban he wore to conceal his abnormal cranium gave him an East Indian appearance, plus an aura of the mystic.

"My position is unalterable," he said, in a calm but vibrantly authoritative tone. "Just as a citizen of any government may relinquish his citizenship in favor of another nationality, I have, of necessity, relinquished even terrestrial citizenship. Mr. Kent here is your Agarthian delegate. I do not sit here in council with you. I am merely an observer. I am the terrestrial deputy of the Elder People, who saved us all from destruction. As their representative I am their Star Warden in charge of this entire Solar System. I speak to you with the authority of a vastly superior race of benevolent beings, and the government of this planet is only one of my present responsibilities. My orders are to help you to govern yourselves, but at the same time to guide you in the fundamental principle of civilization throughout the universe. That principle embodies Man's total *raison d'etre*. It is development from Finite to Infinite—toward godliness, to put it in a plainer sense. The road to Infinite is cooperation and constructiveness. Internal wars and nationalism will not be tolerated. In the event of danger from malignant interstellar forces, I am to exert my powers to defend you, while at the same time helping you to defend yourselves and thus enable you to occupy your rightful place in total civilization.

"For these reasons you must accept the charter. Is that plain enough for you, Mr. Gormski?"

"An ultimatum!" shouted Gormski, jumping to his feet. "Mr. Germain defies the world."

Many delegates raised their voices above the gavel in support of Gormski, but Germain quickly dominated the assembly. He arose to deliver his next words, his eyes penetrating each one who listened to him.

"You have now emerged from the cocoon of your own atmosphere. Terrestrial Man is a new metamorphosis taking wing in the limitless oceans of outer space. This is a form of birth, gentlemen, and I assure you that the mortality rate in such cases is high.

"You have become aware of *contact*. Contact, that is, with interstellar forces. Just as you have been the property of interstellar peoples for ages without knowing it, you can be again. But let me make this point clear to you. You are *not* the property of the Elder People. Rather, you are their wards until you come of age. The dangers, let me remind you, are far from being behind you. They lie ahead. You are not expected to acquire overnight an adequate perspective of the incomprehensible. You are merely expected to accept protection and guidance until you have progressed sufficiently to carry on independently yet in cooperation with universal civilization."

At that moment, a fanatic who had represented himself as a Soviet news reporter suddenly jumped from the Press box and aimed an automatic at Germain. Guards shouted and started running, women reporters screamed, and television cameramen switched gleefully to telephoto lenses.

"Down with the tyrant!" shouted the assassin.

But that was as far as he got. In the next instant he became as rigid as a statue, totally incapacitated. Security guards carried him away.

Gormski was on his feet again, shouting extemporaneously while pointing dramatically at Germain.

"That man is a monster," he cried out. "You see now how invulnerable he is. He paralyzed his would-be assassin. He could have killed him. He could kill us all, from where he is sitting, with no other weapon than that Frankenstein brain of his. I ask you, in all reasonableness, fellow humans, before Heaven—could not such a man hypnotize us all into believing what he says?—by conjuring up the mere vision of alien space ships and filling our minds with fear, forcing the susceptible ones to succumb and hysterically give him all the power over us that he desires? I declare that here before you is the danger and the aggression. Throw him out. Destroy him."

There was a rising hubbub, and many were on their feet shouting at each other. Some reporters dashed out, others stayed on, greedily, while some spectators merely fled. But soon again Germain's even, authoritative voice dominated the loudspeakers.

"That was an insidious plot, Mr. Gormski, designed to prove your point. I would suggest you payoff your collaborator and get the devil out of here yourself. This is an assembly for statesmen, not gangsters."

The Australian chairman banged his gavel. "This confusion

calls for adjournment," he said.

"Yes," agreed Gormski. "And I propose that the first subject on our next agenda shall be the question of the legality of Mr. Germain's presence here, and of Mr. Kent's, as well as of Agarthi's chair in this council and of the proposed Agarthian charter. Until these questions are settled we cannot discuss anything."

There was an immediate response in favor of this motion, although the American and British delegates remained non-committal.

Within both Germain's and Kent's crania resided sealed instruments the size of a pea. Originally, they had been the size of a basketball, but thanks to Dr. Borg's rediscovery of the older method of densification they had been reduced to a size that had enabled him to install about a dozen of them in the heads of Agarthi's leaders. These were micro-telaugs over which they received augmented telepathic messages or transmitted the same, at will. Also, the micro-telaug was the relayer of power transmitted from Agarthian laboratories with which any attacker could be paralyzed.

It was Kent who had paralyzed the fanatic, although Germain could have killed him, as Gormski had claimed, with no other weapon than his own brain. When the assassin had leaped from the Press box, Germain was occupied with a message from Agarthi. Kent received it, too. Borg and Mandir, an Agarthian Elder, communicated with them saying that certain experiments with sub-matter had produced a second order type of energy, and certain results of this discovery had led them to suspect the presence of alien space ships within the orbit of the moon. If their deductions were valid, they were faced with a very advanced foe who could never be detected by the giant network of space-radar screens that had recently been erected by the principal nations of the world. Could Germain use his ESP to see what he could pick up? Germain would, at his first opportunity to concentrate, which would be back at his hotel.

As a squad of reporters approached Germain, Kent asked

him, "You going to let them know?"

"No," he answered. "Not until we get the situation in hand. The nations have such a high opinion of their abilities now that they'd dash out in their new space buggies and pull a Don Quixote on us. Because that's what it would be, a toothpick against windmills. They're babes in the woods, and those who wouldn't be getting themselves killed and throwing every defense we've given them down the drain would be succumbing to mass hysteria. So keep it under your hat."

"Mr. Germain," cried the New York Times reporter, an elderly man with horn-rimmed glasses and wearing cigars instead of a handkerchief. "About that assassination attempt—do you actually suspect Gormski?"

"Or, if you don't think it's just another Russian veto with a kick," said the Los Angeles Times, a younger man with short-cropped sandy hair, "would the motive be political or have some connection with economic pressure groups who have been locked out of the old cartel pastures by reason of your influence in Terrestrial Government?"

Germain paused on his way to the exit with Kent. His keen, dark eyes, as they looked over the trailing crowd of reporters, did not even blink at the flash bulbs of the photographers. "It is difficult for you to remember," he said, "that I am capable of reading such minds as Gormski's like a book, as well as your own. It all follows an old, old pattern, and yet everyone fails to realize that history is no longer repeating itself. There is no precedent for *Now*. The old perspectives are a surface scum. It's not the details but the fundamentals you'll have to grasp before you will be able to even survive in your new environment."

"I COULD strangle that Gormski with my one good hand," Kent told Germain on their way back to the hotel. He glared ruefully at his withered left arm, caused by a death ray one night in Santa Cruz, Bolivia, during World War Three. Pavlovich had done that—Pavlovich who had since died out among the asteroids along with his master, Nicholas I. Since then there had been greater masters to subdue. Interstellar masters. But thanks to the Elder Race, the King of the World, and Germain's surgical mutation, they had survived every campaign—even that hellish space battle out by Eros, which had resulted in that planetoid's complete liquidation.

Germain smiled at his old battle buddy. "Don't worry about Gormski," he said, as their U.S. Government furnished limousine slid through the evening traffic. "He is a mere straw in *this* gathering storm. The main worry is public apathy. The transition from planetary to interstellar status, even though we have not yet made an interplanetary flight, has been too abrupt. Of necessity, the science that Earth would not ordinarily come to know in two or three thousand years has been brought to light, and the people just don't comprehend the significance of their new position. They merely think the promised Millennium is at hand, that Cornucopia has at last turned the corner. They relax when they should be sharpening their wits. But there's more to it than that. I sense a really great danger—"

"You mean those space ships might actually be out there?"

Germain looked at Kent, pensively. "I mean a danger much greater than mere alien space armadas. The cybernetics lab at Agarthi has been working on some interesting statistics connected with the decadence of present-day civilization. I mean—stuff like political corruption, graft, embezzlement, juvenile delinquency, the collapse of moral standards, lower church attendance, the increase of divorces, murders, suicides, infanticides, patricides, perversion, narcotics addiction, et cetera. Do you know what the computers tell us?"

"I know. Decline and fall of the Romans all over again. This is the old cycle again, eh?"

"No. You're wrong. The computers show that the rapid increase of these phenomena cannot be correlated with the maximum probability curves. That means—"

Kent's pipe dropped from his mouth and he caught it in his hands. "Oh, no. Not that again. Not another extraneous influence?"

"I'm very much afraid so," said Germain.

"But good God, we've cleansed the Earth. The old underground interstellar influences were rooted out—even Satanus, himself. What else could—"

"Kent, there is another force somewhere, powerful and dangerous because of its very subtlety, which is attempting to undermine humanity *from the inside*. Suppose—" The limousine stopped in front of their hotel.

"Suppose what?"

"Never mind. It's a long story."

The two men got out and a reluctant doorman nodded recognition. He had already seen the evening headlines concerning the affair at Lake Success. Gormski had succeeded in sowing the dragon seeds of suspicion in the riotous field of world opinion...

THAT night, Germain shut himself up in the bedroom while Kent sat quietly in a chair and read the evening papers. He was suddenly disinterested in the feature news concerning the U.N. meeting, in spite of such glaring 144-point headlines as: GERMAIN HURLS ULTIMATUM!—and: AGARTHI CHARTER ILLEGAL: GORMSKI.

After Germain's remarks in the car, Kent became vividly aware of a much greater crisis hidden between the lines of every common article and advertisement in the paper. He thought: *There's nothing so hidden but the obvious.*

As he read, he could almost hear the thunder of walls crumbling to destruction—the walls of civilization:

Loan Gifts Bared by Air Force Aide—Doctor Kidnapped For Dope—Thrill Party Sex Show Kills Girl Fourteen.

It was not all in the U.S.A. Kent was something of a polyglot and was in the habit of balancing his perspectives with news from abroad. He saw that Europe had its own quota of corruption, murder, divorces and general dereliction. There was an advertisement in a French newspaper guaranteeing that the strip tease girls of a certain burlesque show would take off everything. Guaranteed nakedness.

What topped it off and ruined his appetite for supper was an article concerning a New York suburb, captioned: *Abandoned Church Site to be Improved.*

He read that the half-finished church, because of insufficient community funds, was being cleared away for a large dancing casino and bowling alley, the money for which had been raised through a community owned amusement corporation.

Nothing wrong with dancing and bowling, but it was a gross distortion of relative values to say the abandoned church site was being *improved.*

He flicked on the television set. A loan shark huckster was giving a commercial.

"Why worry about paying the other guy until *you* have been taken care of first?" bawled the huckster, pointing an accusing finger at Kent. "*You're* the guy who does the work to earn *your* money. Be willing to pay *yourself* off before anybody else and I'll show you how you can not only *keep up* with the Joneses... Brother, you can get *way ahead* of them."

Kent turned it off. He felt like he needed a stiff drink. But there was one consolation. Germain had proof that it was an outside influence. It was not spontaneous on the part of the people, themselves.

He clenched his good fist. "Who the hell—" he started to growl.

Suddenly, Germain opened the bedroom door and came out. His face was inscrutable, as usual, but Kent could read him by his attitude. It was very tense. His extra sensory perception had discovered something.

"What did you get?" he asked.

"The next U.N. session won't take up until next Monday, will it?"

"No, but—"

"That gives us four days. Let's go to Agarthi."

"It's a good thing we brought our own transportation," said

Kent, remembering their much photographed space commuter out at Idle Wilde.

"This is that time of great danger of which the King of the World warned me before he rejoined the Elder Race. But he also said—"

"Yes?"

"He also said that when the time comes I would discover powers that I did not know I possessed." Germain looked at Kent intently. "May God help me to find those powers soon."

This unexpected change of plans at least served to confuse Pavlovich. Twelve hours later, when in position to attack, he found that his quarry had left New York, and that he had returned to Agarthi…

CHAPTER SEVEN

AGARTHI City had been built in the heart of Amnyi Machen, a towering peak that rivaled Everest. It had been built fifty millenniums before by the Elder Race.

Lillian Germain, in spite of the fourteen thousand foot altitude of the cavern city, was warm and comfortable in her sunsuit as she stood that day in her garden and looked out over the flowered walls across the tops of low, marble white buildings and at the distant palace where the King of the World had once ruled for two thousand years of time.

A warm glow of thankfulness suffused her being as she looked up at the glowing ball of energy that the ancient interstellar founders had hung there to produce non-radioactive sunlight. In Agarthi, life was prolonged, and in her present state of happiness she never wanted it to end. T he dangers were past, she told herself, and the future stretched boundlessly before her in breathtaking, rosy vistas.

She was waiting for her husband to join her. Now that Agarthi had relinquished Earth Government into the hands of Terra's ordinary citizens, Stephen's terrible responsibility would be diminished.

At this thought she had to laugh. Diminished? That which was left as his responsibility still entailed the whole future of a solar system. Now he would be launching on a program to establish an interplanetary government. She suddenly resented the vastness of this perspective, because recently she had become aware of another future responsibility, which was very small and personal, but which was as important as all the solar systems in the universe.

She was waiting to tell her husband the well-known precious little secret that she was going to—

"Hello, beautiful!"

Before she could turn voluntarily, she was in his arms, and she was necessarily speechless for a full quarter minute by reason of the unhusbandlike kiss he planted on her lips.

"Sorry I've been neglecting you for the past ten thousand years," said Germain, laughing at her confusion. "It seems I've been busy at the 'office,' darling."

"I'm glad the U.N. gave you a breather till next Monday," she said, "even if it was caused by that old stinker of a Gormski. Did Michael come with you?" She had always referred to their mutual friend, Kent, by his first name.

For a moment, Germain had a keen but distant look in his eyes. "He'll be here. I had to send him on a special mission."

Lillian looked deep into her husband's black, far-seeing eyes, still trying to comprehend the magnitude of the mutant brain that lay behind them, the brain on which the distant Elder Race confidently depended—because as a parting gift they had refined Borg's surgery, adding a few improvements of their own. In the knowledge of his power she found comfort and protection, and at the same time she was delighted, as only a woman can be, in the fact that he was in every other way a normal, well-balanced human being and the intimate companion of her life.

"You can't fool me," she told him. "You're worried about something. What is it?"

Germain's face became a stony mask. "Just worries one

must expect in my position. It's the old financial situation," he lied. "Now that we are functioning in connection with the outside world our economy must be balanced. To have money, we need a source of credit-like natural resources. Agarthi hasn't any natural resources."

"What about Steve Rockner's gold mine in the Gobi? You've been working that. Agarthi now has the rights."

"Chicken feed. So is the fifty million a year contract with the United Nations to hand out interstellar science to terrestrial governments. We need other resources, Lil. If it weren't for our secret allies, the Lunar Interstellars, and Janice's treasure—"

All this was connected with previous adventures. A lost colony of benevolent interstellar people had taken refuge inside the moon, ages before, when they learned that Earth was the property of long established malignant interstellar forces. These hidden Lunar allies had suddenly taken a hand in Agarthi's struggles to free the Earth of its secret oppressors. Also, a certain incredible treasure, believed by some to be the legendary treasure of the Nibelungs, had been uncovered in the hiding place of the deposed controllers of Earth and had been given into the hands of the Lunar Interstellars for safe keeping. Agarthi dipped into this on infrequent occasions, but it was difficult to market in the outer world the jewelry of ancient supermen manufactured on some planet of an alien solar system millennia before the dawn of modern terrestrial history— especially considering that it had been designed for a race of giants.

"How would you like to go on a little vacation trip?" Germain asked Lillian, suddenly.

"Where to, my love?" she said, gaily.

"Oh, somewhere local. Say Jupiter or Saturn."

"What?" Her blue-green eyes widened under arched brows.

"Sure. I'm not kidding you, Lil. I'm going to set up a solar government I've got to make some inspection tours. Mars comes first, of course, but there may be danger there, so we'll let the Golden Guardsmen comb that area for the time being. In the meantime, I want to snoop around farther afield. Care to come along?"

"Oh Stephen, I wish you didn't have so many responsibilities," she exclaimed. "Even with your capacities it's such a burden to carry."

"Wait a minute," he laughed. "You forget I have some able assistants. There are all the thousands of Agarthians, headed by Mandir, who are working out the proposed mechanics of the whole Solar Government. Kent is my go-between and Agarthi's representative at the United Nations. Borg and Grange are working on universal industrialization and applications of Universal Power, as well as systems of defense against any possible raids by interstellars. And Rocky is going great guns with the Golden Guardsmen, aided by Stierman, Turner and Brion. What else could I ask for?"

"I know, but——"

"No buts about it," he interrupted. "We're going on that cruise."

"How long would we be gone?"

"Five months, maybe eight or nine. Who knows? We may find something interesting."

"As interesting as a junior mutant?" she asked.

Germain's facial expression, or general lack of it, was in keeping with his Indian physiognomy. His Sioux Indian blood was predominant when it came to showing visibly anything he felt deeply. But in that moment his lower lip quivered.

"What do you mean?" he asked.

"What do you think I mean, dummy? In a few months I don't think I'd better be skylarking around Jupiter."

Germain's dark brows went up. "Lil!" he cried. "You don't mean——"

She laughed and rumpled his hair. "You males are all alike. You all go into the same routine. *Of course* I mean it. We're going to have a blessed event."

Sudden joy changed to dark concern. Germain took her by both arms. "Are you all right?" he asked.

Again she laughed at him. "That's another part of the old line," she teased. "Oh Stephen, you're not at all different from any other man." Then, very quietly, she came into his arms and said, "I'm glad of *that.*"

Germain looked at her expressionlessly. He was weighing her last remark, remembering that she had once feared his mutant brain. Now, thank God, he thought he was no longer a mental monstrosity to her.

"Stephen," she suddenly exclaimed, while her complexion turned a delicate pink. Her eyes widened and her lips parted.

"What is it, Lil?"

For answer, she snuggled very close, gratefully. "You're so kind," she said. "So thoughtful."

"What did I do?"

"You knew all the time you were going to be a daddy and you kept quiet about it so that I'd have the pleasure of telling you."

He knew what she meant. His extra-sensory perception had enabled him only last month to detect a small kidney stone in Dr. Borg, which was dissolved by proper treatment. Yes, he could have known about the baby...

He caught her chin and lifted her face until she looked into his eyes. "I could have known, Lil. But—long ago I decided many things about this abnormality of mine. One of those things was that I had to recognize you as a woman as well as my wife, and that as such you are entitled to—"

She beamed at him, appreciatively. "So you trained yourself to leave me some secrets of my own," she concluded for him. "I told you you were considerate."

"But now I'm going to look into you—into that little head of yours. I see your micro-telaug is still secure." Lillian had one, as did Janice Maine, Steve Rockner, Michael Kent and a handful of other Agarthians. "Is it working all right?"

By way of reply, she concentrated confidently, hurling at him a paralysis beam that would have incapacitated a dozen ordinary men. He closed his eyes for a moment, then he smiled in a reassured sort of way and took her chin again in his hands.

"Just be on the alert, darling. If anything happened to you—"

"Stephen, you don't have some secret information, do you?" She swiftly utilized another feature of the micro-telaug and probed his mind, knowing full well, however, that he could wall off his thoughts at will. Just before he did shut her out, she caught a shadowy glimpse of physically invisible space ships manned by— She could not quite make it out, but whatever manned the ships was not human.

"What are they?" she gasped. "And *where* are they?"

"We've just detected them close by in outer space, about fifty thousand miles," he confessed. "Guess you might as well know as Janice or Rocky would spring it on you sooner or later. They're very advanced aliens, Lil. I tried to reach them with ESP, but they have no minds, at least not what you'd think."

"No minds?"

"They're robots."

"Oh Stephen. You must be mistaken."

"No, Lil, although whether or not they are the instruments of living intelligences remains to be seen."

She stamped her foot and clenched her fists, then bit her lip and turned away from him. He pulled her around to him and saw tears flooding into her eyes.

"Does it have to go on forever?" she pleaded. "The Universe must have been created, for a higher purpose than for this carnivorous cycle of dog eat dog! When will there ever be such a thing as peace and security? When life was simple, the stars were impossibly remote, Stephen. Now that the stars seem to be within our grasp at last, life's simplicity has receded into astronomical remoteness. I *hate* this."

"Lil, honey, I've taught you the Fundamental Law. Creation depends upon the giant swing of the pendulum between construction and destruction. It's the struggle between the extremes that counts. That's what makes existence. Perfection is the end of existence. By that I mean the *death* of existence.

There must be evil to overcome. In that struggle the victor rises to higher stages of development, ad infinitum. We can only hope that it will continue to be our kind that ascends that ever expanding spiral."

She relaxed slightly but did not smile. She kissed him and said, "I am beginning to see why the proposed vacation trip. Actually, you wanted me out of harm's way if Terra is going to be attacked, and at the same time you want to be out behind the enemy so as to find a soft spot and perhaps direct the Golden Guardsmen at the same time. And maybe be in a position to make a run for it to contact the Elder Race again if you need their help."

"I see my mind gets more undressed than yours," Germain grinned. Then the grin faded abruptly and he added, "But this time there'll be no running to the Elder Race. We're on our own."

CHAPTER EIGHT

JANICE Maine was also very much contented with her lot in Agarthi. Formerly a highly trained scientist and spy working against Agarthi, her love for big Steve Rockner had led her on a devious trail back to it, and she had become its loyal ally, as well as Rocky's wife.

She looked about her, drinking in all the peace and pleasure that her senses could bring her in the quiet swimming pool enclosure. The vine-clad, circular wall enclosed the ancient pool, on the surface of which lily pads glistened in stationary repose, like green silk, amongst the pinkish white splashes of color provided by the lilies, themselves. Grass grew between rocks along the water's edge, and in some places blue columbines and gorgeous bird-of-paradise flowers tried to dip their faces in the water. Above, great trees sprayed their leafy branches across the cavern's "sky." Birds imported from many lands throve in Agarthi's scientifically balanced climate, and Janice had accustomed herself to the sight of ruby-throated hummingbirds vying for attention together with keeled toucans and king birds of paradise. Even as she looked above her now she saw two java sparrows, which she could call by name and they would come to her, if she willed it, to be fed tidbits from her hands.

She lay on a bench of imperishable metal, supported by cushions, her coppery hair drying from her recent swim. And she smiled, pensively.

She was simultaneously thankful for and amused at her present unsophisticated reactions whereas a short time ago she had approached this place with the cold, steely mind of an automaton, an international spy for the enemies of Agarthi. But, as in the case of Dr. Borg, who had previously served the Russian dictator, Nicholas, Agarthi had won, and her whole life was dedicated to its purposes—and to Rocky.

As she lay daydreaming on the bench she was unaware of an unusual intruder. It was a two-man space ship, such as were used by Agarthians or the Golden Guardsmen as commuter vessels between their interplanetary dreadnaughts.

But this particular vessel had the peculiarity of only being one foot in length…

It landed on the moss-grown stones near the pool's edge, within ten feet of her. A miniature door opened, and a tiny figure clad in a space suit emerged. Its head was enclosed in a transparent metal globe on top of which were several diminutive electronic devices. Quickly, the Lilliputian figure walked toward Janice.

Janice stirred, turned on her side, and looked dreamily toward the pool, thus bringing the intruder and his ship directly into her line of vision. But in the same instant the figure and the ship vanished. They were both completely invisible.

Then, suddenly, a purplish globe of light began to grow beside Janice, and she sprang to her feet. In an instant her micro-telaug was in action, hurling a paralysis beam at the globe of light. But to no avail. It kept on growing.

And then a mental voice, transmitted also by micro-telaug, reached her mind:

Boy, what a boon to suppressed husbands these gadgets are. No more sneaking in the back way, shoes in hand, no kicking over milkbottles in the dark. You come in the front door, invisible or otherwise, but impervious to rolling pins, cusswords and poisonous thoughts. All you say is: Darling!—take me as I am! And if you really do have to spend a night in the doghouse, you can shrink down to a size where you can get into the darned thing without shoving Fido out into the cold. With these things marriage becomes a tolerable institution for trapped husbands.

Janice bit her lip, half angry at herself for being fooled, half angry at the intruder for his deception. "Rocky," she exclaimed. "If you do that again I'll paralyze you for a month. I'll short-circuit your carrier beam and skin you alive."

The purplish light vanished, and Steve Rockner, in fun space operation uniform of the Golden Guardsmen, stood before her grinning exultantly. He unfastened his globular helmet and placed it on the ground.

"Oh you big ape," Janice exclaimed. She came willingly into his arms.

After a long, satisfying moment, she stood back to look at him. "What are you in uniform for? Are you that close to action?"

"Pretty close," he said, brushing back the flaming mop of his red hair. "You coming with me or are you joining Germain and Lillian?"

A troubled shadow passed over her face. "I was kidding you about the action," she said. "For a moment I had forgotten about the alert warning. Do you really think anybody would dare invade Terra now, with our new defenses?"

Rocky shrugged. "We're still babes in the woods," he said. "We're plenty advanced, technologically, but we lack experience. They can have one thing we haven't and we're in for trouble."

At that precise moment, an alarm was transmitted to them from Agarthi's central laboratories, over the VHF carriers that activated their micro-telaugs.

Council call. This is an emergency. Assemble immediately.

Janice looked at Rocky, tensely alert. But engraved in her

mind in that moment was the image of the pool enclosure where they were. Was this perfect peace to be shattered by a war of the worlds?

Rocky squinted his brown eyes, as though listening for more. In his mind was a vision of the Golden Guardsmen fleet, superman battleships packed with Elder Race weapons and Universal Power, each one of them a quarter mile colossus of destruction. Then he looked at Janice, at once grim and jubilant.

"Maybe this is it," he exclaimed. "Let's go!"

He reached down, replaced his helmet, and drew Janice to him. They were both engulfed in the purplish rays of the relative densifier, and in a moment two diminutive figures raced toward the tiny flier. When they had entered it and closed the door, it took off with a seeming instantaneity that startled a raucous cry out of the birds in the trees...

THE Chamber of Agarthian Elders looked very much like a serrate chamber. A central proscenium with a speaker's rostrum, and a superior rostrum above made of white onyx, two dozen or more plush seats for the Elders arranged in a half moon below, and another half moon section of seats for an audience of neophytes who had not yet become Elders of the Council. Around the walls were mezzanines for the listening Agarthian citizenry.

Stephen Germain sat in a great chair behind the white onyx rostrum. In such a position he automatically represented its former occupant, who had used it for two millenniums of time. Now Germain was the Star Warden of the solar system.

In the inferior chair, behind the second rostrum below, sat thousand year old Mandir, chief of Agarthian Elders. Before him, in the Elders' section, sat the true Agarthian Elders whose average age topped four hundred years.

In the neophyte section sat younger Agarthians in their neophyte robes emblazoned on the back with the famous Sword of Agarthi. Among them sat Earthmen from the outside world who had been admitted to the ranks of the neophytes and had passed the psychic tests and conditionings connected with the Journey through Seven Towers—a mental experience that could overwhelm anyone in the lower I.Q.s but which left the surviving students strengthened by a brand new perspective of all history, philosophy, religion and science, the four walls forming the room in which Man lives. The Journey of Seven Towers had made those walls transparent to the successful neophytes, giving them vistas of the Infinite.

There was Steve Rockner, his space suit removed, revealing the golden uniform of the Guardsmen and his Fleet Admiral's insignia. Beside him sat Janice Maine, her sunsuit concealed by the pastel-shaded street robe common to Agarthian women. Next to her was Lillian Germain, her raven black hair contrasting strikingly with Janice's coppery coiffure. And there was statuesque, ivory-skinned Ingaborg with her nordic blue eyes and white-golden braids, sitting beside David of Ravenoe, also blond and blue-eyed, a chivalric atavism, the cut of his long hair, the set of his jaw and the square of his massive chest reminiscent of the days of King Arthur and the Round Table.

Back of Rockner were the commanding officers of the Golden Guardsmen, among them such outlanders as Greg "Baby Face" Stierman, formerly the Chief of the U.S. FBI, his previous aide, Sam Turner, and former U.S. Lieutenant Colonel George Henry Brion of the O.S.S. Beside them sat the humped, wizened little Russian scientist, Dr. Julius Borg, inventor of Energy Serum, discoverer of relative densification, and the creator of the new Stephen Germain. Beside him was his new found intellectual companion and colleague in superscience, "Little Willy," alias James William Grange, D.S., Ph.D., former technical aide to the O.S.S.

Germain addressed all of them without preamble:

"You have been called together here in emergency session because we are in imminent danger of attack by a very advanced alien force. I will call on certain members of this audience to report their findings. Dr. Borg, will you please report?"

Borg rose laboriously to his feet, a shrunken man with a

large, grizzled head, a pockmarked face and a clay-like complexion. Iron-gray hair, short-clipped, stuck out on his head like the bristles of a brush. Whenever he tried to smile, as he did now, it resulted in a toothy snarl, which was recognized only by those who knew him for what it really was. But his looks did not matter nearly as much as his colossal intellect. His words carried great weight with the Agarthians.

"With the aid of Mr. Germain's extra-sensory perception," he said, "and with the help of certain new apparatus developed by Dr. Grange and myself, which produces a second order type of radiant energy, we have detected the enemy. Also, I must give credit to our friends and allies, the Lunar Interstellars, who have detected signs of the enemy simultaneously with us.

"The invasion force consists of large, extremely fast ships presently stationed some fifty thousand miles out in space. We have counted a hundred of them, although to radar they are invisible."

This statement caused a slight flurry of excitement among the outlanders and the Agarthian neophytes, but the Elders remained calm. All of them were weighing against this announcement the fact that the Agarthian old line fleet consisted of only twenty-five space battleships, that the Golden Guardsmen had a hundred ships, and that "Terrestrial Government" was building about fifty more, of inferior armament. Besides that, there were about a hundred and sixty interstellar vessels belonging to the Lunar Interstellars. Beyond that—nothing, except Universal Power, which was in its infancy. This was perhaps a margin of safety, but its extent depended on the nature of the enemy.

Then Borg hit them hard. "These alien ships are manned by robots," he said. Before a rising tide of startled comments could engulf him, he continued, "The robots appear to be guided by an elusive intelligence that may in some way be connected with the so-called flying saucers."

Young David of Ravenoe, who was better in battle than in a council chamber, stood up to raise an objection. In his new found affection for Ingaborg he had been mentally star gathering and was not up to date with recent developments.

"That's inconceivable," he said. "What can we possibly know about the flying saucers?"

"Plenty," said Borg, snarling affably at his questioner. "Perhaps my colleague, Dr. Grange, could enlighten you. It is extremely *apropos* of the subject under discussion."

While David sat down, to get his arm pinched by Ingaborg in rebuke for his irrepressibility, the slim, dapper figure of "Little Willy" Grange rose to take the floor. He stroked one side of his thin nose, characteristically, and began.

"You have all become acquainted with studies in sub-nuclear physics," he said. "This branch of science has investigated the nature of a type of sub-matter composed of, not protons and electrons, but *protinos* and *electrinos*, some eighteen hundred times smaller than their equivalents in gross matter. The hypothesis that this second order of matter might constitute the substance of the so-called ether and be the carrier medium or magnetic energy as well as other wave phenomena has now developed into strongly substantiated theory. In fact, sub-matter may be the actual substance of *the next plane of existence*." Grange smiled at the reaction of his audience, but went on. "We're getting into deep water, but we've got to, because the flying saucers are either the denizens of the sub-material world or they are a hybrid substance caught halfway between the key, you might say, to the world of secondary phenomena. Sometimes they are invisible, and at other times they appear like an ectoplasmic materialization, reflecting primary orders of waves such as light like so many ephemeral bubbles.

"They have long been a mystery, but our investigations have revealed that they are attracted to any source of atomic energy, as though hard radiation in gross matter accompanied secondary type releases of energy upon which they seem to feed. Or at least they are attracted, for some reason. They also have something to do with magnetic forces and have been observed to become confused when confronted with various magnetic fault zones, which exist on this planet.

"So Dr. Borg and I devised a trap. I won't go into detail except to say that it required an atomic pile and a newly developed, and I might add quite dangerous type, of intermittently cross-magnetizing cyclotron, together with certain apparatus connected directly with secondary wave phenomena. To make a long story short, we did trap a flying saucer, just three days ago, and managed to hold it imprisoned long enough to make satisfactory observations. What we found corroborates Mr. Germain's contentions, that the discs are living, sentient creatures."

The hubbub that ensued brought dozens of people to their feet, particularly the Agarthians in the galleries. But the ensuing discussions brought out the fact that the advent of the aliens in outer space had brought an unprecedented occurrence of flying saucer phenomena in earthly skies. Germain announced that he had detected a high order of mentality in the discs, and that he had sensed in some way he could not describe in words that movements of the alien fleet manned by robots bore a positive relationship with movements of the flying discs. He said that it was of prime importance to continue an investigation into their nature.

Old Mandir reported on strange occurrences in Europe, which led him to believe that some elements of the enemy had already infiltrated into terrestrial civilization. There had been significant disappearances of important prisoners of the previous war, including Dr. Gerhardt Eidelmann, who had adapted captured Elder Race equipment to the purposes of the forces opposing Agarthi. His stature as a research physicist was practically equal to that of Borg's. A mysterious force was beginning to stir in the world, and Agarthi prepared its battle armor.

Plans were outlined as the day wore on. Elder Race machinery was to be set up throughout the world in hopes of ferreting out the nefarious influences they feared. War ray batteries in strategic zones were being converted as rapidly as possible to the use of Universal Power, in order to cover major cities with what they hoped would be impenetrable defenses even against interstellar hordes. Space fleets were to be converted to faster drive, also using Universal Power.

Then came Rocky's assignment.

"Admiral Rockner," said Germain, "you will assume active battle command of the Golden Guardsman fleet immediately. You will enter space at a point opposite to the enemy position and pursue a course around them, reaching Mars in such a way as to avoid all possible contact with the unknown fleet. This is not sparing you the possibility of a major engagement, inasmuch as I have been warned in the past by the Elder Race that this present trouble would someday originate in the area of Mars, and therefore it may be assumed that your probing of the Martian defenses to discover the nature of the enemy's home base may require your heavy armaments more than they will be required in this area. You are to use your own judgment in regard to attack, within limits. If you are not able to determine adequately the nature of the enemy and his powers to retaliate, you are to report to us through Mandir and await further instructions."

Rocky turned to Janice, grinning from ear to ear. He had always loved a good fight, not because he was belligerent but more or less on a sportsmanship basis. It was the challenge to his interest that he responded to most readily, outside of the lovelight in Janice's eyes.

"I'm the battle chief, it seems," he said to her, "and I've got the men and equipment. You've got the scientific know-how. Besides that you're my wife and not to be pampered. Want to come along?"

Janice pretended to snicker. "Benevolent, aren't you? You know you couldn't ever get away with leaving me behind—you big ape."

"*Sir*, to you—lieutenant."

Her blue-green eyes blazed narrowly. "Now look here, Rocky. If you think for one minute that I—"

"Okay. Okay." he exclaimed. "But this is no honeymoon. There's a war on, you know."

David, Ingaborg and Lillian Germain had gathered around them. David was a Commander in the Golden Guardsman organization.

"I believe," said Rocky, to the latter, "you are on special commission?"

"Yes," said David. "Germain and I and Ingaborg and Lillian—"

"Not Lillian," said Germain, joining them. "On second thought, she stays here. But my special mission still stands. We're going exploring. I'm taking my own ship, the *Nova*. There'll be a full crew." He was referring to an ancient vessel originally constructed by the Elder Race itself, which had been the private ship of the King of the World, a titanic dreadnaught built for giants, almost a mile in diameter and now brimming with specialized equipment and Universal Power batteries capable of lighting all the cities of the Earth simultaneously.

"But what about Lil?" objected Ingaborg, putting her arm affectionately about Lillian's waist.

Just then an Agarthian technician confronted them, addressing Germain. "There has been some strange interference, sir. The master telaug controls show a blowout somewhere. Somebody's micro-telaug has been burned out."

Germain's deeply tanned face was impassive, except for a slight lowering of his brows over dark, glittering eyes. "The enemy," he said, "is stronger than I thought. Moreover, he is in our midst."

"What do you mean?" queried David, as Dr. Borg hobbled up.

"I mean," said Germain, "that one among us who possesses the micro-telaug now is no longer one of us. That person, whoever he may be, is masquerading as an Agarthian or a Terrestrial, but he is—what shall I say? An *alien*. However, now that he is aware of our cognizance he is no doubt clever enough to conceal himself and the present crisis does not leave us sufficient time for a laboratory controlled investigation. I suggest that we allow the alien to reveal himself by his own actions."

They all looked at each other. Germain and Julius Borg remained expressionless.

"Stephen," said Lillian, "I don't like the idea of being left behind now."

Germain pressed her arm tenderly. "An old friend of ours is going to take you under his wing," he said. "In your condition you've got to—"

"You mean—Michael?" Lillian's eyes suddenly lighted with pleasure. "Is he back from that special mission of yours?"

"Something tells me he is. Let's go find him."

So Germain and Lillian went out of the Council Chamber to meet their oldest, most trusted friend, Michael Kent, a man who had grown up with them, loving Lillian competitively with Germain and ultimately coming to love them both more than each alone. He was their most intimate mutual friend and ally…

Behind them, Dr. Grange remarked to Dr. Borg, "There are only a dozen micro-telaugs in operation. We ought to be able to run a check on each one."

Borg was looking at Germain's departing figure. "I suspect there won't be time," he answered. "Not now."

"What do you mean? It would only take a half-hour at the most. Surely the danger isn't as imminent as all that."

And Rocky added, "Germain doesn't seem to be that worried."

Borg snarled in a friendly way. "That's when he's *really* worried. Right now I'll bet his ESP is spread thin from here to the alien fleet. What do you think he's holding onto Lillian's arm like that for? Mentally, he's walking on a glass tightrope, expecting it to break any second."

"I think I'd better round up my boys," said Rocky, referring casually to ten thousand of the most highly trained and specialized fighting men in the known history of the world.

Janice went out with him.

Borg turned to Grange. "We'd better take our places in the war labs…"

MICHAEL Kent appeared to Lillian in the antechamber like a clear portrait out of an old trunk, brown eyes, curly brown hair, pipe and all. It was reassuring to her, carrying her back to her childhood.

"Michael," she said, kissing his cheek, "you're a sight for sore eyes. Here we are in the middle of a nightmare of unrealities and uncertainties and you pop up as real and reliable as—as grandmother's teapot!"

Kent shrugged significantly at Germain. "How do you like that? So now I'm nothing but an old pot."

"Have you looked over the lab?" asked Germain, expressionlessly as usual.

"It's such a fortress it scares me even when I know you're on my side," Kent answered. "She'll be safe there if anywhere on the planet. I don't see how anything could touch her there."

"Is Yvonne there?" Yvonne was Kent's younger sister.

"On the job. Every time she reads that mental tape of yours she goes around like a somnambulist, a superscientist not knowing a damn thing about what she's doing. It's kind of weird, as though she were a split personality."

Lillian frowned. "Do I have to weather this storm cooped up in that superman's castle?" she complained, referring to a specialized laboratory Germain had built atop the Pacific island of Guam, with the permission of the U.S. Government. Why he had built it he had explained to no one except the Elder People who had left with him alone certain equipment, which they could entrust to no one else, and there he had worked with mysteries for which human speech had not yet found words.

"Well, there is more than ourselves to consider, Lil," he answered her.

She blushed, unable to argue back.

Both Kent and Germain were in a hurry, pressed by the gathering storm of events that involved more than the safety of

Terra, itself. But Germain took him aside and talked with him.

Which was an excuse for having the chance to examine him, internally. As he talked casually, his extrasensory perception was inspecting the other's micro-telaug. It appeared to be in perfect condition. He probed the other's mind and found nothing out of the ordinary, other than an honest anxiety for his friends and for civilization as a whole—plus a grim anticipation of the lesson that the present emergency was going to give to the U.N. and one Mr. Gormski.

"Something is bothering you," said Kent, eyeing his friend closely.

Germain laughed. "A lot of things are bothering me."

"I mean—something about me."

"No, but I *am* bothered by a presentiment that, well— something is escaping my attention that shouldn't."

"*That* is bad. I'd be afraid of anything that could escape *your* attention."

"That's just the point. It's there, somewhere, like the missing piece in a puzzle. And I'm looking for it because something tells me it's the most dangerous link in this whole mess."

"You know," said Kent, "the outside world still knows nothing about what's hanging over their heads. Aren't you going to warn them at all?"

A slight smirk shadowed one corner of Germain's mouth. "Their super radar screens can pick up every meteor between here and Luna, so what the screens won't pick up would be unbelievable to them. They would laugh, accuse me of hoaxing or having hallucinations. They might even make me mad, and as one of the Agarthian Elders I'm supposed to be the master of my emotions—but sometimes I feel like going on a scalping party." He grinned as he always did when joking about his Indian blood, which was actually a throwback to a Sioux woman three generations removed. "Seriously, though, my main fear is that they might actually believe me and go off half-cocked in their shiny new space navy, and that would be curtains. It would be just as well if they believed this whole thing was a hoax until we get a grip on the situation. Their crews are uninitiated. They'd be liable to commit suicide if they took it upon themselves to meet the enemy once they were aware of him. If they do get the news, try to convince them when you get back to the U.N. Monday that they must accept our guidance. Give them every proof you can. Try to hold them to the Emergency Clause of the Charter. They must follow Agarthi's command or they'll get their fingers singed off up to the arm pits."

"Well, I'd better be getting Lil out of here then," said Kent. "I think I can make it back to Guam in about three hours."

"Take good care of her," said Germain, extending his hand.

And to his wife, in an adjacent room of the palace, he said, with sheer telepathy, unaided by micro-telaug: *This is not goodbye, dearest, I'll be with you.*

Lillian Germain could believe that. She knew her husband.

But neither of them knew Izdran of a Thousand Lives...

CHAPTER NINE

ORDINARILY, Lillian would have expected of her husband that he say goodbye to her personally, but Germain knew she would understand by this very omission that the circumstances were far from ordinary. She would ask no questions and go with Kent. His reason for getting her away from his presence would probably be obvious to her, too, he thought, but he couldn't help that. The fact was, he expected any second to be attacked personally by the alien or his agents. Logic told him that without any ESP. He was the Star Warden here.

As soon as Kent left him he made a dash for Mandir's chamber of meditation. He knew the old man had gone there, but more than Mandir he needed the chamber, itself. It was sound proof and telaug proof, which meant that even the extraneous thoughts of others could not penetrate here, nor could augmented psychic influences get in. Moreover, lighting effects and acoustics there could minimize the biochemical interference of conscious thought and leave the subconscious unhampered for controlled operation.

The gray headed old mentalist lost a slight fraction of his practiced composure as Germain dashed in without warning.

"I have sensed the existence of a very grave emergency," he said to the younger man, "and your presence here is proof enough. What is it, Stephen?"

"Very little time to talk," retorted Germain. "I seem to be the focus of an attack. Get to Borg and Grange and have them work out that secondary interference screen. I am staying here."

"Just as you say," said Mandir, quietly. "But I shall retire immediately to the King's old chambers and join forces with you, if this attack is to be mental. It's too bad the psychic ray has not been remounted. Perhaps we could—"

"It's more than mental," said Germain. "Think of—of—"

"Yes?"

"Of ectoplasm—not just the supernatural idea, but a substance which is a concentration of submatter, a physical manifestation. Much that is about to happen is totally new to our experience." Germain, like Izdran, was equipped with the seventh sense, which unlike the intuitive "sixth sense" (ESP), gave him within a limited degree an actual fourth coordinate perspective.

"What are you going to do, then?" asked Mandir.

"Add something new, myself. You have delved into autosynthesis or *faith* power, haven't you? Not the religious sense of blind *faith*, but the basic, metaphysical nature of faith. One of its manifestations is levitation."

"Yes," said Mandir, his dim eyes beginning to glimmer with academic interest. "Twice I achieved levitation. The King did it easily. What are you getting at?"

"Faith power is based on the fact that any given set of results arises from a given set of causes and that, conversely, if the mind can perceive as an absolute reality a synthesized set of results for which there was no original cause, that *cause* will come into being in order to match the results. In other words, if I could perceive strongly enough the result of my being transported elsewhere, the cause of that transportation would have to come into being in order to match that result. In short, what I am after and have been close to achieving is mental teleportation. I am going to have to perfect it now. So leave me here and contact Borg and Grange at once."

IN substantiation of Germain's presentiments, an astounding circumstance developed in the city of Agarthi. Without other than Germain's own warning, a medium sized, disc-shaped space ship materialized before the palace.

It was approximately one hundred feet in diameter, and twenty feet thick. It was smooth surfaced, without rocket tubes or fins or observation blisters. It hung suspended in space for a moment, and then it settled quickly to the ground.

Immediately, Agarthian defenses went to work on it. Disintegrators came first, with no effect. Sonic heat and death rays were equally futile. Telaug beams could not penetrate its psychic screens. But the televisibeams brought back to all operators the spectacle of ten, three-eyed robots working at the command of an ordinary Terrestrial. The latter was a big man with bushy eyebrows and a thick, Slavic physiognomy.

This is a projection from outer space, came Germain's thought to Telaug Control. *But it is no mere image. It is physical, a sub-order materialization, and it can do damage. I am asking the laboratory to locate the source of the projection, which will be invisible to all primary waves. Attack on the secondary level. All primary energy will be useless against the attacker until you scramble his second order screen.*

An attempt was made to contact Germain further, but he threw up around his chamber a shield, which nothing seemed to be able to penetrate. He and Borg knew something immediately, which the rest did not. Borg, Germain, Lillian and Kent were the four who knew that man on board the alien ship, but Lillian and Kent were gone from Agarthi. Germain and Borg had glimpsed him briefly as the televisibeam image was relayed over the micro-telaug carriers.

The man was Sergeyev Pavlovich. Germain and Borg had assumed him to be dead, for they knew that when he escaped from Terra in the ship conceived of by Germain the Elder People had set a trap of death for him and Nicholas and the rest on board. By some unimaginable piece of luck, Pavlovich had escaped—but then Germain's seventh sense had not been so sharp in those days.

But if Pavlovich had returned, it was highly possible that Nicholas, also, had come back. Both Borg and Germain shuddered at the thought of the mad dictator returning to Terra armed with the superman technology of an alien world—no doubt Mars. This would explain strange occurrences in Europe, particularly the disappearance of Gerhardt Eidelmann.

Eidelmann! A tremendous scientist who once adapted Elder Race weapons to the purposes of the detrimental interstellars! What would be a more logical move on Nicholas' part than to acquire Eidelmann?

That combination was bad enough, both men thought, simultaneously, but there was more. Whoever was behind Nicholas with this alien technology had a stake in Terra also. There would be an alien mastermind, as well. And where was *he*?

Germain thought of the telaug operator who had reported one micro-telaug blown out. They had not had time to inspect all possessors of the micro-telaug. Yet one of those people was now a mere mask for the *alien*.

For one brief moment, Germain was an ordinary human being. He was envious of the world beyond Agarthi, where life went on undisturbed, as yet, by the tremendous influences being brought to bear on its destiny. Regardless of adverse world opinion, the responsibility for the world was here on his own shoulders, and he was not any too certain of the outcome, inasmuch as his seventh sense perspective of the future was only based on probabilities, and these swirled before him indefinably. In spite of his mutant mentality he was only a neo-interstellar being—far from being a god.

And in the midst of it all, a personal enmity. Pavlovich. He had locked arms with Pavlovich in physical conflict. Indirectly, he had defeated the man, disgraced him, destroyed his every hope. Pavlovich hated him. Nicholas' strategy again was obvious. He had sent the big Russian on a suicide venture to obliterate him and remove one big obstacle from his goal of world conquest.

WHILE Borg and Germain entertained these thoughts and the Agarthian garrison stood at bay, the alien ship opened. Out of an airlock marched the semi-tangible sub-order images of five robots . The airlock closed behind them and they proceeded into the palace.

A platoon of palace guards confronted them, firing at the weird materializations with cruder, more physical weapons than previously. This time they used explosive bullets, and for a moment it seemed that there would be some effect produced on the intruders. Two of the robot forms wavered, quivering like an image out of focus, or stricken with interference. One of them collapsed into nothingness.

But then the invaders used a new weapon. It was not physical paralysis, but mental. Telaug Control blew half out of commission trying to protect the victims. The telepathic robots paralyzed the minds of the defenders, seemingly possessed of an inexhaustible source of power from somewhere. The third eyes of the remaining four automatons blazed with this alien energy as they continued toward their goal into the interior of the palace, while Borg and Grange worked rapidly, in grim, silent accord, deep below in the tremendous interstellar laboratory that the Elder Race had left at their disposal. They knew they were racing against the slimmest margin of time, for the advantage was all on the side of the enemy.

The Agarthian defenders next made the mistake of trying to grapple physically with the robots, only to find that their substance could thin out or densify almost into the semblance of gross matter, and many there were who fell dead with broken necks or crushed skulls at the hands of the inhumanly powerful robots. And the worst development of that encounter was that the robots acquired disintegrators from the defenders. With these they marched on Germain, himself.

Telaug Control, Mandir, and perhaps Borg were aware of a few lightning swift tests Germain had made. Releasing his screens for a fraction of a second, he had probed the robots with enough lethal psychic power to kill a platoon of them if they had been human. But he had found no response there, no effect. If there was mentality there it was of a different order, or *frequency*. He shot that clue to Borg and then closed his screens quickly. That word *frequency* was a clue for Borg and Grange, but there was pitifully little time to work on it.

In the meantime, Steve Rockner sprang into action with two of his ships. He had seen the effect of explosions upon the images. He had seen the effect of the counter-weapon—psychic paralysis. He knew his ships were equipped with psychic screens as well as a battery of the world's most specialized weapons.

The two dreadnaughts, densified to mere ten foot miniatures but packing an irresistible power in terms of mass and momentum, simply peeled off out of the cavern's "sky" and plowed through the materialization of the alien ship.

The image went out like a bubble, but to the chagrin of all watchers the four robots remained inside the palace. Then the ship image reappeared before the palace, rematerializing as if nothing had happened.

Borg telauged to Rocky over a secret carrier that was keyed to penetrate his screens: *You can't do anything here. Follow your orders and head for Mars. The source of our trouble is undoubtedly in that area. Contact the Lunar Interstellars. We're calling for all the help we can get. Now get going!*

But Germain—came Rocky's thought. *I can't leave a buddy in a jam, Borg.*

If he can't take care of himself there's nothing you or the Guardsmen can do. There's more at stake than Germain. He gave you orders. Carry them out.

Anchors aweigh came Rocky's reply.

Which was a significant little remark. While the four robots closed in on Germain, one hundred sleek, powerful, super-equipped space warships wearing the gold-emblazoned symbol of the Sword of Agarthi on their prows, emerged through a shaft in the towering side of Amnyi Machen, and many intelligences, friendly and unfriendly, between Terra and Luna, were aware of their headlong plunge into the bottomless sea of outer space. These same intelligences were also aware of twenty-five mighty space battleships of the old interstellar class rising out of Agarthian depths—mile long fortresses built on the Elder Race pattern.

Unfortunately, this action also alerted the quasi-established Terrestrial Government. Agarthian operators were besieged with messages from the capitals of the world requesting an explanation. When they were finally informed that an alien invasion was imminent, they soon suspected that it was an Agarthian trick. Some nations merely alerted their new space fleet units, while others acted more rashly. The latter sent their ships into space to meet any challenge on the part of Agarthi. Obviously, it was Gormski's influence again, based on the reminder that Germain had hurled an ultimatum at the U.N.

To many a Terrestrial the sight of their own space warships over their heads was comforting and a source of newfound pride, but to Borg and Mandir and Germain it was a mess. This was not counter-aggression. It was sheer exposure to the twice invisible enemy lurking out there in the depths of space.

Except for the Golden Guardsmen and the Lunar Interstellars and the old line Agarthian fleet. Perhaps in that direction lay salvation. That and what Borg and Grange were working on in frantic haste.

In the midst of all this, four robots found the door to Mandir's meditation chamber, behind which Germain stood at bay. Four robots possessing psychic eyes, cold, impassive, intent on their goal. They were not trying to capture Germain.

He knew that now. They were on a mission of destruction. In their interlocked mentalities was one driving impulse: *Stephen Germain must die.*

But Germain had no intention of dying. Fear could result from not knowing what to do in an emergency. Germain felt no fear because he knew what he was doing. In fact, he was the only one who felt that his was not a stand against death but a trap for the enemy. Not a complete trap. He would not be able to trap the robots, but in the struggle he might be able to gain important knowledge pertaining to the nature of the enemy. And that was what he was after, for otherwise he was sure he could have been elsewhere.

He had foreseen, long ago, the need for such a special citadel as this chamber. He only regretted that it was not yet hooked up to the Universal Power generator in the war lab. Still, its ray screens were powered by nuclear energy, and all the man-made electrical energy in the world would have been impotent before those screens.

The robots apparently could not bring with them, into their strangely projected materialization, the physical accoutrements necessary to penetrate his screens, so they resorted to a very simple method of approach. They used the disintegrators they had taken from the guards. Not against the screens, which would have been futile, but against the structure of the palace, itself. They disintegrated the floor and carved out a cavern beneath it. Conductor cables parted, and the screens collapsed. Before Borg could transmit a power beam to substitute for electronic conduction, the robots blasted into the chamber.

It was then that Germain duplicated a feat, which had been achieved heretofore only by members of the Elder Race. The weapons in the robots' hands suddenly changed their physical location. They were found days later in shrubbery surrounding the palace.

The robots were not defenseless, however. They had wrung the necks and crushed the skulls of half a dozen Agarthians. And Germain was made of flesh and blood. So they closed in on him.

Still he knew that he was safe, having made certain successful experiments before their arrival. So he probed them and studied them in frantic haste.

The robots brought into play their psychic paralysis, which at first he sought, experimentally, to resist. If the force had been transmitted by a living brain it would have made no headway, but Germain knew it was powerfully augmented, so he did not waste his energy resisting it. He knew it could only paralyze his conscious mind, but since his subconscious mind had long since become voluntary he carried on almost unhampered, although physically he could not move a muscle.

Pavlovich, he thought at them. *Desist at once or you're done for.*

He knew that though the robots were not human their activator was. And he knew that activator's psychology.

At once his subconscious mind was filled with augmented human thought. And with that thought came the impression of hate, triumph and vast amusement.

At last you die, Germain. Make way for the New Order!

That was all Germain wanted. Extra-sensory perception raced back along that human thought line, and in an instant he telepathed to Borg: *Position of enemy ship—five hundred miles, at ninety degrees, straight on.* Before he could give Pavlovich the deathblow, the latter's psychic screens chopped him off.

And in that instant, the robots closed in. But just as they reached for Germain in one corner of the chamber, he disappeared.

In the same moment, he reappeared behind Borg and Grange, down in the war lab. Removed from the influence of the psychic paralysis, his conscious faculties were as suddenly regained.

"Have you got it yet?" he asked them.

They looked up at him in astonishment and elation, but there was absolutely no time for exclamations. They subdued their questions and emotions in view of the press of circumstances, like the proper Elders that they had become.

"We've been synthesizing the necessary harmonic pattern," said Grange, "and this will have to be it." He threw a switch and Borg worked four vernier adjustments while they watched the second order oscilloscopes, scopes that could give a sine-wave fix on frequencies ranging above a million megacycles, close to the border of light waves.

"This is better than an interference scrambler," said Borg. "The enemy screen is limited to around a million megs. We can scramble and penetrate by means of oscillations between inferior and superior frequencies on the second order level produced by sub-nuclear excitations on the basis of higher harmonics built up from the basic frequencies. Watch..."

The new televisibeam, operating on secondary type energy, brought them a wavering, ghostly image of Pavlovich's screen out in space. As they watched, the great sphere of energy ripped open, and suddenly there sprang into view on the primary type radar screens a clear indication of the ship, itself.

Without speaking, Germain made a lightning swift movement and threw in the Universal Powered war ray switches. But in the same instant, Pavlovich covered himself with an incredibly powerful first order screen. He split it open just one fiftieth of a second to retaliate with a new weapon—demagnetization. A quarter mile chunk of Amnyi Machen flashed into nothingness, but it was mostly snow and ice, precipitating landslides outside Agarthi that lasted for two days.

Before any further damage could be done, the alien ship retreated, because its titantic screens, powered from some central source elsewhere, had begun to weaken under the impact of irresistible Universal Powered disrays from Agarthi. And in that retreat they saw another weapon of the enemy. It was super velocity. The ship virtually disappeared, from the point of view of ordinary vision. But Germain's ESP followed it, unable to reach Pavlovich because the psychic screen was out again.

"That must be inertialess drive," ejaculated Grange.

"It is," said Germain. "We've got to work fast. Duplicate your present weapon and equip every ship you can. All ships must be able to break the secondary type screen, and they must be able to 'see' the enemy in all encounters. Transmit your information to the Lunar Interstellars as well. Janice is with the Guardsmen. She'll be able to direct their technicians."

"This has all been recorded," said Borg, "and Agarthian technicians are already working on sub-nuclear assemblies, which can be rocketed to all our ships in robot fliers. I'll send extras for the Lunar boys. The Agarthians can take over from here. Grange and I want to go out in our lab ship and work on the flying discs in outer space. There's something there we have to track down."

"I think you're right," said Germain. "They may be a clue to the source of the alien control." At that moment Mandir came into the lab, and Germain turned to him. "You are in charge here," he said. "We're leaving. I'm taking the *Nova* at once."

"Congratulations," beamed Mandir, enthusiastically. "You have achieved auto-teleportation. That was wonderful."

"What about the robots?" asked Germain.

"They have dematerialized."

"I thought so." Germain's forward jutting brows lowered as he faced the other three. "Friends," he said, "this is no picnic. The world, the solar system, perhaps *more than that*—" they knew he had something definitely in mind when he emphasized the last three words, but he was non-committal—"stands at the crossroads in this moment. And may God help us."

"God helps him who helps himself," said "Little Willy" Grange, stroking the side of his nose, thoughtfully. "And by that token He should be disposed to give you a lot of assistance, Germain."

Borg snarled appreciatively at this remark as Germain left the laboratory...

*   *   *

BALD and myopic Gerhardt Eidelmann started nervously but swiftly regained his composure when Nicholas materialized in his prison cell in Berlin. He recognized Nicholas as anyone might have recognized Adolf Hitler under similar circumstances. He had never known Nicholas personally, but he knew him for what he was—ruthless and capable, a born tyrant, conqueror of kings, and murderer of all who would stand in his way.

"I thought you were dead," he said, trying not to give the other the satisfaction of having been impressed. Inwardly, he burned with curiosity and wonderment.

"They all thought I was dead," replied the materialization, now no longer in evening dress but in his old, resplendent uniform he had worn as master of thirty nations, complete with the original Star of Honor medal and his cape of royal purple. "But the world will soon know that I am very much alive."

"What are you doing here?"

"I have come for you," said Nicholas. "You are very necessary to my plans."

"Why?"

"Because you understand interstellar science. Outside of the actual Agarthians, Earthmen who have that knowledge are fewer than the fingers of my hand."

"I can name them," said Eidelmann. "Myself, Stephen Germain and Julius Borg."

"Precisely. Do you wish, voluntarily, to join forces with me and delve into such science again, on a much larger scale than before?"

"Your object?" queried Eidelmann, trying to contain himself in his growing elation.

"World domination. What else?" Nicholas' gray eyes flashed with the old light of confidence and triumph. "Earth shall be mine again, and this time permanently. What you and I can set up on this globe will stop even an interstellar invasion. Even the solar system will be ours and all its worlds, from Mercury to Pluto."

"What have you got?" queried Eidelmann, cautiously, for he knew the illusions of the megalomaniac, and he could only share in such dreams on the basis of facts and figures. He was a cold-blooded scientist, unmoved by mere aspiration.

Then Nicholas lay at the feet of Gerhardt Eidelmann, social outcast and international criminal, the kind of world that Eidelmann the scientist could appreciate. "I can prove this," Nicholas told him, his eyes blazing with enthusiasm. "I have a space armada, an army of telepathic robots, magnetic disintegrators, invisibility to all primary wave phenomena. I possess subnuclear equipment, psychic paralysis, inertialess drive—everything you will need as a basis for expanding the potentialities into armaments that will be invincible."

"You did not acquire this all by yourself," said Eidelmann. "Who's in it with you—Martians?"

"No. It is a secret race, which now dominates the planet, Mars. I have been on Mars for the past year, and I dare say I've made good use of my time there."

"What of *them?*" queried Eidelmann, persistently. "What's their cut?"

"They want it all, naturally. But just as naturally I intend that they shall have nothing. With your help I hope to get possession of Universal Power. Once we have it they will be powerless, and I'm sure they may even be destroyed. In fact, they must be destroyed. They are not human."

To any intellect lesser than Eidelmann's, all this would have been incredible, but logic told him that if Nicholas could prove half of what he claimed there was a good chance of realizing his dreams.

"All right," he said. "When do we get started? Can you get me out of here?"

"If I had one of those old teletransporters you used to work on, it would be easier," replied Nicholas, "but the Agarthians picked them all up. Anyway, just stand by for a few moments."

The international prison in Berlin was taken by surprise when a mysterious space ship suddenly appeared out of nowhere. All guards were mentally paralyzed. Three-eyed robots blasted their way in to Eidelmann's cell unmolested, and he walked with them out to the ship. Before superior space war equipment could be brought into play in the Berlin area, the ship was gone.

And so Eidelmann began his new career under Nicholas, returning conqueror...

There were many others who were approached secretly by Nicholas' growing forces, in many cities and countries. Within a few days, willing cooperators were alerted and began to be equipped with the instruments of a super science. There was no need for propaganda machines or cold wars this time. The evidence and the power were immediately at hand, and those who coveted personal advantage were quickly bought over to the cause of mass enslavement to the benefit of the few. The new *Politburo* was on the march.

WITHIN a week, Eidelmann reported to Nicholas, on board their hidden Nrlanian ship in eastern Russia.

"I have been working extensively all the robots," he said. "They are obviously controlled by some central source of power located on or near Mars. If we can locate that central control and take possession of it, we have the robots. If your assumption is correct, that the true Nrlanians are few in number, stripping them of their central control and their robots will practically leave them helpless. Of course having a control over their central is tantamount to having victory over them, but that, may be harder to acquire than their robots. There may be alternatives. I am working on a substitute control here on Terra, with the help of a number of myoid aides your men have helped me to create, I'm quite sure we can take over robot control without capturing the Nrlanian central—or at least we can control all the robots in our command. I think that's the right direction to take."

"There may be more to Nrlanian Central Control than we imagine. I want Universal Power. If the Nrlanians strike at us, we'll need it—and we'll need that Zero Bomb you were working on in the old days. What about that?"

"My notes on that are still available, but I had brought my

experiments to the point where the computations showed irrefutably that the Zero Bomb would be suicide to use, inasmuch as it would precipitate a propagating chain reaction in stable matter, resulting in the instant destruction of the planet, itself. The thing requires further research and as a matter of fact I have two of my best nuclear physicists working on the math right now."

Nicholas thought: If Earth won't submit, or if the Nrlanians think they're going to take it from me, I'll use the Zero Bomb and make a string of asteroids out of the planet. But he said, "What about Universal Power?"

"Your robots seem to be doing a good job in that direction. They've raided several Terrestrial plants and uprooted the whole outfit in each case. It's dangerous using them for the job, however. Obviously they would not be permitted by their Central Control to steal Universal Power if that control thought we could use it against the Nrlanians. The conclusion to be drawn is that they intend to use it, themselves."

"I doubt that we will give them that chance," replied Nicholas, tonelessly. His fists suddenly clenched. "Damn Pavlovich for a blundering idiot. The whole world is alerted now and Germain, instead of being dead, is at large. No telling where or how he may strike in that Elder Race ship of his."

"And there are the Golden Guardsmen, the Agarthians, the Lunar Interstellars, and the Terrestrial fleets," put in Eidelmann unconsolingly.

"We can handle mere space armadas," said Nicholas, confidently. "It's Germain I'm worried about—and *Borg*. Where is he?"

"He may be busy arriving at conclusions similar to ours. My experimental ship is almost completed, according to reports from my construction division. With it we should start locating Central Control and catch the Nrlanians napping before Germain or Borg beat us to it. That, I think, is the final key to everything."

"I am giving that operation top priority," said Nicholas.

"When can you be ready?"

"In about three more days. I have all the industrial facilities of Irkutsk isolated for that exclusive task, and three full robot crews—"

"I want that ship in forty-eight hours!" interrupted Nicholas.

"We can't do the impossible—"

Nicholas stood up and stamped his booted foot. "We *are* doing the impossible," he shouted. "I want that ship ready in two days."

"Then give me another crew of robots."

AT that moment an orderly rushed in and clicked to attention before Nicholas. He handed him a secret dispatch from the electro-observatory at Cheremkhovo, whose town was also in the hands of the robot fifth column and Terrestrial collaborators.

Nicholas looked at the interlinear decoding of the dispatch, smiled coldly, and handed it to Eidelmann.

Eidelmann read:

TERRESTRIAL GOVERNMENT FLEET ATTACKING YOUR THIRD FLOTILLA.

Eidelmann looked up. "So the trick worked," he said. "Revealing a portion of the fleet to their radar drew them out where you want them."

"I want you to watch this," said Nicholas. "We'll watch it on our own screens." At the same time he put on a helmet made of fine silver mesh. He worked the controls of a type of transmitter, which Terra had never seen before. "My third flotilla is going to step on an ant," he said.

Nicholas closed his eyes and concentrated grimly for about a minute. Thanks to Nrlanian science, he was able to transmit a multiple order to twenty-five hundred robots in twenty-five superdreadnaughts of the void.

But in that same instant, Eidelmann was astounded to observe a miraculous change that suddenly came over the Russian orderly, who had remained in the room. The expression of deference vanished from his face, and he suddenly looked at Nicholas with an inhuman gleam in his eyes.

It was those eyes that Nicholas saw when he opened his.

"Remember," said the orderly, in a strange voice, "that I am omnipresent. You can never deceive me."

Nicholas blanched, then quickly recomposed himself. He knew that Izdran had penetrated his camp.

"What—who is it?" gasped Eidelmann.

The orderly turned to him. "I am Izdran," he said. "What would any of you be if I suddenly withdrew the activating power from the robot fleet? Just remember you need me. Don't make the childish mistake of underestimating the Nrlani."

Nicholas impatiently removed his headpiece. "This is just another cheap demonstration," he said. "There's work to be done. Now leave us alone."

"Perhaps," said the orderly, "you would not be so sure of yourself if you knew that the deception you plan will be valueless to you even if you succeed."

Nicholas raised one eyebrow but said nothing. He only glared back at the orderly.

The latter smiled gloatingly. "You humans are such playthings," he said. "Your little emotions are so transparent. All your senses of value are relative, never specific. All that which you desire—power, wealth, victory—would be nothing, Nicholas, without the one little keystone that must ultimately support the emotional arch of your triumph."

"What in the hell are you talking about?" shouted Nicholas.

"Lillian Germain."

For the second time, Nicholas blanched. He stiffened, and his hand went to his radium pistol at his belt. Instinctively, he suddenly sprang in front of the orderly and clutched him by the collar, anger making him blind to reason, for the gesture was futile as far as Izdran was concerned.

"You have her," he exclaimed. "Tell me where she is!"

"Or you'll *what?*" The orderly's eyes blazed with an inhuman light.

"I'll blast you and your stinking sky city out of the solar system. Now tell me where she is!"

"You'll do exactly and precisely what you are told to do," came the cold reply. "When you are ready to come to reasonable terms, after your work is done on Terra to *our* satisfaction, you can have her. Not before."

Suddenly, a startled orderly was looking at Nicholas and wondering what had happened. And in another moment he was even more startled, because Nicholas broke his nose with a blow of his fist. Eyes filled with tears of pain, and with the lower half of his face overrun with blood, he stood there stiffly but trembling in his fear and bewilderment.

Eidelmann half rose to his feet. "What the devil—" he protested.

"Get out of here," shouted Nicholas, knowing that Izdran had ceased possessing the soldier. The latter ran bleeding from his presence.

Nicholas paced the floor in a blind rage. He clicked on intercoms and telecasting equipment, barked orders to all strategic offices on board and on land and yelled at Eidelmann in between.

"Assign your best scientific aide to the project of taking over robot control from Nrlanian Central. You get on that special ship of yours personally and get it done. I want direct control of the robots, and I want to know where Nrlanian Central is hidden. If we find it, we won't try to take it. That's a little suicide task for my expendable friend Pavlovich. I want a Universal Power unit installed on his special ship. He may not know it, and I hope he doesn't, but a Universal Power unit packs more potential explosive power, if it's shorted by a collision, than ten hydrogen bombs. Enough to blow a moon out of its orbit."

Suddenly he stopped pacing and looked with widened eyes at Eidelmann.

"Moon!" he exclaimed, as Eidelmann suddenly caught onto the same idea. "A Martian moon. What a fool I've been.

Maybe we can narrow our search down. Central Control might be either on Deimos or Phobos."

"*Dass lasst sich leicht denken,*" Eidelmann murmured, half aloud, in his own language.

"What was that?"

"I said there's plenty of work to be done..."

CHAPTER TEN

NICHOLAS had a temporary villa established near his ship, on the outskirts of Irkutsk. Here, among other human equipage attached to his growing command bivouac, was Trinha Llih.

She was in negligee that night preparatory to retiring when Pavlovich came brazenly into her room. It was his first appearance since Mars.

He paused for a moment to look at her, his eyes taking her in hungrily. Then he strode across the room and pulled her into his arms, kissing her and holding her so tightly that she gasped for air.

"Let me go," she exclaimed, in her own tongue.

"You're mine," he exclaimed, heatedly. "Nicholas has everything else. Besides, I've got plans and you're a part of them."

Suddenly, Trinha relaxed in his arms and smiled up at him. She had come to her shining world of Panh at last, and she had seen enough. To her it was dirty congestion and a mass of confusion in the midst of impossible abundance. Moreover, the gravitation wearied her, forcing her to spend a large part of her time lying down. But she had not been entirely idle . She wanted to return to Mars, and she still had her dream of vengeance against Nicholas. Pavlovich, it suddenly occurred to her, might be her only ally.

"You startled me so," she said. "Where have you been? Did you get Germain?"

"No, but it's just as well," he answered. "Germain's going to keep Nicholas and the Nrlani occupied while I lay my own plans."

"What are your plans?"

"One of them is to get rid of Nicholas and take over where he left off. What do you think of that?" His brown eyes glared at her challengingly.

She smiled in a peculiarly Martian way, with a sweetness that was deadly because it was ice cold. "I hate Nicholas," she said. "I'll help you destroy him."

Pavlovich's brown eyes went up a notch. "How could you help me?"

"You want control of the robots, don't you?"

"Yes, but—"

"Eidelmann has been preparing a second control. He plans to control them from here."

"You mean—independent of Nrlanian control?"

"Yes. And I know where those new controls are."

Pavlovich grinned in triumph. "You show me where," he said, "and I'll promise you Nicholas' head on a silver platter."

"I wouldn't serve it to a *krnar*," she exclaimed, fiercely.

"Where are Eidelmann's new controls?" he persisted.

"In the basement of this house," she answered. "I've been there several times. They know I'm a Martian and don't speak their language, but what they don't know is that I understand everything. I know what they're doing down there. They can't fool me."

Pavlovich looked down into her face, curiously. "How could you understand everything in a place like that?" he asked.

"I don't know," she said. "But I do. Take my word for it. The controls are there and they are almost completed."

"I'll find out. If what you say is true, I have a chance against Nicholas and the Nrlani, too. Trinha, are you with me?"

Controlling her revulsion, she kissed him.

And far away, somewhere, that little scene caused a very inhuman entity to laugh. It was a laugh one might have expected of someone who had just won another move in an intricate game—like chess...

*   *   *

THERE was one more item Germain had to attend to before he sprang into action. That was Lillian's safety. He entered the meditation chambers of the King and made full use of his prodigious mind.

Far across Asia his perception expanded, out beyond the China Sea and the Philippines, to Guam.

Auburn-haired Yvonne was in the laboratory citadel there, perched high on old Com Mar hill, overlooking Asan and the reef-whitened sweep of the sunlit ocean. Yvonne was not a scientist, but she could act as one. In the lab was a thought tape taken from Germain's mind. If she forgot how to operate the mysterious equipment there, she had only to repeat a reading of the tape, and again she was Germain's right hand at the controls. They were dangerous inventions, untried before by mere Terrestrials, and he had made it clear to her and her brother, Kent, that she would be risking her life if she were ever called upon to use them. But she had begged for the chance to work for Agarthi. It was her personal contribution to the new world Germain was trying to build—and protect. He had chosen her deliberately because of her inability to comprehend what she would be operating if called upon to handle the equipment. This was to provide for the failure of any enemy attempt to read her mind, because the mental tape was treated to make an ephemeral impression only, which would fade each time she accomplished her purpose at the controls. On the tape was only the secret of how to operate the equipment. How or why it worked or what it actually did was Germain's secret, alone. He and the Elder People's. For that equipment was the result of a type of reasoning and a cosmic point of view, which even Borg or Mandir had not yet conceived of.

In the midst of her daily routine about the place, Yvonne was suddenly aware of Germain.

Where is Lillian?—he asked her.

The girl's hazel eyes widened in fright. She had never been able to accustom herself to Germain's manifestations of mutant intelligence.

"She—she never arrived," responded Yvonne, instinctively terrorized because of the necessity of talking to nothing but the air.

You have her direction finder, persisted Germain. *Turn it on.*

Obediently, the girl hastened into the laboratory and found a familiar little switch, which she turned on. A large electron tube began to glow with a bluish light, and a subtle hum pervaded the vast room. At the same time, a multiple loop antenna began to gyrate above the tube. Beside the switch, a small ammeter kicked feebly into life.

Fix the position—came Germain's thought. *Calibrate.*

Quickly, Yvonne threw another switch, and a vernier scale leaped into life. She manipulated a manual control, affecting the antenna and the vernier needle immediately responded to the lesser deviation of the ammeter.

Then, just as suddenly, everything went dead.

A screen has been thrown up, came Germain's tense thought. *What a fool I am. Kent was not Kent at all. He is in the hands of the enemy. And so is Lillian!*

"What do you mean?" cried Yvonne, frantically. "Where are they?"

No time to communicate with you on that point. I'm going after them. In the meantime, keep a finder on me, and keep Lil's finder activated. Stand by for further instructions. And one thing more...

"Yes?"

Turn on the Chronoperceptor.

Yvonne's aquiline face blanched as she looked up at a two-story mass of sub-nuclear equipment that would have staggered the imagination of any normal human being. Up to this point she had been operating straight Terrestrial type gear. But this was Elder Race equipment. The Chronoperceptor loomed above her, enigmatically, like the gateway to a world that lay beyond the era of Man. She feared it, but she moved to obey.

She threw in more switches, and a prismatic display of colors began to dance in the room to the tune of harmonic effects in the atmosphere, which seemed to be akin to the very music of the spheres...

IN the meantime, Germain's perception raced elsewhere, afar into space, following the lead given him by Lillian's finder before it went dead. He detected a fleeing ship by virtue of its secondary screen, which he could not penetrate, and beyond it lay a gigantic screen, miles in diameter. There was something there of tremendous import, and he was determined to investigate it in the flesh.

Minutes later there arose from the remains of Amnyi Machen's peak a titanic vessel on the prow of which was engraved one word: *Nova*. Inside, in addition to a picked Agarthian crew, were Germain, David and Ingaborg.

And soon in its wake followed another special ship engaged in a separate mission, bearing Borg, Grange and a laboratory of equipment, including their new flying saucer trap.

Beyond them lay the unknown enemy, and out there in the great darkness were the Golden Guardsmen, the Lunar Interstellars, the Agarthians, and the inexperienced Terrestrial fleet. Behind lay Agarthi, commanded now by Mandir. And there was the whole world, waiting for new triumph and a further step toward the Infinite, or for defeat and slavery.

The battle was on...

CHAPTER ELEVEN

SAMMY, you sell newspapers. You ought to have an idea about what's goin' on. What d'ya think?"

High-powered traffic thrummed along Main Street where the car tracks used to be. There were no more streetcars. There were helicopter commuters.

Sammy thought: Thank God there's still hot dogs. I can understand hot dogs. And coffee. They can raise our taxes and feed us all the bull they want, but we won't take any substitute for coffee.

He sank his teeth into his hot dog and chewed a while, watching Pete, the car lot attendant, and old cockeyed Jules behind the counter. They were ordinary earthy guys who were - just as mixed up as he was.

"We got Universal Government now," put in Jules, reflectively flipping Pete's hamburger over on the griddle. "So how come there's war emergency? Who's fightin' who—and *what?*"

"Well," said Pete, "it's Nicholas again, or at least they think. He wasn't satisfied with startin' World War Three and running most of the governments on Earth. When they chased him clear off it he picked up some ammunition on Mars. Now he's back with ships and an army."

"Mars," snickered Jules. "Next you'll be swallowing that bunk about robots."

"That's what they *say,*" Pete insisted. "He's got a whole army of robots, and they run his space ships, too. If that's not so, why did we just send out all our own ships—the new space fleet that all our taxes went into? I tell you, we're in danger of extra-cerestial regression or whatever it is they call it in the papers."

"With Universal Power?" sneered Jules. "We can wipe out everything."

"Don't be so sure," said Sammy, at last. "You know what Stephen Germain told them at the U.N. By being able to go to other planets we put ourselves in danger of being attacked by stuff that's way over our heads. I think we should let him and Agarthi have their Emergency Clause in the Terrestrial Government Charter. I think we need their help. In fact they're probably going to help even if we don't want it."

Jules' crossed eyes glared. "Sammy, I should have poisoned that hot dog. You're a sucker like the rest of them. I think Gormski's right—Russian or no Russian. He told the U.N. that Germain might stage a war of the worlds or make us *think* we saw strange space ships, just to get us to accept the Emergency

Clause. If we had, he'd be our dictator right now. I think this scare is all a thing cooked up by Germain. He's a mutant. He's not one of us. We gotta stick up for our rights. You talk about Nicholas. He just wanted to rule the Earth. Germain calls himself the *Star* Warden. That means he's trying to glom on to the whole damn solar system."

Pete drank coffee and shut up. He had seen this kind of argument start brawls every day for the past three days. It was worse than arguing about the World Series. Now *there* was something he would rather talk about. Baseball. Thank God there was still baseball. *That* he could understand.

"I think it's all over our heads," said Sammy. "If I was a candidate for World President, my platform would be: 'Give the world back to the people.' Right now it's for the birds. Not even the politicians know what's cookin'."

"Hey," Pete exclaimed, pointing at the side entrance of the bar next door. "Millie has finished her act."

Sammy looked through the entrance and saw Millie the burlesque queen, seated on a bar stool with a drink in one hand and a cigarette, plus a holder, in the other. Her dress was above her knees, showing a yard or so of white flesh composed of calf and thigh. Her legs were crossed in a deliberately provocative pose as she watched Pete.

"Pete," said Jules, reproachfully, "you got a wife and three kids. Why don't you layoff Millie?"

"Christ," said Pete. "Could you? She's gorgeous."

"Yeah," said Sammy, "but I don't like it when it's so easy to get. Come to think of it, though, it ain't like the good old days. Everything's easy to get these days."

An indefatigable troop of Salvation Army workers came by, singing the Battle Hymn of the Republic. A young girl came to Pete rattling a tambourine.

"Give a gift to the Lord, brother," she said.

Pete grinned, sarcastically. "Who's *He* payin' taxes to?"

An enraged evangelist behind the girl overheard him. "Repent ye!" he shouted. "For the day of the Lord is at hand!"

"Why don't you crack-pots give up," exclaimed Pete. "You're all a broken record."

"Yeah," put in Sammy. "Heaven's probably got troubles enough these days without crack-pots trying to save the likes of us. G'wan, beat it."

The evangelist straightened his shoulders and led his troop onward, to the beat of a forlorn sounding drum. They sang:

"I have read a fiery gospel, writ in burnished rows of steel:
"'As ye deal with my contemners, so with you my grace shall deal;
"'Let the Hero, born of woman, crush the serpent with his heel...'"

*   *   *

AT LAKE SUCCESS, the quasi-established Terrestrial Government reconvened its Supreme Council. Michael Kent, the Agarthian representative, had the floor. Not that his legality had been cleared. Soviet representative Gormski and other Eurasian colleagues would not recognize Agarthi as a member. But the Council had voted to hear his version of what had happened since adjournment on the previous Wednesday when Germain had given his ultimatum that they must accept the Emergency Clause.

"It is very *apropos,*" said Kent, before a battery of microphones and TV cameras, "to quote Mr. Germain on one point brought out in the last session. He said: 'You have now emerged from the cocoon of your own atmosphere. Terrestrial Man is a new metamorphosis taking wing in the limitless oceans of outer space. This is a form of rebirth, gentlemen, and I assure you that the mortality rate in such cases is high...

"'The dangers, let me remind you, are far from being behind you. They lie ahead. You are not expected to acquire overnight an adequate perspective of the incomprehensible. You are merely expected to accept protection and guidance until you have progressed sufficiently to carry on independently yet in cooperation with universal civilization.'"

106

Kent looked beyond the light banks, out at the dark crescent of humanity that was his audience—representatives of all the nations of the world. What could they know of the *real* facts? How could he convince them that they were only cattle compared to the alien force with which Nicholas the First had somehow become connected?

"To be brief," he continued, "Agarthi has already been attacked. Our own forces have been dispatched to meet the enemy."

Gormski rose to his feet and demanded to have the floor, which the Chairman granted. "If this is so," he almost shouted, "then why did not our giant radar screens, capable of detecting every meteor from here to the moon, detect this enemy fleet?"

There was applause and laughter, but Kent interrupted. "Because of a science unknown to you. These aliens use a second order type of energy, which screens them against all primary types of energy including electro-magnetic waves."

"Then why," shouted Gormski, "did not Agarthi warn the nations of the Earth that this danger faced us all?"

Again there was applause. Kent took a big breath.

"Because," he said, "Germain did not want to send you to slaughter. You should not have dispatched your fleets. They will be destroyed."

Gormski winked at several of his colleagues and smiled derisively. "May I remind you, Mr. Kent, that Universal Power is as far beyond atomic energy as was the latter beyond chemical energy? We have bought from Agarthi the indisputable super science that you claim was given to you by the so-called Elder Race. Each of our space warships is now equivalent to Earth's total armaments of only a generation ago. And there are *thirty* of them patrolling the void at this moment. Do you suggest that the forces of the Terrestrial Government are totally inadequate and that only your own forces could protect us?"

"I do," Kent's gaze was even, unperturbed, confident. "You are inexperienced—babes in the woods. And worst of all—you are over-confident."

Mr. Balfour, the U.S. representative, requested the floor.

"May we ask," he said, "just what your own forces consist of?"

"You may," replied Kent. "Of the Agarthian old line fleet of Elder type ships there are twenty-five. Your ships are fifty thousand-ton vessels. The Agarthian ships are two hundred and fifty thousand ton vessels, equipped with apparatus that your most modern physicists would need a year of additional training even to begin to comprehend. The very specialized Golden Guardsman fleet consists of a hundred vessels, each of which is equivalent in destructive power to your entire fleet. You have often raised the question: How can Agarthi support a superior armaments program when the combined tax income of the world could only build thirty Terrestrial Government ships? The answer is, gentlemen, that we have been riding heavily on reserve resources left us ages ago by the Elder Race. Now those reserves have been depleted, and that is why we have had to sell Agarthian science to the outside world on the basis of fifty million dollars per year. There are other resources, also, of a nature which I am not permitted to describe, but as time goes on we will actually need Terrestrial Government appropriations to continue the work of making Earth safe in relation to interstellar civilization. However, to continue. There is also another force, an ally of ours, an ally in whose existence you do not believe. The Lunar Interstellars, a benevolent colony of interstellar people who took refuge inside the moon ages ago when they discovered Earth was secretly in the thralldom of malignant interstellar influences. When Agarthi opened warfare against those malignant forces, the Lunar Interstellars joined forces with us and the Elder Race to make Earth free of secret bondage for the first time in thousands of years. Now, in the face of this new and perhaps even greater threat, the Lunar Interstellars have joined us once more, with a hundred and sixty magnificent vessels that would make yours look like covered wagons."

Gormski sprang to his feet, characteristically. "This is

preposterous," he shouted. "It is again a hoax to inspire fear and to promote acceptance of the Emergency Clause whereby Agarthi could rule us all in the event of extra-terrestrial aggression."

"Then what of Russia's present predicament?" put in Kent. "Has not Nicholas returned, backed by this alien force, determined to take the Earth again? Can you deny that everything from Baku to Kharkov has been taken and that Irkutsk is dominated at this moment by an alien warship and an army of robots?"

"That Nicholas has returned from hiding we do not deny," said Gormski. "But robots and alien space armadas are questionable. Can't you recognize propaganda when you see it?"

"Would Nicholas, who is Germain's sworn enemy, collaborate with him in this 'hoax,' as you call it, to inspire fear of extra-terrestrial aggression?" queried Kent.

"Gentlemen," interposed Dr. Jorge Calaveras, the Peruvian Chairman, in Esperanto. "This is getting us nowhere. Mr. Kent was originally given the floor to inform us of the nature of the enemy, according to Agarthian investigations. So the Chair is calling upon Mr. Kent to give us that information."

Kent looked at all of them. "How can I explain that which you could never understand?"

"Explain yourself, Mr. Kent."

"An alien force, perhaps dangerous even to the Elder Race, itself, has emerged from age-long secret hiding. One of their weapons happens to be the much discussed flying saucers."

There ensued a burst of laughter, but he continued. "Doctors Borg and Grange, working in the Agarthian laboratories, succeeded in trapping one of these flying saucers. They are not ships, gentlemen. They are living, sentient creatures. Their movements have a direct relationship with the movements of the alien fleet we have detected. We believe them to be under the control of the unknown robot masters. We do not know what they can do, but we have reason to believe that they are the enemy's greatest reserve weapon."

"Assuming for the moment, that what you say is true—" The Chairman's opening remark was interrupted by derisive laughter. "Only for the sake of argument," he protested, pounding with his gavel for order. "What does Agarthi think is the source of this hidden enemy? Is it Mars?"

"We believe that Mars is only a part of the picture. The robot masters, themselves, may come from another plane of existence."

Gormski was on his feet again. "In other words, Mr. Kent, you propose that Heaven, itself, is our present enemy?"

It was an obvious slap in the face and it touched off the Irish in Michael Kent. Why not give them the works?—he thought. We're the ones who'll have to fight their battles for them.

"Heaven," he answered, "is not our enemy. But the enemy may be a threat to Heaven."

Half the Council was on its feet booing. "He's mad!" "Throw him out!" "He's wasting our time!" "This is an insult to our intelligence!"

Kent was thinking of the cybernetics lab in Agarthi and of conclusions of which Germain had informed him. He remembered Germain's exact words: "I mean a much greater danger than mere space armadas... I mean—stuff like political corruption, graft, embezzlement, juvenile delinquency, the collapse of moral standards, lower church attendance, the increase of divorces murders, suicides, infanticides, patricides, perversion, narcotics addiction, *et cetera*... The computers show that the rapid increase of these phenomena cannot be correlated with the maximum probability curves based on human nature... Kent, there is another force somewhere, powerful and dangerous because of its very subtlety, which is attempting to undermine humanity *from the inside*."

And then there were Dr. Grange's remarks regarding flying saucers, before the Agarthian Council: "The hypothesis that this second order of matter might constitute the substance of the so-called ether and be the carrier medium for magnetic energy as well as other primary wave phenomena has now developed into strongly substantiated theory. In fact, sub-matter may be actual substance of the *next plane of existence...* The flying saucers are either the denizens of the sub-material world or they are a hybrid substance caught halfway between— the key, you might say, to the world of secondary phenomena..."

"I propose," said Gormski to the Council, "that we strike Mr. Kent's latest remarks from the records and that we dismiss Mr. Kent from this session of the Supreme Council. I propose further that we concern ourselves with examining the emergency as *we* know it and arrive at sober decisions affecting a practical method of defense."

The motion carried and Kent left. An uncontrolled rage filled him. The coming battle, he told himself, would teach them a lesson, if Earth survived at all.

* * *

THAT night in his hotel room he made use of his telepathic communicator that had been placed surgically inside his skull. Relayed through Agarthian augmenting equipment, his call reached Yvonne, his sister, who kept a lonely vigil in Germain's own laboratory citadel on Guam.

How is Lillian? he asked, referring to Germain's wife.

Michael! came Yvonne's augmented thought. *You never brought her!*

Are you crazy? I was just with you yesterday, and I left her there.

No, Michael. Germain communicated with me. He thinks you were possessed by an alien intelligence and were given a false memory of what you did. Lillian is gone! Germain made me use her direction finder and it located her—until an alien screen blocked it.

Sweat beaded suddenly on Kent's forehead. *Where is she?* he telepathed.

Somewhere in space. She has been kidnapped by the enemy. Germain has gone after her in the Nova. Michael, I'm scared. Why don't you come here?

What have you got to be scared of, Yvonne? In that place you're safer than anyone else on Earth. That lab's lousy with Elder Race gear—the genuine stuff.

That's just it. Germain made me activate some of it. He made me turn on the Chronoperceptor. It scares me, because when I read the mental instruction tapes here I gather that this Elder Race machine is building up some kind of "tertiary" field that's surrounding the entire planet. I gather what it's supposed to do, but I can't put it into words. Maybe there are no words for it. But it's too much responsibility to carry alone, Michael. I need help. Germain was angry when he had the Chronoperceptor turned on. He would not have risked it otherwise.

Kent reflected that the Elder Race equipment to which his sister referred was something, which only Germain understood. This was the first time it had ever been activated, to his knowledge. Therefore, the lab on Guam could well be one of the most important cogs in this whole affair. Now that the Terrestrial Government Council had rejected him he had no further assignment for the time being.

I'll be there he told Yvonne.

Besides, he thought, Lillian's and Germain's direction finders were both on Guam. Maybe he could help at that post more than at any other. And he remembered—Lillian had just announced to Germain a precious little secret concerning herself.

No wonder Germain was fighting mad.

CHAPTER TWELVE

ACROSS the world, on the outskirts of Irkutsk, lay a round, gray shape a quarter mile in diameter and three hundred feet thick. It was Nicholas' flag ship, a Nrlanian vessel built by robots and Gdjinhji slaves in the subterranean work cities of Mars. From it had marched that army of telepathic robots, which had since turned Irkutsk into an industrial slave city. In many Russian cities, from Baku to Kharkov, other Nrlanian vessels rested, and robots worked tirelessly, all under the control of Nicholas the First. But what bothered Nicholas and his chief aide, Dr. Gerhardt Eidelmann, was the fact that the control they maintained over these robots and ships, as well as the balance the Nrlanian fleet hanging above them in outer space, was theirs only by the sufferance of their allies, the Nrlani, who lurked somewhere between Earth and Mars in their floating city and worked through their hidden Central Control.

Near the space warship at Irkutsk was a villa, in the basement of which was a laboratory guarded by robots. Here Nicholas and Eidelmann, dressed in hooded, black radiation garments, were ready to draw an ace card out of their sleeves...

"Just give me another ten minutes," said Eidelmann, "and the power banks will be sufficiently charged to jam the Nrlanian beams."

He peered through thick eyeglasses at a fifty-foot power panel fed by Universal Power. Nicholas paced the floor.

"I don't see how we can fail," he said, his gray eyes gleaming in anticipation of his new acquisition of power. "In a few minutes the complete control of the local Nrlanian fleet and all its robots will be cut off from Nrlanian Central. And if the remainder of the Nrlanian ships approach us as near as the orbit of the moon we'll control them, too. They will he ours. Think of it, Gerhardt. Even the Nrlani will be helpless. It's like—like cutting off their arms!"

His face clouded. He remembered having looked upon a Nrlanian once. Izdran of a Thousand Lives. And he thought: What the devil would a thing like *that* need arms for? He had never told Eidelmann about it. Pavlovich and Trinha Llih, the Martian girl, had also beheld Izdran in his true form. None of them had ever brought the subject up again. It wasn't something a human being would care to talk about. The Nrlanians were anathema to human life. He shuddered.

"Hurry it up," he grumbled, darkly.

On the side of the lab opposite the new power panels were banks of relay controls and several televiewers. On one of the screens was a scene of destruction in outer space, relayed to him by his flagship. As another Terrestrial Government ship blasted into nothingness before the onslaught of the activated robot flotilla, he smiled mirthlessly.

"The imbeciles. They can't touch our screens. It's like shooting fish in a barrel. They haven't the slightest knowledge of second order energy. In a few hours the Terrestrial Government fleet will be nothing but cosmic dust."

"I wish I could say the same for the Agarthians, the Lunar Interstellars and the Golden Guardsmen—not to mention Borg and Germain," put in Eidelmann, still watching his meters.

"They do not possess second order equipment, either," retorted Nicholas. "Hurry it up, will you?"

"Look," said Eidelmann. "The banks are charged. When I throw the switch on the transmitter here the Nrlanian bands will be jammed." He threw the switch and a soundless, tingling vibration filled the room. "Now here goes our key carrier locking the robots to their new Central Control." He threw in another switch. "They are yours, Nicholas."

"No they aren't. I'll take them." The two men whirled around. "Hands in the air, Nick."

IT was Pavlovich, and behind him was Trinha Llih, smiling at Nicholas with her ice cold Martian smile, her eyes blazing triumph. Pavlovich carried in one hand a regulation radium pistol, and in the other a Nrlanian dis-gun with which he had dispatched the robot guards.

"Sergeyev!" shouted Nicholas, scowling at him. "Don't be insane..."

Pavlovich grinned sardonically, his fat brows closing in on the wart between his eyes. "I've never been saner in my life." he answered, "Get your arms up."

As Nicholas and Eidelmann slowly raised their arms, they both took a deep breath. Without knowing why, Trinha breathed deeply also, as though guided by an alert instinct.

In the next instant, the two men's armpits seemed to explode. A black smudge filled the room even as Pavlovich fired his radium pistol. Then he fell forward, coughing violently.

As two dark figures hurried toward them, Trinha, still holding her breath easily because of the oxygen rich terrestrial air she had taken in, snatched up Pavlovich's weapon and fired it again. The resultant explosion dropped one figure to the floor, and the other staggered, falling into a corner…

Not knowing what she was doing, she groped her way along the control panels and flipped a toggle switch, whereupon the ventilating system whirred into greater activity, clearing the air, and she dared to take a breath.

When visibility was good again, she saw the inert body of Eidelmann on the floor in the center of tile room. Pavlovich shook his head and struggled to his knees. They both looked at Nicholas.

Blood ran from his nose and ears as a result of the side blast from the radium bullet's explosion. Slowly, his wits were returning. He began to be aware of what he was looking at.

As Trinha lifted the robot control headpiece from its rack and put it on her head, Nicholas reached for his gun, and Pavlovich made a dive for him. Nicholas' knee came up and caught him in the throat. He rolled to one side, stunned. And Nicholas drew his gun.

Then he froze, staring.

In the doorway stood a telepathic robot, its center eye glowing. Nicholas knew what that glow meant.

"No!" he shouted, suddenly paling.

He aimed at the robot and fired.

The blast inactivated it and made it fall with a crash, but three more stepped over it. They walked toward Nicholas. He sweated, fired again, damaged two of them.

Then two more appeared. Nicholas tried to fire again but found difficulty in using his arms. The mental paralysis was setting in.

"No!" he screamed. There was a steel door behind him. He managed to turn and blast it open, and then he stumbled through the opening.

Pavlovich sat up again; staring at the robots, the blasted exit door, and at Trinha, who still wore her control headpiece.

"Send them after him," he yelled. "He'll get away!"

Trinha removed the headpiece. "Let him go," she said. "What can he do now? This is the new Central Control."

Pavlovich rushed toward her. "Give me that headpiece, you fool."

She thrust it behind her, her chin up and eyes blazing. "Leave Nicholas alone," she said. "You do what you want with the robots and the fleet. I've helped you. My reward is having Nicholas live to taste his defeat."

"But he's still got his agents…"

"They can do nothing. You have power over the Earth." Temptingly, she finally held the headpiece toward him.

Pavlovich paused, eyes suddenly gleaming as he looked at it. *"Da,"* he said, lapsing from Martian into Russian. He brushed a mop of hair off his forehead. *"Da.* Give it to me. I'll take charge from here."

As he concentrated on his new toy, Trinha started to make an exit. At the door of the lab she turned to look back at Pavlovich, who was now oblivious of her.

"Da," she said, mockingly. *"You* take over." And with that she left him.

*   *   *

BUT there was Eidelmann's special ship, which was not robot controlled, and of which Pavlovich knew nothing. While the latter played empire, Nicholas rounded up Eidelmann's top aides in the control room.

"Eidelmann is dead," he told them. "Pavlovich now has control of the robots and the fleet. But we're not finished yet."

The way he stared each man down they could believe him. "I believe we have one bargaining point left to us."

"And that is?" Dr. Reinsch, tall, lean, with a wiry, white crop of hair, was Eidelmann's chief nuclear physicist—had been in the old days of the Nazi new underground movement when Eidelmann had played with Elder Race machinery.

"You know what I'm talking about," replied Nicholas, "because you are now the greatest living authority on the subject. You helped Eidelmann build the first Zero Bomb."

Reinsch's face clouded over. "Of course," he said. "Even today the sub-assemblies of that bomb exist, and I could put them together, but it is not a useable weapon. It requires—"

"Forget the refinements. If the bomb will work—"

"But you don't understand. In its present form, if it were detonated, it would start a progressive chain reaction in stable matter, destroying the entire planet in a small fraction of a second."

"Precisely. And that's what we will do," said Nicholas.

"What? Destroy the Earth?" Reinsch's brows went up, eyes wide in amazement.

Nicholas' gray eyes blazed. "If Earth will not surrender, including Pavlovich and his forces and all the forces and allies of Agarthi—I will destroy it. The Zero Bomb you will assemble immediately. You will also need to connect its detonating mechanism with a slow timer set to trigger the bomb within one hundred hours. Controlling the timer I want a VHF receiver with traps on it to receive only my own secret frequency transmitted from the flagship here at Irkutsk. I want remote control over that bomb no matter where I am in the solar system. Once everything is set, I'll issue my ultimatum demanding complete capitulation of everybody or I'll neglect to reset the timer and the Earth can go up in smoke."

"You're...you're a madman," retorted Reinsch, his face quite livid with rage and disgust. "I can't place in your hands the power to destroy the Earth. No man could be entrusted—"

For answer, Nicholas calmly shot and killed every man in the room—except Reinsch. As the latter stood there sweating, Nicholas trained the pistol on him.

"It is not a question of trust," he said, quietly. "It is a matter of obedience. You will do precisely and only what you are told to do. Now where are those sub-assemblies for the Zero Bomb? I'll give you exactly three astronomically timed seconds to start talking."

Reinsch looked at the bodies lying on the floor. Many of them had been close colleagues. He had just had dinner with two of them.

At the crisp count of two, he started talking...

* * *

"WHAT slobbering idiots," raved Rocky. "That's the trouble with not getting better organized in time. Who gave the Terrestrial Fleet the order to attack?"

Stierman, heavy set, powerful, dark-complected, only stared gravely into the televiewer. He and Brion and Turner, all flight commanders with the Golden Guardsman fleet, had come to Rocky's flagship for a quick, personal conference on strategy. Their position was by now closer in to Mars than to Terra.

But down there between Luna and Terra they could see the catastrophe develop. Janice, in spite of her hard training, could hardly suppress tears of consternation.

"It's massacre," she said. "The Terrestrial Government Fleet is lost."

Rocky held his red-thatched head between two, ham-like hands. "Ye gods," he moaned. "Let's hope the Agarthians know better. Those robots pack too much stuff. We've got to complete our secondary projectors before we can hope to break their screens. How soon will the project be finished, Janice?"

"We'll be within range of Martian war rays, if any, before they'll be ready," she answered. "The Agarthian Fleet and the Lunars are deployed all over space between here and Terra, also converting to secondary projection."

"What's the latest from Borg and Germain?"

"Nobody knows where the *Nova* is," put in Brion. "I don't blame Germain for not telling us his position. If anybody would have second order screens by now, he would, and if he's invisible to the enemy, why spoil the advantage?"

"Borg and Grange have contacted the Lunars and they relayed the message on the coda-beam," added Janice. "They have found out a lot about the flying discs. They are creatures that live in space, and they are dangerous. They are definitely connected with the enemy."

"That's a big help," said Rocky. "What are we supposed to do about it? Nothing we've got will touch the critters because they are better than the old soldier. They don't just fade away. They fade *out*, completely. And we can't out fly them when they become nothing. But what harm can they do, actually?"

Stierman said, "Borg has intimated they may be the Sunday Punch, held in reserve. We don't know what they can do—yet."

"So what's the immediate plot?" queried Turner.

Rocky told him. "The only thing we can do until we're *really* ready, is to approach Mars and very gingerly probe its defenses."

Stierman raised a pair of thick eyebrows. "Fortress Mars may not be on Mars at all," he suggested.

"*That* we've got to find out," said Rocky. "So back to your ships. And remember, we're scouting, not attacking. Don't be like those Terrestrial Government monkeys. I'll break the neck of the first officer who tries to show our big right arm."

Which might have been a questionable threat, inasmuch as "Iron Man" Stierman had broken a few muscular necks, himself, having been Terra's leading exponent of judo, plus a few other manly arts. Brion and Turner were also very big time professional trouble deflaters. But on the other hand they respected Rocky's threat for two reasons. First, he was their commanding officer and a regular Joe.

Secondly, he was six feet six inches in height and weighed two hundred and sixty pounds. They had seen him manhandle hardy thugs as though he had been playing Ping-Pong. It was not for nothing that Agarthi had gone out of its way to adopt big, fun loving, fight loving Steve Rockner to handle ten thousand of Terra's most capable fighting men—most of them battle experienced commandos and pilots from World War

Three who had flocked to Agarthi from all over the world in response to Michael Kent's recruiting efforts.

"But Steve," exclaimed Janice. "Can't something be done for those poor things? They're simply being slaughtered..."

"Brother!" said Rocky, watching the televiewer. "They say Pride goeth before a fall, but this is a case of idiotic, boneheaded stubbornness going before the Diluvium. Agarthi *must* be taking over under the emergency. They'll order a retreat. If they don't, Terra's tin can space fleet will be destroyed, and the world will be in the hands of the enemy before we get back. Already half of Europe seems to be in the hands of Nicholas, according to Agarthi's relay-casts we got half an hour ago. He's on the march again. But we'll stop him, for one good reason."

"And that is?" queried Stierman. Rocky brought his big fist down on the chrome-molybdenum flange of the control panel. "We've *got* to, that's why."

"Any additional orders?" queried Brion.

Rocky looked from Brion to Stierman to Turner. They all avoided his eyes and seemed to slump, mentally if not physically.

"All right," he came near to yelling at them. "I suppose you think *I* like it. I know you'd rather be fighting than pussyfooting around out here, but orders—"

"Rocky," interrupted Stierman. His blocky, muscular hands rippled with tension, as though they would have been happy snapping a few vertebrae. "Put this on record as speaking out of turn, but I'm going to say it. As the erstwhile Chief of the FBI, I made a reputation with the underworld by one sure method. Fight one fire with two. Papers, reports and investigations had their place, but the main thing was *drive*. We didn't case a 'joint.' We barged in and tore it apart and found out what was in it. Right now one of our ships could take over Earth. So with a hundred ships, we'll be able to tear hell out of Mars and find out what's there without losing time. I suggest—"

Rocky was on his feet, pacing back and forth in front of them. "Listen. I have a hunch that when the green light comes through, you are going to get more than a bellyful. It's going to be more than you want. It's going to be big, final, decisive, involving Earth, Mars, the solar system—human civilization. So let's not go off half cocked. Damn it. If it weren't for the responsibility—if it were just us 'girls,' I'd like to go in if it was barehanded. You *know* that. So bear with me until that second order stuff is ready. Now get back to your ships. Densify and deploy widely. That way we'll be harder to detect harder to hit, harder to hurt. And of course," he added, "turn on the invisibility. It's only first order stuff, but it may add to the enemy's confusion."

IT was difficult, as a matter of fact, for hidden enemy detectors to keep track of a great fleet of space ships that suddenly deployed out over thousands of cubic miles of empty space and then became miniature. Under the influence of Borg's relative densifiers, the electrostatic and magnetic nature of every electron and proton in every ship was altered, causing molecular structure to shrink, creating miniature dreadnaughts only ten feet in length.

At which point they also became suddenly invisible to light and all other primary radiations.

Such ships were hard to find, impenetrably dense, swift, dangerous. The enemy was more wary of them than it was of the vast Agarthian warships or the sleek, mysterious vessels of the Lunar Interstellars. But every possible movement of Terra's multiple forces was being watched. Almost every ship was registered in the depths of intricate, hidden machines—thanks to the flying discs.

All except one ship—a swiftly moving vessel indetectably enshrouded in second order invisibility—the *Nova*...

CHAPTER THIRTEEN

GERMAIN admired Ingaborg and David. He was glad they were both on board with him. Their quick, healthy nerves were what he needed most right now. Eyes glued to the second order detectors, their nimble fingers were poised for almost instantaneous action above controls that would flood the new generators with oceans of Universal Power and rotate the screen frequencies all over the spectrum so that nothing would have a chance to penetrate.

"It's too quiet," complained Ingaborg, almost in a whisper.

"That's natural," commented Germain, as he continued to tinker with a new second order instrument he had invented. A silver wire mesh helmet was attached to his head and to the instrument. "It's instinct. We're close under enemy guns, like a submarine at the bottom of an enemy harbor. If we weren't indetectable they'd probably blast us out of existence. So we're quiet."

"That's not why I'm quiet," put in David, never taking his eyes from the bank of meters and signal lights before him. "I'm speechless at the thought of this floating city out here in space. I thought the *Nova* was the biggest man-made object in the solar system, but this fortress stretches for miles. It's like a planetoid."

"A deadly fortress of alien science, which is inimical to human civilization," added Germain. "It may be *the* stronghold of the principal enemy."

"You mean—the robot masters?" This from Ingaborg.

"Yes."

"What is our next move?" asked David.

"That will depend on this instrument," Germain replied, suddenly grim again at the thought of Lillian.

"What is it?" asked Ingaborg.

"A psychic heterodyner."

"A what?"

"It works something like a signal generator, generating harmonics of normal human thought, and also it can receive such harmonics, or intermediate frequencies, all on the second order level. I'm trying to find the thought band on which these aliens operate—if any."

"What do you mean—if any?" asked Ingaborg.

"Maybe it's not thought at all, as we know it."

"What about Lillian? Do you think they've taken her here?"

Lights flared before Ingaborg and David and they tensed, watching the gyrating detector needles.

"I think they've found us," said Germain. "Change position and densify."

Swift fingers flew across the signal buttons and Agarthian engineers elsewhere on board moved to obey. The gigantic vessel leaped across two miles of space. And one minute later it was only twenty feet long.

"I've got to try my luck again," said Germain to Ingaborg and David. Since their *relative* sizes were the same, they could not see that they were now Lilliputians. They only knew it from experience. "Set the screens at one point seven two eight nine three six million megs."

After a few seconds, David said, "All set. Better act fast before they catch our frequency."

A light of triumph sprang into Germain's dark eyes. "I've got it," he exclaimed.

If a pin had dropped it would have sounded like an I-beam. They could all hear each other breathing, and the ventilators hissed faintly. To know that primary and secondary invisibility as well as densification might not yet be enough to evade the tremendous enemy over their heads, that they might all be blotted out in the fraction of a second, and that one of their number—Germain—was for the first time tapping the very thoughts of inhuman intelligences that sought their lives, was almost too much for taut nerves.

Then Germain jumped as though he had been struck. He fell off his seat onto the deck, writhing, holding his temples, and the wire mesh helmet rolled from his head.

David sprang to his feet, but Germain held out his hand, waving him back . "Keep to the controls! Rotate the screens!" Ingaborg did this as he said it. "Full speed for Mars. Quick…"

Almost before he could draw another breath the operators astern had thrown on the power and the ship leaped away on its long journey.

"What happened?" came a logical question from David, back at the controls. "Are you all right?"

"I—I had to take a big chance," Germain grunted, as he pulled himself back into his chair. "They found me and let me have it—a psychic ray, on their own frequency. But I found that frequency, and I traced the source of their control. It's all recorded. In a minute I'll have all the coordinates and we'll know exactly where their Central Control is located. It is *not* in that flying city."

"What thoughts did you catch?" asked Ingaborg.

"All the thoughts of the enemy."

This time, Ingaborg looked away from her controls to stare at Germain.

"Yes, do you know how many there are?—the total number of the enemy, outside of the robots and this Central Control, whatever it is?"

David, too, looked at Germain to catch the answer.

"Seven intelligences. Nothing more."

"Seven?" This was from both of them.

"Yes. Seven members of a lost race of inhuman monstrosities . I gather that the Elder Race once destroyed their world, which is now marked by the asteroid belt. The whole key to their present power lies in their Central Control."

"And Lillian?"

"I say I caught all the thoughts of the enemy. I should have said I caught the *thoughts* of all the enemy, not *all* they were thinking. But I don't think Lil is in the city. Wait..."

He was bending over his invention. "The location of Central Control is—"

*   *   *

IN that moment, blackness struck them, along with vertigo. The thunders of a thousand Maelstroms smote their minds and they were vaguely aware of being buffeted about in space like a ship in a hurricane.

All but Germain. After the first second of shock he regained his special faculties and became sharply aware of the fact that the enemy had struck a very powerful blow.

Then his mind was assailed by Izdran. Germain's mental feathers ruffled instinctively and he sought to gain his full stature but was somehow weakened. He struggled with Izdran as though caught in the cloying webs of a dream.

He was aware of a monstrous, shadowy entity that laughed at him derisively while playing at spider and fly. However, when he realized that the other was merely trying to communicate with him he became receptive, struggling to remain alert for deception, like a lightly drugged panther.

Then came visual illusion—a coppery bowl of a sky over his head. Below, immeasurably distant, was a flat world spreading outward in all directions without horizons, its only feature being fire. Red and yellow flames, reaching hungrily upward as though from the surface of a titanic sun.

Germain stood on a bare, round disc fifty feet in diameter. The disc floated motionlessly in space, suspended between coppery sky and flaming world below. Not far distant was another disc supporting Sergeyev Pavlovich. Pavlovich did not see him. He was gazing over the edge of his disc platform at the fire below, and though there was no sensation of heat he sweated.

Pavlovich was also aware, as was Germain, of Izdran. The latter was simply a ball of light poised motionlessly above them.

To Germain it meant that Izdran was duo-psychic, controlling two minds simultaneously, allowing Germain to be aware of Pavlovich but not enabling Pavlovich to see him.

Germain asserted himself slightly by creating the illusion of a comfortable chair for Izdran to see. He sat down in it and hurled the first thought:

I presume you are merely attempting to communicate. What has Pavlovich to do with all this?

Instantly, Izdran answered him by cutting him in on his

communication with the Russian:

Pavlovich, you exult now in your possession of separate control over the robots and the fleet, as well as Universal Power—not realizing, of course, that through the medium of the Martian girl, Trinha Llih, I maneuvered it that way in order to deflate our erstwhile collaborator, Nicholas.

Germain had little time to wonder about this turn of affairs, because of Pavlovich's reply. The latter appeared to accept, at last, that his present environment was the product of illusion. He straightened up, regained some of his confidence, and Germain caught his sarcastic reply:

In that case you've given me what I want. Thanks very much. You thought you set a trap, but it seems I ate your fatted calf. The robots and the fleet are mine—and so is the Earth. You fumbled with the lynx, Izdran. Now beware of the tiger. You'll soon have Germain on your neck, or what you use for a neck, and I'm depending on the two of you to destroy each other and save me the trouble.

Suddenly, Pavlovich's disc platform became a mere open pattern of thin girders. Pavlovich yelled with fright and fell across a gap between them, clutching at them, trying to save himself from falling into the flames below. And Izdran calmly replied:

My dear Pavlovich—the sprawling, inefficient, destructive and parasitic form of life known as human shall be obliterated from the universe, and all Germain's delusions of high purpose and godliness in Man shall implode into cosmic dust to clear Creation for a new beginning. You are both mere mice squealing in the darkness of your own stupidity. Germain is even now feeling the weight of our greatest weapon, which nothing can resist, as is every space ship that Agarthi and Luna can muster against us, and your captured Nrlanian and Terrestrial Government vessels will also be useless if they emerge too far into space, as they would automatically meet with the same fate, becoming but lifeless derelicts, flotsam adrift in the grip of solar gravitation, ultimately becoming fuel for the fires of Sol. You have had your little try to best us and you have failed—all of you. We have use for you Terrestrials just as we have use for the Martians, but only as a temporary front. If you continue to exist at all it will be merely to serve us, then be destroyed utterly. We are not asking you to surrender. That is completely immaterial. Whatever any of you may choose to do, your era is at an end.

Pavlovich scrambled to his feet, standing astride two girders, and he replied: *You sound like all this has gone to your head. You're crazy. Nobody could be that sure of himself.*

The lacework of girders thinned to half the previous number, and Pavlovich struggled again to maintain his footing.

Your era is at an end, telepathed Izdran, *even if we make no further effort to curb your present actions. If you disbelieve me, let me ask you a simple question: Do you know what happened to Nicholas?*

Germain tensed, sensing that all this was not mere propaganda. Before Pavlovich could reply, Izdran answered his own question:

Nicholas is in space flight, in a secret vessel built by Eidelmann. For my own amusement I have left him intact to get through to his goal. He carries remote controls, which hold the power to destroy or save the Earth. Somewhere on your planet is a very deadly bomb—one that will propagate a chain reaction in stable matter and thus destroy your world instantly even as ours was destroyed by the Elder Race long ago. Soon you will hear from him, as will the remaining Agarthians on Earth. He will give you an ultimatum: If you and all the peoples of the Earth do not surrender, along with the Agarthians, Germain, the Lunar Interstellars and the so-called Golden Guardsmen, he will permit that bomb to detonate.

Germain received the relay of Pavlovich's startled thoughts: *Where is that bomb? We've got to deactivate it!*

Izdran's psychic laughter was not a pleasant experience. *This has become a very interesting little game, hasn't it? Now why should I spoil it at this stage? Nicholas has killed Dr. Reinsch, who was the only other living human who knew the bomb's location. Now only Nicholas knows. I could find out by tapping his mind, but I don't want to be tempted. Let him have his power piece. From where I sit, the game is loaded with very entertaining suspense—especially in view of the fact that when Nicholas gives his ultimatum I shall have the Agarthian ships, the Golden Guards-men, the Lunar Interstellars and Germain and Borg all gagged so that they cannot reply even if they wish to submit. Mistaking their silence for defiance, he just may be megalomaniac enough to allow the bomb to explode.*

But Earth... came Pavlovich's frantic mental cry tinged with quaking fear. *Earth will be destroyed...*

Izdran's doubly relayed thought returned like a hammer blow, contemptuously: *What is the Earth to me or my kind? One puny obstacle to be brushed from our path—a dustmote lost in Infinity. It is quite expendable, so why not let Nicholas save us the trouble?*

At that moment, all the girders supporting Pavlovich dissolved and he plummeted, screaming, into the flames below. Germain knew that the Russian would wake up somewhere with a bad headache and the vivid memory of a nightmare.

He addressed Izdran: *Where is my wife, Lillian?*

Ah yes... The little mutant speaks. I thought I'd need her to play my game with Nicholas, but that is no longer necessary. She is alive and well, Germain. And I will tell you where she is, just to add interest to our little game. She lives now in the heart of Central Control. Now why don't you try to find her? Izdran laughed. *Or is the mutant afflicted with altruism? Would he rather find Nicholas first? The bomb, you should know, was set to detonate in one hundred hours unless Nicholas decides to change the settings through his remote controls. Where is Nicholas, Germain? The Earth has only hours to live. And where is Central Control? You think you know where it is. It would be amusing to see you try to reach it, or enter it. Only Martians can enter Central Control, Germain. Any other form of life would be destroyed. I'm going to make this an experiment. I'll give your wife just sufficient air to last her until the Zero Bomb detonates on Earth. When Earth dies, so does she. Now you can't very well serve two loves simultaneously, can you? Whom do you value more, oh hero, born of woman—the people of the Earth, or your wife? The board awaits you, Stephen Germain. It is your move.*

Rage filled Germain. He tore Izdran's disguise from him even as Izdran removed the disc platform from under his "chair." But Germain did not fall. He chose to remain exactly where he was, sitting in the chair, suspended in the center of Izdran's illusion.

He saw Izdran and his mind reeled. But there was no time to wonder about such an inconceivable form of life, a thing conceived on a basis foreign to human concept.

Izdran, he telepathed, *you and your six companions are going to die.*

The blazing globe was back, disguising Izdran again. And once more the Nrlanian laughed. *But the chessboard, Germain. Have you forgotten the queen piece? And the black bishop—Nicholas? It is your move, Germain.*

CHAPTER FOURTEEN

TRINHA Llih finally mastered the controls of the televiewer and located Eidelmann's space ship. She had no way of interpreting the Doppler-principle triangulator in front of her, but she reasoned that Pavlovich's small Nrlanian flier was traveling many miles per second in the general direction of Mars.

She had traced Nicholas, after several days' secret investigation, only to see him take off in a hurry. As Pavlovich's hidden ship had been emptied of its robot crew, she had been able to steal it without fear of its coming under Pavlovich's Central Control. She dismissed the thought of possible pursuit by any of Pavlovich's robot controlled battleships, because she knew that such a move would lose the Russian a ship to the Nrlani once it emerged into the range of their own control. In the meantime, there was Nicholas to think about. His unexpected escape in an independently controlled space ship was not her idea of the kind of defeat she had planned for him.

"You know, Trinha, I think you and I have the same idea."

She turned, swiftly, reaching for her radium pistol, but not swiftly enough. A man's hand swept the weapon out of her reach, and she looked into the muzzle of her own weapon. Then she screamed.

"Eidelmann!"

He stood there glaring at her, smiling only with his mouth, as bald and myopic as ever, but unscarred. "When you saw me last," he said, "I was a shattered corpse."

"You were dead. *Dead...*" she exclaimed, brokenly, in the limited Russian she had been able to pick up while on Earth.

The other shrugged. *"That* Eidelmann *did* die," he answered.

"But I am another Eidelmann."

Her eyes widened. Her hand went to her lips. She paled and drew away from him, her pulse roaring in her ears.

"It is a long and complicated story, which you would not understand," he told her. "To make it short and simple, there was a machine, long ago, with which I experimented. It was not my invention. The Elder People built it. It was called a tel-etransporter. It transported physical objects by *broadcasting* them. Naturally, I experimented with the obvious. I built multiple receivers. With such an arrangement I once produced a multiple army for a new Nazi Germany—the famous *Doppelganger* troops—troops without number. In spite of that army, Agarthi succeeded in defeating us. All Elder Race equipment was taken from us, and those of us who survived were imprisoned. However, I was not entirely imprisoned. Not even Nicholas knew that I was, myself, a *Doppelganger*... While he freed one of me, my second counterpart worked as an independent agent elsewhere, yet knowing everything that was happening to my other self. When the first Eidelmann was killed, it was a matter of logic for the second one to take over. Consequently, here I am. I followed you, because I correctly assumed you would know where this ship was concealed. And now it seems we have a common interest—to overtake Nicholas."

Trinha understood little of all this. Her practical mind was groping through the temporary chaos of her thoughts, which had been wrought by the hurricane of fear that had broken upon her at sight of Eidelmann. But now she was reasoning that Eidelmann could be of help to her, ghost or demon though he might he, because he had good reason to be on the other's trail. That he might take over where Nicholas would leave off, in the event of the latter's ultimate defeat, was immaterial to her. The main objective was Nicholas.

"Take over," she told Eidelmann, finally. "Why should I argue?"

"That's more like it," said the German scientist. "It would

be quite unintelligent of us to act like two stubborn mules and pull against each other when we're both after the same stack of hay."

Trinha could not understand all he said, but she could understand the little dot of light that was centered on the screen of the televiewer. That was Nicholas' ship, and it was headed straight for her own planet. She could understand that she hated Nicholas. He had betrayed her people, herself, and her sacred dreams. Death was too good for him, but if all else failed—

* * *

"IZDRAN," said Prahl, accusingly, "you are cheating." He was looking at the same screen that occupied Izdran's attention. "You are letting the Martian girl and that resourceful German get through the barrier. They may be able to liquidate Nicholas if you don't turn the discs on them, and if Nicholas dies the Zero Bomb will be out of control."

Izdran might have laughed, but his seventh sense was bothering him. "The stakes in this game may have risen to vital proportions," he said. "I don't like the future picture. So I'm throwing an extra piece onto the board, but I'm letting it make its own moves. That's not exactly cheating. And what if I am? Are we becoming moralists at this late stage?"

Reflectively, Prahl replied, "It is, perhaps, later than we think. I don't like this game. It makes light of our objectives."

"On the contrary. If we can't rule Earth we might as well see it destroyed."

"But have you forgotten what else will be destroyed if Earth goes?"

"My friend, in *that* house there are many mansions..."

* * *

IN the next instant, Germain was aware of being back in the

control room of the *Nova*. He would have discounted much of the illusion just experienced had he not possessed a seventh sense that warned him very definitely of total cataclysm. In spite of his self-control, a cold, nervous sweat beaded his face.

There was nothing to do but fight, so he said a prayer and set to work with every cell of his mutant brain.

He looked about him in the control room. The lights were out, but his extrasensory perception went exploring. There were Ingaborg and David, sprawled unconscious.

At first he thought they had struck their heads against something, but when his ESP carried his mental vision through the ship he realized that the entire crew was unconscious.

Then why not himself? For the first time he was aware of the terrible strain he was under just to remain conscious. Something seemed to be draining his mind of energy—the same mysterious force that had somehow affected all electrical conductors on board and deadened the Universal Power generators.

What had Izdran said to Pavlovich?—*Germain is even now feeling the weight of our greatest weapon, which nothing can resist, as is every space ship which Agarthi and Luna can muster against us.*

Did that mean—?

"*No,*" he exclaimed aloud, shaking his head to clear it of the terrible vision of almost three hundred ships scattered over millions of miles of the dark void—*lifeless derelicts, flotsam adrift in the grip of solar gravitation*—and of Earth in the grip of Pavlovich, only to be destined to destruction, or at least to slavery and eventual extinction at the hands of the robot masters.

And Lillian!

His mind leaped outward only to meet a restricting wall that dimmed his perception. It did not hinder him entirely, but it was hard to get through.

Carefully, he sought to discover the nature of that wall. It clung to the *Nova* like a mass of jelly, and he soon knew what it was. Simultaneously he knew what every other ship from Terra or Luna looked like at that moment.

A massed cluster of flying discs completely covering

everything. Obedient to Nrlanian Central Control, they had penetrated even second order screens, and now they were exerting their mysterious powers in order to immobilize all resistance.

Again he tried to examine the peculiar creatures, and again he was confronted with an alien thing that seemed unfathomable. But now he suddenly became aware of features he had not detected before. The discs were all mental power, but passive unless controlled. They were lethal when activated by outside volition. And that outside volition was Central Control.

He felt his pulse increase as he envisioned this tremendous instrument lying in the hands of the Nrlani. By methods perhaps similar in principle to those Berg and Grange had used, they had trapped the discs for centuries and conditioned them to respond to Central Control. Wandering through space, they were very adequate extensions of the Nrlanian central brain—a cold, inhuman intelligence expanded to the size of a solar system. The thralldom of millennia of time in which Earth had lain secretly at the hands of malignant interstellar powers seemed insignificant when compared to the magnitude of this.

He shuddered and then made a new effort to concentrate.

If there was to be any chance of salvation, he had to get to Central Control. To the devil with Nicholas, for the time being. If he could get to Central Control and find a way of entering the place he could perhaps accomplish more than he could by choosing any other course of action, and at the same time he could rescue Lillian. As for the threat of the Zero Bomb, he was thankful Izdran had not been able to probe the secret depths of his mind. There were a few hidden pieces which he, himself, had installed on Izdran's treacherous chessboard.

In the meantime, he had to act fast. If he remained a prisoner inside the *Nova* he would soon succumb to the terrible, draining force being exerted upon him by the discs.

WITH an alarmingly difficult physical effort, he staggered through the companionway and along A-deck toward the lifeboats. Then he came to a stop and shook his head. What was he doing? Leaving Ingaborg and David?

For a moment he thought clearly again. Yes, he was leaving them—and all the crew—to rescue them later if there was still time, or to leave them to their fate if there was not. He could not consider himself, or his friends, or even Lillian.

That was the hell of being a straw god. More and more people depended on you. People? No—worlds, a solar system.

And here he was staggering around in the pitch dark—

But dammit. No use trying the commuter boats. They'd be as dead as anything else.

Yet he had to get out. *Had* to...

He staggered on again, his ESP dimming at times so much that he had to grope through the dark with his hands.

Toward the space suits and the airlock. If he could just bailout of the ship and get free of those damned discs, he might be able to think—maybe reach somebody, or even effect an astral projection—anything rather than lie down now.

He reached the suits and got into one of them. The air valves worked because they were mechanical rather than electrical. That was something, at least.

But when he tried to activate the ship's airlocks to go outside he realized that the pneumatic devices inside were dependent upon electrical valve trips.

No action. The ponderous doors of the lock might as well have been a mile thick. He couldn't get out.

He fell to his knees, his space mitts scraping down the apathetic metal before him, and his deepest instinct brought to his lips a single faint cry of remorse.

"Lil, honey. Lil..."

Then he paused, suddenly rigid. In his mind was a picture of himself in the palace at Agarthi, trapped by Pavlovich's robot images.

Autoportation!

He lay down on his back and assembled his thoughts, knowing that even if he succeeded he would die unless he could include the spacesuit, as well.

Calm now, he thought. Every muscle relaxed. Heart slower, breathing diminished.

There. Now build the faith image. Myself, in this suit, outside, a mile away—probably as far as I can project—looking back at the *Nova*. Get it clear, clear—*clear*... Ready, relax...

In the next instant he was aware of the cold hissing of oxygen from his tanks, a very conspicuous sound when one is falling free in interplanetary space.

Falling swiftly, that is, toward the surface of a planet.

Approximately five thousand miles below he beheld the mottled pale green and red topography of Mars, toward which he was hurtling at an indeterminate speed. He knew that the inverse square law was not working to his advantage as he fell ever deeper into the field of the planet's gravitational influence. Then, too, there was the *Nova* with its helpless human cargo. In a matter of hours it would dig its grave beside his own down there.

Unless he could do something...

CHAPTER FIFTEEN

FAINTLY, the message was received, first on one band, then on another. Operators in all parts of the world began to notify their respective regional governments. The regional headquarters, in turn, appealed to the Terrestrial Government Council at Lake Success. It was Nicholas' ultimatum.

Ironically, Gormski was chairman at the time and it devolved upon him to read it to the Council:

"Furthermore," the ultimatum concluded, "unless an answer is received from Terrestrial Government, from Pavlovich's provisional occupation government, from Agarthi, from the Lunar Interstellars, from the Golden Guardsman Fleet and from Germain, himself, within the next twelve hours—Earth will cease to exist..."

Gormski's usually pasty complexion was ruddy just now, and

he stared at his audience through his bifocals, defensively. "This is followed by some technical data," he mumbled, "concerning the wavelength to use in communicating with Nicholas. He is on Mars."

Council members were on their feet, shouting, and Gormski was pounding the gavel for order.

"If you had not opposed the acceptance of the Agarthian Charter and its Emergency Clause—" began some of the accusations, directed at Gormski.

But he was prepared for this. "One way or another," he said to them, "the same effect has been achieved. Germain and his forces have set out to defend us exactly as he would have had we accepted the Charter in the first place, yet we are still at an impasse. The Terrestrial Government Fleet has been half destroyed, and the other half has been captured. Half of all Eurasia is under the dominance of Nicholas' invading forces, now headed by this Pavlovich. Agarthi itself stands at bay, and we hear nothing of our saviors who sought to form a chastity belt across the stars against the ravishment we were warned to expect. I say we should contact Agarthi and Pavlovich simultaneously and concur on this matter, inasmuch as our destinies appear to have reached a common denominator."

Gormski had early been indoctrinated with an old political principle: "If you can't lick 'em, join 'em." A second principle provided for a two-faced attitude, so that one face could be saved merely by presenting the other to view.

"Particularly," he added, "we must contact this Pavlovich to determine whether or not we should consider this new threat as the outburst of another Carpet Eater or as something to be taken seriously. Since it is apparent that Pavlovich had muscled in on Nicholas' territory and the two are at desperate odds, Pavlovich would not be willing to surrender along with the rest of us unless he knew for a fact that the ultimatum could be made good. Agarthi's opinion in this might also be valuable, and their facilities might be more capable of communicating with Nicholas than any that we now have at our disposal.

Thus, by attracting the Council's, attention to these new considerations, Gormski simultaneously provided himself with a loophole for past errors and acquired new stature as a leader. Secretly, however, he conceded that Germain had been sincere, as well as Michael Kent. He wondered where they both were at that moment...

AGARTHI and Terrestrial Government appealed to Pavlovich simultaneously for an opinion, and it was soon forthcoming.

"The Zero Bomb exists," his message read. "I have already transmitted to Nicholas my own message of surrender. He has replied that he is not as much concerned with our capitulation as with Germain's and that of the Golden Guardsmen. As yet they have not replied, and he gives us all just six more hours."

Terrestrial Government representatives stormed the gates of Agarthi in person, including Gormski. But to all their pleas and inquiries and demands, Mandir made the same reply.

"If Germain and the Guardsmen, together with their allies, the Lunar Interstellars, can do nothing, then nothing remains to be done..."

Churches, shrines and hilltops began to overflow with praying and wailing multitudes. There was less wailing and praying at liquor bars, however, because many a proprietor was giving out free drinks.

Towers, steeples and buildings supporting large clocks came into prominence as millions of people watched what might be the last hours of existence dribble inexorably away into nothingness...

*   *   *

THE second terrestrial vessel to acquire second order screens was the laboratory ship carrying Dr. Grange and Dr. Borg, together with their small crew of Agarthian specialists. Painstakingly, under a cover of second order invisibility, they had combed the void for signs of the discs, ceaselessly making adjustments on their giant trap and simultaneously watching all fleet movements as well as they could.

It was not until the Nrlanians struck, however, that they began to discover what they were after. When they witnessed the envelopment of several Lunar vessels by the flying discs, they moved into action.

"The discs may be able to penetrate our screens, too," commented Grange. "Which means that we had better capture one and see what makes it tick before it is too late."

"I have made one concrete observation," said Dr. Borg. "The reason we did not see discs out here until now is that they were all too highly attenuated. Now they have densified into our own plane."

Just then, the alarm rang on the trap, and they rushed to see what they had caught. Donning lead-lined suits, they admitted themselves into the antechamber from which they could observe, through glass panels, the atomic pile and multiple cyclotron apparatus that formed the trap. There were second order controls, which they now manipulated in order to wrap a triple screen around their prisoner.

They could see the disc through the panels. It floated above the cyclotrons and pulsed with light and colors, as though struggling to get free. Beside Borg, several types of special motion picture cameras were whirring automatically, as were spectrographic and electronic analyzers and stroboscopic floodlights of various types.

Before either scientist could congratulate the other, however, the disc merely attenuated until it was mist, then nothingness.

"You see," said Borg, through the radiophone in the helmet of his suit. "I tell you they can travel from one plane to another. Grange, I think I know the answer..."

"You'd better have an answer quick," replied Grange. "The discs will soon overtake us like they are overtaking the fleet."

"We are equipped with the relative densifier," continued Borg. "Why don't we reverse its field action and instead of densifying—*attenuate*. Maybe we could—"

"Borg! You've hit it! That would enable us—"

"To follow the discs to their source and find out a lot of other things—maybe even stumble upon the home stamping grounds of the principal enemy."

At that moment, signal lights in the antechamber caused them to get back into the main body of the space ship. An Agarthian captain was impatient to communicate with them.

"The differential analyzer readings have been relayed from Agarthi," he said. "Nrlanian Central Control is definitely located on the Martian moon, Deimos…"

* * *

"WHAT in Purple Blazes is coming off around here?" shouted Rocky.

"What's the matter?" asked Janice. She had just come back from a tour of the battle stations and her coppery hair was loose, framing her pale, smudged face in a ruddy halo.

Rocky looked at her. "Don't interrupt me at a time like this," he pleaded.

Her hands went to her hips and her chin went up. "I *beg* your pardon?"

"Oh you know what I mean. When I'm trying to figure something out and my think-gadget is plugging away on all two cylinders and you come walking in with your assets showing I blow a gasket and lose my bearings. I'd call *that* an interruption."

She knew he was trying to be sweet, but the strained look on his face told her this was no time for play. She came and leaned over him, with her arms around his neck.

"What's old think-pot worried about?" she asked, casually glancing at the instrument panel before him. Not that she took their present situation lightly. She had merely made a habit of keeping up the local morale.

"Think with me, honey," he said, "and fast. All hell's

breaking loose. My indicators on the ether fleet units are blacking out all over the place. The enemy just *can't* be knocking them off like that, Janice, unless this is the end of the universe or something."

"What do you mean? Let me see." Immediately she became the trained scientist again, her keen eyes analyzing the indicators.

"Discount the Terrestrial Government Fleet," he said. "What didn't get fried is cooked. All captured by Nicholas. But the Agarthian fleet consisted of twenty-five supers, the Lunar Fleet started out with a hundred and sixty, and there's our own outfit with a full hundred ships, not counting the *Nova* and Borg's special job. So you read the board and figure it out."

Janice was reading the board—and growing pale.

"Good Lord, Steve. The blue signals are on the Agarthian band, aren't they?"

"Right!" Rocky was sweating. "Read 'em!"

"Only ten left, Rocky! And the red signals—you can see them go out. The Lunar Interstellars are blacking out about one every ten seconds. It *can't* be right..." She reached for the intercom switch, but he stayed her hand.

"I've checked Electronics," he said. "We're metering perfect. No, Janice, something big and very unfunny is chopping us down all over space. Wait—here's Stierman calling in. Maybe he's got something. Go ahead, Greg."

Stierman's dark-browed visage flickered strangely on the visiscreen, as though they were looking at him through water.

"Well?" he said. "What's your idea—or are we going to be sitting ducks?"

"I thought *you* had an idea," said Rocky.

"I have," replied Stierman. "This is their big weapon—and that may mean—"

"The discs," ejaculated Janice.

"You're right," said Stierman. "They're doing something we can't understand. You can see what's happening to the ether by our warped reception. Such forces may really be able to cripple us. We've got to act—but what's the plan?"

"Steve, may I take the floor?" Janice requested.

"Beautiful, if you've got an idea, take a couple of decks and all the bulkheads. We're listening."

"Whatever it is that's knocking out those ships, it's not localized. Its effect is too widespread. And if you'll note the other fleets' positions on your tri-coordinates you'll see that it's sweeping our way like a tidal wave. We have the slim advantage of having been forewarned. Not knowing what may work nor having time to investigate, I suggest three plans of action to be tried simultaneously by three sections of our own fleet. One plan might have a chance and at least a third of us would come through."

"Don't stop now," said Rocky. Stierman's face was inscrutable as he watched her on his own screen.

"Plan One," she said. "First group full speed to Mars and land. Maybe this stuff operates best out here and you'd be safer on the ground, even if this plan precipitates an engagement with Martian forces.

At least those forces will be physical and not composed of flying discs. On all our own ships, the second order screens are practically in the testing stages, and I think Group One could complete their conversions even under battle conditions and have a chance to survive—*if* the discs aren't operating on the planet, proper. Plan Two: Second group densify to maximum smallness and make a run for it—maximum survival acceleration. Maybe density will do the trick and high velocity will help. The density may reduce the surface areas of the ships and not give the discs enough to work on to be effective. Plan Three: Third group also densify, but remain stationary and bail out in the commuters. In the small boats you may be able to hide out and come back later to see what happened to the ships, themselves. I've got a hunch every ship in each of the fleets is tickling a signal light somewhere on an enemy control board, but a sudden plethora of small commuters would confuse the issue—and the discs aren't miraculous. They can't be everywhere. What do you think?"

"Sweetheart," said Rocky, "you just made a sale. It's good. I'll buy it. What do you say, Greg?"

The shadow of a grim smile tugged at the corners of Stierman's mouth as he looked at Janice approvingly. "It's good," he answered, "provided I can lead Group One. My second order screens have just checked out. I'm ready for Fortress Mars."

Rocky barked orders at his recorder. "Plan One: Ships 101 through 133." Number 101 was Stierman, and Rocky grinned at him as he said it. "Plan Two: Ships 134 through 167. Plan Three: 168 through 200."

"But what about 100?" asker Stierman. "That's you."

"We're going to be real fancy," said Rocky. "I've just been listening to some relay data out of Agarthi. If anybody gets a chance, look us up on Deimos." Deliberately, he snapped Stierman off. And in the next instant he put the recording of their decision on inter-ship code broadcast, preceded by the call signal identifying official orders. The he turned to Janice.

"Sweetheart—get some of the boys together and rig me *direct* controls on one of those remote controlled U.P. bombs. Don't ask why. No time. Get!" Whereupon he spanked her where only prerogatives dare to land. And she got.

"Electronics," he barked into the intercom. "Bring us up to normal density." He switched to Navigation. "Lunar ship seventy-two is closest to us and still intact, but won't be intact in about another couple of minutes. Watch it in the visiscopes and tell me what hit it. I'll be in Locker A. *Janice!*"

She had paused to hear his order somewhat puzzled. "Meet me in Locker A," he told her. "We're in this for better or for worse, aren't we?"

Her blue-green eyes probed his. "Yes, Steve, but—"

He sprang to his feet and led her out. "No time for buts. Let's go. I want those direct controls on a U.P. bomb. Better weld on a couple of cargo rings. Work like lightning. No time to talk. See you."

He left her, taking the ramp below toward Locker A, where

the special Golden Guardsman space suits were stored.

HE had just climbed into a suit when Navigation reported.

"It's the flying discs, sir," said the Navigator. "Completely engulfed the ship. Lost communication within thirty seconds. Their power just faded out."

"Thanks," said Rocky into his pace phone. "We'll get it ourselves in about thirty minutes, maybe less. Before that I'll give Electronics the signal for densification. By that time I'll be outside on a U.P. bomb and you'll be on your own, but at maximum density you'll have such reduced hull area that the discs may not be able to be entirely effective. You'll have Universal Power and you may still be able to hobble along. Follow us to Deimos if you can."

"*Us*—sir?"

"Yes. My wife will be with me."

"But—surely you're not going to—"

"No, no suicide run, but a U.P. bomb is the fastest thing we've ever produced. We might outrun the discs and get to the source of trouble on Deimos. Of course, if worse comes to worst—"

"Yes?"

"No time to talk now. Let's get a move on."

Within twenty-five minutes, Janice met Rocky in Locker A. He had been outlining a plan of action to all sections onboard, but when she came in he cut it short and handed her a suit.

"In you go," he said. "Is our chariot ready?"

Her eyes told him she knew what he was planning. "Yes, Rocky, it's ready. And I love you for including us both. So much more wonderful and big of you than trying to be a hero by yourself and leaving little wifey behind…"

"Heck, you'll be safer out on that bomb than here in a minute or two. Let's go."

"For luck, honey." She kissed him.

He grinned, then clapped her helmet on her. When she saw him next, through her faceplate, he was not grinning. He was pulling her in frantic haste toward the bomb chutes.

"When we get on the bomb, we'll densify and be small enough to go through the chute with it. Then I'll signal the ship to densify."

"It may seem strange to think of it at this time, but I wonder where Germain is?" said Janice.

"No time to wonder. He's a superman and I think he can take care of himself, but if you and I are going to survive we'll have to be more primitive about it and struggle like hell. Now come on!"

*   *   *

GERMAIN soon noticed that his fall toward Mars, as well as that of the *Nova*, was swiftly developing into a lateral drift, and he wondered if he and the ship were to become satellites. As he drew to within a thousand miles of the planet's surface his ESP leaped downward in exploration.

He was aware of the crystal ridges that brought water from the poles by osmosis. In fact, he could make out a few with the naked eye, or at least their general direction, because of the belts of vegetation that followed them in most places. He wondered if the ridges were a result of natural geographical formation or actual intent by the Martians or long-forgotten ancestors who had dabbled in a science unknown to modern physics. Certainly the crystal ridges were more practical than the supposed canals, which would have presented too much water surface for evaporation under conditions of light gravitation and thin, dry atmosphere.

He was intrigued by various ancient ruins, which he perceived only by means of his ESP. In many places he detected clusters of pyramids. They stood in pairs, always a large one with a smaller one beside it. Perhaps the Martians were moon worshippers, or their ancestors had been, he mused. A large pyramid for the larger appearing moon, Phobos, and a smaller one for the more distant moon, Deimos.

Strange, he thought, that out here he should be indulging in comparative archaeology and ethnology. But the thought persisted that on Earth there were also pyramids and that in the distant past there had been both moon and sun worshipping pyramid builders. He remembered the persistent custom among Western Hemisphere Indian cultures of using the two horn symbol, or the two feather symbol, for the legendary "Twin Stars." The Apaches, the Incas—

But what was happening to him? Was he getting feeble minded out here in space? Worlds were at stake and he was wool gathering.

He forced his mind to alert objectivity and probed Mars with more practical intent. His sensory projection was able to penetrate through underground robot defenses and see the bustling slave cities, now converted into fortresses and space ship hangars, largely manned by mentally conditioned Martians. One glance told him that here were the factories and arsenals of Mars, but for the Nrlani this was *not* their own front line of offense and defense. That would be Deimos and Central Control—or would it?

Suddenly, he was aware of a distant fleet of thirty-four ships skimming with lightning rapidity over the surface of Mars, and he could swear they were Golden Guardsman vessels. In the next instant he was sure of it, because Martian defenses fired on them and closed their screens, and many a Nrlanian warship, manned by robots, emerged from subterranean hangars to engage in combat with them. He knew simultaneously that these particular Guardsman ships had secondary screens, and he breathed a vast sigh of relief. Now they could operate—at least against Fortress Mars. They were fast versatile, powerful and deadly, even against Nrlanian ships, as was soon made evident by the successful blows he began to witness. Good for Rocky! That was one way of killing two birds with one stone—escape the discs by attacking Mars, itself. But where were the other contingents of the fleet?

He probed space telepathically. If some ships were out here

and had survived the disc attack he would implant in the minds of their crews the command to pick him up and try to rescue the *Nova*, which was now definitely caught in an orbit.

Suddenly, something flashed past him but was lost to sight in the maze of blazing stars that formed the firmament like a jagged wall of coral at the bottom of an endless sea. It might have been a meteor—but he knew that it was not.

He also knew that it was coming back toward him. Soon he could see it again, and his worst suspicion was confirmed.

A flying disc...

*   *   *

NEITHER Nicholas nor Trinha Llih nor Eidelmann were aware of the *Chess Player* as their two ships maneuvered in toward Mars through robot detector screens unscathed. Nicholas was so intent upon his preparations for the ultimatum that he had failed to detect his pursuer, and so he landed his ship, near a large Gdjinhji trading city where five crystal ridges converged among at least a hundred pairs of ancient pyramids. Knowing Mars as he did, he knew he had little to fear from a surface town, and as he had come with few personal provisions he had an idea that he would have to avail himself of the town's facilities. Aside from this, there was a much more vital consideration...

Trinha knew that town. It was Zridhn Nor. She told Eidelmann about it and explained to him what Nicholas already knew—that it was the subterranean cities they had to stay clear of. The surface ones were relatively harmless. Zridhn Nor was situated at that point on the planet's surface where night was beginning to descend, so under cover of approaching darkness they moved in behind the outlying pyramids at a point opposite the side of the town where Nicholas had landed, and where Nicholas, at that moment, was hurling his ultimatum at the Earth.

The populace, large at this particular season, had been

attracted by the sight of the large terrestrial space ship built on Nrlanian lines, and their smaller vessel had apparently gone unnoticed. It was then they remembered that they had turned on their invisibility hours before.

"I have a plan," Trinha told Eidelmann. "You would be very conspicuous, but I would not. These are my people. I know their customs and speak their language. You want your own ship and you want Nicholas out of the way. What I want is Nicholas, himself. He's up to no good, and if we leave him alone he may accomplish what he's after. I intend to stop him. He would not have landed near the city if he did not intend to enter it for some reason. When he leaves the ship, I'll be there. If you distrust me, you can watch me in the televiewer."

Eidelmann handed her the radium pistol. "I'll work with you on that plan," he said. "But don't try any tricks. I need certain equipment on board that ship. If you try to take it I'll have to blast you down. Agreed?"

Trinha agreed...

HOURS passed and the night grew late, but still Nicholas had not emerged from the ship. Hundreds of the Gdjinhji tribesmen had taken up a vigil at a respectful distance and some had even prepared jars of *grabdal*, believing that the Nrlani had arrived to do business. Trinha mingled inconspicuously with the women, easily taking up the regional pattern of conversation as though she had never left Mars and visited Panh, Guardian Star of the Twin Moons. It was a relief to her, physically, to walk under the influence of the lighter gravity of her home planet, to breathe its rarer air and feel the lightening of her blood. She preferred Mars to Earth, even if it did mean being sold, eventually, to the highest bidder. It was tribal law. But it was something she could understand. This was her home.

Suddenly, lightning seemed to flash in the sky. They all looked upward, startled, as lightning was rare. The first flash was followed by several others, and in another minute they heard thunderous reports, as of gigantic explosions. Then several long, sleek ships swept low over Zridhn Nor, glowing in pale bubbles of energy as they screened themselves from attacks emanating from higher up. A circular ship, recognizable at once as a robot controlled Nrlanian battleship, started to pursue the intruders, but suddenly it flashed blindingly into extinction not two miles away.

It was then that Nicholas emerged from his own ship and faced them. Bewildered, they looked at him as though for an answer. Confidently, then, he walked among their campfires, one hand resting lightly on the butt of his radium pistol in his belt. Taking full advantage of his previous experience on Mars, he spoke to them in their own tongue.

"What you see above you is the answer to the warning I gave you some time ago at Druhdrui," he said. "I came among you then explaining that I was the ruler of Panh, but I warned you of the usurper, Stephen Germain, who was planning to come here and subjugate all of you. These are his ships now. He is so powerful that he challenges even the Nrlani."

The tribesmen gasped, finding it difficult to conceive of such a power. And they were afraid. Trinha knew this was the effect Nicholas was seeking. Her eyes narrowed, recognizing in him now the same, crafty deceiver who had taken her virgin dreams on a golden platter and thrown them to a pig—Pavlovich. Her hand crept under her outer garments and closed on the cold handle of her concealed weapon.

"But I, too, have acquired new power," continued Nicholas. "I have within my hands the power to blast Panh out of the sky and destroy it forever unless it surrenders. I have come among you to organize you to defend yourselves and to aid me in occupying Panh."

Convenient to his strategy, the story of his previous appearance at Druhdrui had gone before him and gained proportions. They knew him. It was not long before one of the more prominent merchants had invited him to his trading post to eat *charnhr* cheese and warm himself with *bhurra* liquor.

Excitedly, the crowd followed, and Trinha mingled with her

own people. She had merely hated Nicholas on a purely personal basis until now, but his remarks concerning the possible destruction of Earth added new impetus to her intentions. She did not hate the Earth. It was a great, ponderous world teeming with billions of people who were probably as innocent of any intent to conquer and enslave as were the Gdjinhji. As for the battle going on now in Martian skies, she hoped that the Nrlani could be destroyed. She had seen Izdran, and that had been enough. She recognized the avenging ships of the Golden Guardsmen as an extended arm of the Earth people, seeking to free the entire solar system of slavery worse than death. Certainly she would trust them more than she could trust the likes of Izdran, or Nicholas and Pavlovich, or Eidelmann and his fanatic group. If these strangers in their sleek, fast ships were enemies of those she hated, then they were friends to her.

Now she knew that to bring Nicholas merely to his knees and see him suffer defeat would be selfish. She was going to capture him and bring him to Eidelmann, but now the picture had changed. For the sake of Earth, she thought, Nicholas would have to die...

CHAPTER SIXTEEN

THE disc had detected Germain, and now it was coming to investigate. Out here in the depths of space it was difficult to judge the size and distance of an unfamiliar object. Knowing, however, that the discs were approximately two feet in diameter at normal density, he judged this one to be about fifty feet from him, closing in slowly.

It looked exactly like a giant amoeba now, semi-transparent and with a dark nucleus, like a malignant eye, in its center. He was reminded of early spear fishing days off the coast of Southern California when he used to surprise schools of squid in the kelp beds and they had looked at him out of the dark depths with their great eyes like this—utterly alien, voiceless, resentful of his intrusion into their own element.

For the first time since his metamorphosis into a mutant, he was assailed by fear, because here, at last, was the unknown, and he did not know what to do. There was only one faint ray of hope. The other discs had confronted him en masse. This one was alone. It was a case of his mutant powers against the unknown and unmeasured powers of this alien creature that had been spawned in the deadly cold of the void or, perhaps as Borg and Grange suspected, in the fission heat of the sun's core.

They were passive by nature, but deadly when motivated. This one was apparently motivated like the rest, because it had taken an interest in him. Perhaps it was even now intent upon sucking from him his life's energies and leaving him to drift with hundreds of derelict vessels down the space road to fiery destruction.

The disc seemed close enough to touch him. He swung the air-bloated arms of his suit at it but missed it. At the same time it came nearer and he saw that it was much larger than he had anticipated. In fact, it seemed suddenly gigantic, until he realized that he was densified, measuring not more than an inch in length. This time he knew it was upon him, trying to envelop him in its substance. He swung about again, and the substance of it parted like a diaphanous web, only to reassemble itself again. It seemed more of a spiritual substance than material. A link between first and second order matter, or a manifestation of both, he could not tell.

Suddenly it had densified, too, and its substance became tougher, enveloping him in earnest. He soon began to feel that sickening drain of energy that he had felt before. He struck back with all the psychic power he could generate, and he was elated to notice a lessening of the deenergization. He struck again, mentally, pouring into the disc what would have shorted the nerve dendrites of ten human nervous systems.

In another moment, he was completely free, and he saw the disc drifting aimlessly away to his left, expanding slowly into a broad, ghostly, amorphous thing that was transparent against the blazing backdrop of the firmament. He had blocked its outside control. He thought swiftly. Here was pure mentality with not enough intelligence to be inhibited unless acted upon by an outside force. If he could implant in it a powerful post-suggestion it might be able to affect others of its kind and make of his hypnosis a chain reaction. But he knew that even if he succeeded it would not work fast enough. One was not enough to start with. He needed hundreds of them. But hundreds of them would mean his own defeat.

Still, this one contact with a disc had implanted in him the tiniest germ of an idea, so formless yet that he could not quite discern its final outline, but his seventh sense told him he should develop it. Something titanic in its proportions. He concentrated, trying to follow the one premise established: That the discs were pure mentality devoid of inhibiting fears or pre-conditionings. From there, where could his reasoning take him? He concentrated, knowing that he was on the trail of something of immeasurable consequence. Then he realized that this was not the time or the place for prolonged meditation, so he ef-ficiently assigned his problem to his subconsciousness, knowing that in that indefatigable workshop the solution would be arrived at in due time and present itself without warning, whenever it was ready.

Another idea intruded at that moment, and he yelled, "Hey!" He tried, mentally, to recall the disc. It might be the means of getting him out of this orbit. His flying carpet to safety. But when he probed it, it fled, not into space, but into another plane. It attenuated into nothingness.

"HEY yourself!" came a human voice into his ears. It was from his space phone.

"What? Who's calling? Where are you?" His mind raced outward and soon discovered the long, ominous shape of a U.P. bomb, which was exclusive ordnance of the Golden Guardsmen. He was aware of two people traveling with the bomb, but he could not see them with his ESP. He struggled to turn in space, and finally he saw the bomb with his eyes. On top of it were two space-suited figures one inch high, lashed by a thread-like cable to two large cargo rings.

"If you're thumbing a ride you're in luck," came Rocky's voice. "Because I think we're the only tourists within a couple of thousand miles."

"Oh Rocky," Germain heard Janice's impatient voice. "You'd make a bad pun if you were being boiled in oil. Is this a time for such perversion—I *ask* you..."

"No. I'm incurable. Hey, Germain! We're coming alongside."

Germain quickly surmised what had happened to Rocky's flagship and what Rocky had done to escape the discs. He also knew now that Rocky was not leading that task force below against Fortress Mars. But the U.P. bomb interested him. With direct controls on it, and equipped as it was with the almost inexhaustible power that propelled it, they could navigate back to Earth if they did not starve or die of thirst, or, which was more likely, of asphyxiation. Certainly they could make a safe landing on Mars if they were not spotted or shot down first.

But there was another possibility.

"Where do you think you are going on that thing?" he asked Rocky.

"Haven't you been reading your mail? Central Control is on Deimos. Want to come along?"

Germain grappled for the line that came drifting by him, and soon he was pulling himself down to the surface of the relatively gigantic bomb. Rocky, to let him get in close, had lowered the rocket's meteor screen.

"This isn't the safest means of transportation," he remarked. "Get that screen out in a hurry."

"It's out there. You're lucky you weren't hit floating around unprotected like that."

"This is a ticklish means of transportation," persisted Germain. "If that screen should fail and a meteor should get through—"

"We wouldn't even know it, what with all the 'Kingdom Come' this baby carries—but the people around Alpha Centauri might. It'd be like a *Nova*. Incidentally, where *is* the *Nova*?"

"It is out of sight now, because as Mars' third satellite its period of revolution is less than that of Phobos, and that's traveling. In view of the vital business at hand I'll have to investigate her later, even if she is a sitting duck for Martian defenses. We can only pray that your Guardsman ships down there give them enough to occupy their attention until we get some things straightened out, ourselves."

"Weren't David and Ingaborg with you?" asked Janice.

"Yes, but I think they're all in a state of suspended animation. Just now, what is more important than Central Control is Nicholas. I've got to locate him."

Briefly, he related his mental experience with Izdran. Nicholas, he believed, had gone to Mars.

"But what about Lillian?" asked Janice.

"If I can attend to Nicholas immediately, there may still be time to reach her. Rocky, take us as close in to Mars as you dare. I'm going to do some concentrating."

With primary screen extended to protect the bomb as much as possible, Rocky navigated close in, even penetrating the upper reaches of the Martian atmosphere. Suddenly, the three of them became aware of several curious looking objects drifting near them. They reminded Janice of nerve cells she had often examined under microscopes, except that these measured perhaps two feet in length. Beyond these were others, and as their eyes sought these latter their vision adapted itself to further distances. They began to make out literally hundreds of the strange, drifting objects. It was their first glimpse of the Martian djurnur pods.

"What are they?" asked Rocky.

"I hope they are not cousins to the flying discs," remarked Janice.

"Rocky," said Germain, "I'd like to capture one of those. There's not much time to investigate, but there's one over there that we ought to be able to catch. I want to take a close look. It may be important."

Unlike the discs, the pods did not increase their velocity or attenuate, nor did they appear to have any volition of their own, although they were all moving in one direction without sufficient air currents to propel them. Germain increased his size and was able to catch one easily. Then he reduced his size again, simultaneously reducing the pod with him. The three of them looked at it.

"It's vegetable matter," he said. "Some sort of giant seed pod containing a hermetically sealed air chamber." He noted that at the base of the hollow chamber there was a glittering encrustation of crystals. Something bothered him about the pods, but he had little time to reflect on it.

"They are merely a part of the Martian biological cycle," he remarked. "Perhaps unimportant to us just now."

Janice, however, took the pod from him and had a close look, herself. In the meantime—Germain began to concentrate on the planet below him. Rocky and Janice did not bother him. This sort of thing had happened before. They had a good idea of what he was doing. His extra sensory perception was actually combing the surface of Mars.

It was natural for Germain to discover Zridhn Nor with its great cluster of pyramids right on the equator. In the same instant he was aware of Nicholas' large ship on the outskirts. Since Eidelmann had his smaller vessel in secondary invisibility, Germain could not penetrate his screen, but he was aware of the presence of the latter ship by virtue of its protective envelope of second order energy. Finally, he singled out the mentality of Nicholas, himself.

NICHOLAS was standing in the trading booth of Ilyan Ranl, Zridhn Nor's most prominent trader. He was in the midst of a preliminary speech of propaganda when he became aware of Germain's gigantic mentality. It was nothing more than an awareness, but Nicholas recognized it for what it was, as it had happened to him before, both in connection with Germain and Izdran.

He paused in his speech, paled, then staggered slightly. Ilyan Ranl, a slender, elderly man, stepped forward solicitously, noticing with some surprise that the Earthman had instinctively gripped the handle of his strange weapon.

"Are you ill?" he asked.

Nicholas shook his head, waving him away. He was sweating, eyes staring unseeingly ahead, while Trinha, watching from the outer darkness, wondered if he could have become obsessed by Izdran.

"Just a momentary dizziness," he gasped. "Long journey— wait a moment—"

Germain's insistent thought thundered through his mind: *Where is the Zero Bomb? Tell me its location or you die.*

In dubious triumph, Nicholas thought back, shakenly: *Why don't you read my mind, Germain? You can't find what you want, because, I prepared myself for this. Do you think I would be cheated of my only weapon at this stage? Have you forgotten that hypnotists are easily obtained on Earth? I have had them wipe from my mind my own knowledge of where the bomb is located. Once I knew where it is, but now no one knows. You can destroy me, yes, but if you do so you destroy the Earth. In less than an hour the bomb will detonate unless you surrender along with the Guardsmen and the Agarthians and the Interstellars. Only I am in a position to activate the controls that will reset the timer on the bomb. This is your last chance, Germain. Upon you rests the destiny of Earth.*

UNABLE to stand the suspense any longer, Janice interrupted Germain. "Did you locate him?" she asked.

"He is an idiot," replied Germain, quietly. "This is going to be easy. Just a minute…"

He concentrated, and soon Nicholas was insulated from his own volition.

You will proceed at once to your ship, commanded Germain. There you will deactivate the bomb by means of your remote controls. After that you will remain in that village and entertain the natives as the village idiot until you can be taken into custody. Now go quickly.

He was aware of the other's response. Nicholas left the trading booth, followed by a wondering populace. Under complete hypnosis, he started back toward the ship.

Germain's subconsciousness was bothering him concerning a mass of apparently disconnected facts, which seemed to cry out for synthesis. His seventh sense gave him a presentiment that something vastly important would be arrived at if he could extrapolate certain observations into a logical conclusion. As Nicholas started back toward the ship, Germain turned his attention briefly to the Martians, themselves. Then he was distracted by the awareness of the second order screen surrounding the smaller ship in which Eidelmann waited on the outskirts of Zridhn Nor. He was in the midst of concentration on this latter mystery when Rocky interrupted him.

"*Look out*," he yelled. "Here comes an enemy destroyer."

The three of them saw a medium sized Nrlanian warship hurtling upward toward them.

"Full speed to Deimos," commanded Germain. "Hang on tight!"

UNKNOWN to Germain, it was precisely at that moment that Trinha Llih leveled her radium pistol at Nicholas and fired. The explosive bullet hit him directly and detonated. The crowd following her suddenly drew back. Some of the women screamed at the grisly sight of what had been Nicholas I, Prince of Panh. His shattered remains left no question even in Trinha's mind that he was definitely, irrevocably dead. She could not quite know the echoes her single shot was making in the halls of History. Like the passing of Ghenghis Khan, Napoleon, and Hitler, Nicholas' death marked the end of certain bloodied and smouldering chapters. Also, she could not know that this assassination had precipitated a chaotic concatenation of events that would be unprecedented in all the *memory* of human and humanoid civilization in Creation. Hers was not the shot heard round the world. It was to be heard in two planes of existence!

Now for Earth the hourglass was emptying fast, and Germain was unaware of it. He had been confident that Nicholas would reach his remote controls in ample time to deactivate the Zero Bomb. Instead, somewhere on Earth the timer ticked perilously close to the point of detonation. And *more* than Earth was suspended from that point…

Trinha was only vaguely aware of being surrounded by her fellow Martians and disarmed. She was remembering a night that seemed immeasurably long ago, in which she had dreamed that her Prince of the Sky had come at last. She remembered being in Nicholas' arms, inside her father's trading booth at Druhdrui. In that moment she had offered him her virgin youth and all her hopes and dreams. Then he had thrown her to Pavlovich. She had sworn that she would be revenged, and this was it. But it was neither sweet nor bitter. It was a nothingness.

When Eidelmann maneuvered his ship over the nearby pyramids in full visibility, however, she became more conscious of what was going on. The tribesmen of Zridhn Nor held her captive, but they paused now to look at this new ship.

"What is that?" they asked her, as it landed alongside Nicholas' ship.

"Only another enemy, just as was this beast I have slain," she answered. "It is not a robot controlled Nrlanian vessel. An Earthman pilots it, but an evil one."

"One can infer from your statement," said Ilyan Ranl, "that there are good Earthmen. Who are you to know these things? You are of the Gdjinhji."

"I think I know who she is now," said another. "She is that same Trinha Llih who accompanied this Nicholas and his companion into the sky city of the Nrlani, according to the story told us by old Grlahn."

"Is this true?" asked Ilyan Ranl.

"Yes," she replied, "and I have learned many things. Since I am one of you, you should believe what I say. Nicholas was a treacherous enemy, and so is he who pilots that other ship."

"But what of the strange ships that do battle with the Nrlani?" asked Ilyan.

"They attack our oppressors," she answered. "As our liberators they cannot very well be our enemies."

"Look," cried another tribesman. "The stranger enters the other ship."

They saw Eidelmann enter the larger ship, but it was too late to stop him. In another minute, the vessel rose above their heads and hurtled straight up into the sky.

There was not much time to deliberate on the possible intentions of Eidelmann, because in that moment ten Earthmen walked into Zridhn Nor. They were dressed in the uniform of the Golden Guardsmen. Sam Turner was at their head.

The Gdjinhji tribesmen started to back away, warily, as they advanced, but the Earthmen smiled and made signs of peace. Trinha also reassured her people that the strangers were friends.

"I believe," she said, "that you are seeing for the first time the true emissaries of that Stephen Germain of whom Nicholas warned us. That he warned us against them is a guarantee that they are our allies."

Immediately, the problem of communication presented itself, but finally it was discovered that Trinha spoke a little Russian. In Turner's group was a Polish Guardsman who spoke fluent Russian. Through this medium Trinha learned that one of the deadly Guardsman ships had landed nearby under secondary invisibility to undergo repairs as the result of skirmishes with the slave city fortifications. Turner and his men had observed Eidelmann's flight in both ships and had come to Zridhn Nor on foot to investigate the possibilities of picking up some quick transportation. They were referring to the smaller Nrlanian vessel, which now sat idle on the outskirts. When Ilyan expressed surprise that they should expose themselves to a Nrlanian vessel, since they could not know if it were manned or not, Turner explained that his own ship was close by and that Zridhn Nor was directly under it's ray guns.

When Turner questioned Trinha concerning her surprising

knowledge of a Terrestrial language, she related to him some of the things that had happened to her. When she showed him Nicholas' remains he and his men gave a cheer and all shook hands to celebrate. The ex-dictator's death was a great milestone in the system wide clean up campaign, which Agarthi had launched. But news of Eidelmann troubled him.

Turner asked about the small Nrlanian flier and Trinha told him, through the interpreter, that she could show them how to use it. In fact, she wanted to accompany them if they would promise to track down Eidelmann. Turner was well aware of what Gerhardt Eidelmann's capabilities were. This was the first news he had had concerning the German scientist's whereabouts since he had escaped from the international prison in Berlin.

"You're welcome to come with us, beautiful," he said. "We'll be glad to trail *that* character. It'll keep us busy until our own ship has been repaired, which will take about a week if we're lucky."

Trinha, of course, could not understand English, but she could understand and respond to the world of meaning that shone in Sam Turner's laughing, brown eyes. That language needed no interpreter.

Ilyan Ranl communicated with Turner through Trinha and the Polish Guardsman. "Nicholas warned us against Stephen Germain," he said. "It seems that you serve him. Who is this man, actually, and what should he mean to us?"

Turner grinned when he finally understood the other. "He's the only man with the answers," he replied. "If he hasn't got the answers, then we'll all be working for the Nrlani. The best thing for you and your people to do is to organize yourselves into disciplined groups of fighting men who will be able to help us out if you are called upon in the near future to do so."

It was just after Turner and his men, in the company of Trinha Llih, took off on the trail of Eidelmann that Mars felt its first earthquake in thousands of years. They were unaware of the quake, but they did notice the sudden disappearance of

Deimos. One minute it was there, racing through the Martian skies on its appointed course, and in the next minute it had disappeared as though it had ceased to exist. Then they observed that Earth's moon was no longer spinning about the Earth. It was far from its course and beginning a slow fall toward the sun.

These were but the outward signals of the beginning of universal pandemonium...

CHAPTER SEVENTEEN

THE timer on the Zero Bomb had been only thirty minutes away from detonation when it set in motion the last great piece on the Chess Board. It was Germain's hidden piece—the Elder People's gigantic Chronoperceptor on Guam.

Michael Kent and his sister, Yvonne, became aware of it simultaneously. The latter had just finished preparing them a light lunch in the laboratory's well-provisioned kitchen when she heard the alarm bell. Her brother called her and she rushed into the lab.

Michael Kent stood there beneath the two-story machine and looked at Yvonne, questioningly. Under normal operating conditions, the Chronoperceptor produced prismatic colors in the atmosphere accompanied by weird harmonic effects that sounded like music from another world. But now the tempo of color change and sound had increased startlingly. The colors brightened insistently at the visual extremes of red and violet, and the sound was like the maddened scream of a living giant. Above it all, an alarm bell rang.

"What is it?" yelled Kent to his sister. "Do you know what it's supposed to mean?"

She motioned him toward the mental tape machine, signifying that Germain's own instructions might be of some help in this case, and Kent lost no time in following her suggestion. Both of them had read the tapes several times, but so much of it had been so incomprehensible that they had given up trying to interpret it.

Before he could finish adjusting the cathode helmet of the tape reader to his head, however, the Chronoperceptor spoke to them.

"Look at the screen," it said, in a bellowing voice. "What you see is the future, one hour hence."

A panel slid away on the face of the machine and they beheld for the first time a screen that gave them a three dimensional image of a scene that brought a scream to Yvonne's lips.

They saw nothing but flame and chaos and pieces of Earth flying in all directions. They saw the moon slip from its orbit and start its fall toward the sun. They were aware of millions of shattered or bloated bodies of human beings and animals drifting dead through space.

"It—it's the end of the world," exclaimed Kent.

"Mother of Heaven," cried Yvonne. "Don't let it happen!"

The machine robot continued speaking to them. "Owing to the nature of the entire Space-Time continuum, tampering with time and its interconnected chains of Cause and Effect is prohibited. However, in such an emergency as this it may be left to humans to decide what to do in regard to the salvation of their own planet. As a robot built by the Elders I cannot make a move to tamper with the future, but you could take that responsibility onto yourselves. I am only to warn you that even if your alteration of the immediate future should save the Earth it will establish a structure of probabilities, which never existed before. If you wish to accept this responsibility in the name of the civilization, which you represent, you are at liberty to activate the Time Aura that now encircles this world and all that is associated with it for a distance of approximately five thousand miles outward from its surface."

The colors and the sounds had subsided during this speech, and another panel slid back, disclosing a control panel to their view, which was at once incredible and self-explanatory. There was a vernier control, a simple toggle switch, and a large lever. Obviously, Germain had worked on this panel, himself, because there were nameplates in English. Everywhere else on the Elder equipment any nameplates or decals bore incomprehensible symbols. The nameplate on this panel said: TIME AURA— *operate only on instructions from robot.* The vernier scale indicated hours. Beneath the vernier the toggle switch was mounted between two small decals saying *Future* and *Past.* The large lever was apparently a switch, because its decals merely said "On" and "Off."

To both humans who stood there looking at the panel, the silence in the room was worse than the noise that had preceded it.

"*Michael,*" exclaimed Yvonne, looking at her brother with widened eyes. "What should we do?"

Kent sweated. "There's so damned little time," he complained. "If that thing can throw the whole planet into the future or the past— Wait a minute..." He approached the panel, speculatively. Gingerly, he touched the vernier control, turning it experimentally. He set it twenty-four hours back. Then he snapped the switch to *Past.* "If we can go back to yesterday at this time," he said, "we will have that much more time to figure something out."

"Oh Michael, I—I don't know. We're playing with things that are so far beyond us—"

"The end of the world isn't far beyond us," he warned. "Something has to be tried, and fast. Germain wouldn't have set this thing going if he hadn't foreseen the possibility of its being needed. The thing's all set. I'm going to pull the switch." Fearing that further meditation might result in a change of mind, he yanked the lever to the "On" position...

THE Time Aura actually consisted of a thin layer of electrons, far out from Earth but enclosing it completely. Those electrons were in very rapid motion, approaching the speed of light. Suddenly, the spherical vortex that they composed spun beyond the speed of light, and Three Dimensional Nature rejected the entire envelope, throwing it along the only coordinate where anyone thing can exist in two places at once—Time. With the envelope went the Earth, which it contained.

Earth changed position on its orbit. It now occupied a place where it had been twenty-four hours previously. Its satellite, which was not contained within the Aura, was lost. Detached from the age-old centripetal chains that had held it, it began to drift into the grip of Sol.

But to Earth's inhabitants the only thing that had changed was that the moon was gone. Other than that single, titanic event, they were aware of only a few minor phenomena such as a temporary epidemic of ordinary earthquakes and tidal waves, followed by a complete cessation of the tides.

Michael Kent and Yvonne wondered, too, about the moon's strange antics, and they feared for the fate of the Lunar Interstellar civilization existing within its interior. But they were unaware that they had caused this change, inasmuch as they now had almost twenty-four hours to wait before the alarm bell would ring on the Chronoperceptor. To them, their activating the Time Aura was an unknown event in the future.

Inasmuch as the Zero Bomb lay within the Time Aura, it, too, was thus automatically set back twenty-four hours. To the rest of the solar system, Earth was one day late. Its effects were felt on all the minor planets, and Jupiter lost two of its moons in the changing stresses of gravitational imbalances. On the sun, new sunspots swirled angrily and solar prominences licked out a hundred thousand miles in protest against the unprecedented event.

While in another plane of existence even greater chaos ensued...

*   *   *

THE U.P. Bomb proved to be faster than the Nrlanian warship following it, but magnetic energy is propagated at the speed of light, and the bomb's three passengers were aware of being exposed to the enemy's disrays. The bomb's screen was proof against meteors and other physical objects, but not against energy-propagation weapons. So as they sped so fast toward Deimos that it grew in their eyes with appalling rapidity, they wondered why they had not been snuffed out already.

"Rocky," said Germain, in a constrained tone of voice that showed fare emotion. "We can't outrun that thing. There's only one alternative left."

"If you mean what I've been hoping you don't—" began the other.

"There's no other choice," retorted Germain. "If we pass Deimos and race into outer space, the Nrlanian will knock us off at a distance, anyway, and Central Control will continue. With our fleets out of the running and only a small part of the Guardsmen on Mars, the enemy can take over the solar system. Civilization is more important than we are."

"But you can't mean—" Janice started to exclaim.

"I do!" shouted Germain. "Knock Deimos out of existence."

The bomb hurtled toward the outer moon, but Rocky's great hands gripped the controls tensely, undecided, eyes glaring at death. "Hell, let's take a chance," he protested. "We might get out of it and live to come back at Deimos later. Those robots' guns may be stuck."

"*We* are expendable," insisted Germain. "As your Star Warden I command you to ram Deimos."

Janice made a last, desperate appeal. "If nothing else, Germain, think of Lil, and—and—"

"My wife," said Germain, "is *on* Deimos…"

Janice gasped audibly but was at a loss for words. The calm of death was already settling on Rocky's mind. "If that's the way you see it," he said, grimly. "I hope to God you're sure there's no other way—because here goes. It was great while it lasted. Everything, that is…" He reached behind him and squeezed Janice's knee.

In the instant before they reached their target, they were aware of the sudden arrival of another ship on the scene. They recognized it as Borg's special laboratory ship, which was battle geared almost as heavily as a Guardsman warship. They knew it had no time to fire at the pursuing Nrlanian ship, but they could see it trying to cover their bomb with its secondary screen. Too late to change course. Too late to take advantage of the arrival of a friend. They hurtled toward death with Borg trying to make sure their sacrifice would not be in vain, trying to keep the enemy from detonating their vehicle before it hit its mark.

In the next instant, Deimos suddenly became a mist, then attenuated into nothingness. They shot through the space where it had been.

"What the—" Rocky began, but was cut off by an urgent communication from Borg.

"Coming alongside," he said. "Prepare for magnetic grappling. That's Guardsman equipment you're riding. Who are you?"

Rocky began to reply, but again Borg cut him short. "Thanks, Germain. Stand by with that telepathy. We may need it. Very little time…"

As the lab ship came in close, they were aware of a beautiful pyrotechnical display about a half mile distant, like a displaced Aurora Borealis, and they knew that the Nrlanian vessel was playing havoc even with Borg's second order screen.

"All right, Germain," said Borg. "You've read my mind. Guide the others. Here we go…"

The U.P. bomb had by now fallen into the grip of the ship's magnetic grapplers and it came gently but firmly to rest against the hull. Suddenly, the stars around them began to fade and they seemed to be shooting into the depths of a luminous nebula.

"What gives?" shouted Rocky.

"Attenuate to normal density and Borg will do the rest." Germain's mind reached both his and Janice's. There was no time for telepathic communication in the form of word meanings. He only gave them a swift panorama of events, which were now transpiring. Borg had discovered the secret of attenuation. They were attenuating now into the hidden plane where the Nrlani had taken Deimos and Central Control to save it from destruction. Evidently the Nrlanian robot controlled vessels from Mars were not equipped to follow, because this maneuver was definitely leaving their pursuer behind.

Rocky, irrepressible as ever, was about to say something when they suddenly attenuated to a point where the other plane came into focus. The action which ensued almost instantaneously after that first glimpse of what lay ahead was principally the result of Germain's quick mental grasp of the situation, his split-second decision, and his psychic control of every Terrestrial mind, both on the bomb and inside the ship. For that one, decisive instant, Germain's mind commandeered every control.

A broad countryside spread out before them, replete with barren looking mountains, a few small streams, and a meager growth of forest in several places. The whole scene was illuminated by a gigantic sun that glowed only with a pale, silvery light. So pale it was, in fact, that star and other, closer celestial bodies could be seen beyond it. Germain took special note of a nebulous chain, like a tattered cloud, far out between them and the sun. Directly above them raced Deimos, receding outward into second order space. Directly below them spread a strange looking city composed of ancient stone buildings and tents and other, crystalline structures, all surrounded by ancient pyramids. Some people, apparently Martians, lay face down in the streets, obviously terrorized by the sudden appearance of Deimos so close overhead.

But what occupied Germain's immediate attention, as well as Rocky's and Janice's and the others on board the lab ship, was that tremendous object that was suspended neither above nor below them but directly in their path. A huge, Nrlanian sky city, the defenses of which found them at point blank range, inasmuch as each was within the other's screens.

Such was the situation that had to be grasped and acted upon in a split-second if there was to be any chance for survival...

THE next thing Rocky and Janice knew, they were floating in space but drifting back toward Borg's ship, which was already densifying. As it did so, they, too, began to denisfy, and the scene before them began to be obscured by the luminous mists. But the last thing they saw was the U.P. bomb sped on its way by Rocky at Germain's mental command. It drove straight toward the Nrlanian sky city, which started to move to avoid it, for even if there had been time to detonate it the explosion would still be effective. The Terrestrials knew it could not escape the bomb, and they pitied the residents of the strange city below.

They were only half way back to their own plane when they were buffeted by a gigantic hand and sent reeling along the borders of unconsciousness. It was a backwash of the interplanar stresses created by the explosion of the U.P. bomb.

"Wow," exclaimed Rocky. "That just about blew off my tatoos."

Janice hugged him desperately in an effort to keep from getting lost in the mist, just as they both felt their feet touch the hull of Borg's ship.

AS Borg's ship materialized in normal space, approximately fourteen thousand miles above the surface of Mars, the outer airlock opened to receive the three space-suited figures that clung to its hull. They lost no time in entering the vessel, for two reasons. First, they were nearly out of oxygen. Secondly, they sighted three Nrlanian vessels, which began to converge upon them, immediately after they made an appearance.

There was a third reason, which Rocky refrained from mentioning under the circumstances. He was hungry...

Borg and Grange and the Agarthian crew were a welcome sight to the three adventurers, but there was not even time for handclasps, much less for conversation or a discussion of the unprecedented experience they had just shared. Just now there was a space battle to attend to. Germain took command, with

Rocky, Borg, Grange and Janice at his side.

They recognized their original enemy, as the three ships were of a slightly different size and type, although having in common a distinctly Nrlanian design. The largest ship, a stranger, appeared to hover over the scene as though undecided. The medium sized Nrlanian warship they had first encountered, however, came charging in with the full power of its ray weapons concentrated upon the Terrestrials' secondary screen, and again space was filled with the pyrotechnics resulting from opposed fields of force. The third Nrlanian vessel was much smaller than the other two but apparently packed more than ordinary power, because it remained boldly within battle range and, in fact, slowly closed in.

Just as Germain was about to try a dangerous combination of inner and outer screen frequencies in order to get through with a heat ray, the smaller Nrlanian flier drew in close to the Nrlanian warship inside its screen, and in the next instant it had blasted its fellow out of existence.

"Well I'll be kicked to death—" Rocky started to exclaim.

"That flier is manned by friendly allies," observed Germain, quickly. "Hail them."

In another moment they had Sam Turner on the visiscreen. Rocky greeted him with a whoop of joy and started to interrogate him. Turner was brief and to the point. They were on Eidelmann's trail. That large ship above them was Eidelmann. He was using the ship, which he had built in Russia for Nicholas.

"Wait a minute," interrupted Germain. "If that's Nicholas' ship, where is Nicholas?"

Sam Turner grinned. "Strange that I forgot to give you the good news," he said. "Old Nick is dead!"

Exclamations started, but Germain waved his hand for silence. His dark eyes glared intently at Turner's image on the screen. "Where and when did he die?" he demanded to know. "I mean, was it before or after he entered his ship?"

Turner raised a quizzical brow, puzzled. "He got it before he reached his ship. Here—" He turned and pulled Trinha into the field of vision. "See this little Martian gal? She's Earth's first Martian ally. Nick and Pavlovich brought her to Earth. She had a beef with Nick and followed him back here. When she saw her chance, she shot him down."

Janice and Rocky looked at Trinha with both interest and admiration, but Germain seemed to be extraordinarily excited. His hand trembled as he adjusted the visiscreen's focus control.

"Do you know what that means?" he asked. "At the moment Nicholas was shot he was moving under my own hypnotic control. He was to have deactivated the Zero Bomb."

"*Himmel!*" exclaimed Janice, inadvertently lapsing into her native German. Her hand went to her lips and she stared at Rocky.

"That might explain the strange actions of Earth's satellite," remarked Borg. "We have observed that it is falling toward the sun. However, Earth seems to be intact."

Again, Germain waved them all to silence. "Friends, some of the threads of rhyme and reason have come unraveled in physical nature. I am afraid that the Chronoperceptor on Guam has gone into action." None of them, with the exception of Borg, knew what the Chronoperceptor was, so Germain continued. "Elder Race equipment. It would have been able to foresee the destruction of Earth by the Zero Bomb and guide Yvonne in activating the Time Aura which it generates. Earth has been thrown backward in time. It is late on its orbit, which would explain the moon's present actions. But there is something else—" He was remembering the nebulous chain he observed in the firmament of that other plane where they had encountered the Nrlanian sky city. His eyes widened in horror. "Earth's own secondary plane," he exclaimed. "Like the moon, it has become displaced. Physical Earth changed position on its orbit, but the higher plane, deprived of its denser center, must now be dissolving."

"Pardon me, sir," said Turner. "You're quite a bit ahead of me. One thing I can understand is that Eidelmann is right on top of you. He's dangerous and specially equipped. Hadn't we better—"

"No! For God's sake don't destroy that ship," exclaimed Germain. "It contains the remote controls of the Zero Bomb. If we can deactivate the bomb, the Chronoperceptor will not go into action again. Otherwise, periodically, Earth will backtrack on its orbit and eventually unbalance the whole solar system. We've got to capture Eidelmann. Wait. Drive inside his secondary screen," he ordered Borg. "Once inside, I'll take him mentally. It's our only chance."

"And a long one," commented Rocky. "He probably packs Universal Power."

Borg's ship moved swiftly. When Eidelmann saw it coming inside his screen, he was about to fire a disray when he became aware of Germain. In sudden fear, he moved another control, instead.

Whereupon, they saw his ship suddenly attenuate and disappear.

"Good Lord," exclaimed Rocky. "He's got an attenuator, too."

"Very brilliant man," commented Dr. Grange, rubbing his nose. "He deduced its possibility independently—and succeeded. A parallel discovery, Dr. Borg."

"Do you know where he's going?" put in Janice. "He's after Central Control."

"What are we waiting for?" asked Borg.

Germain glanced at Rocky. "Can you answer that question?" he asked him.

Rocky's healthy brain clicked furiously for a moment. Then he grinned. "I think it would be a good idea for me to get transferred over to Turner's ship and get back to Stierman's task force on Mars. From there we convert our densifiers and prepare for Project Heaven. *Nicht wahr?*" He looked at Janice. "I take it Germain is piloting this wagon back into the upper plane to haggle with Eidelmann over Central Control, and in the meantime there'll be some Nrlanians up there to take care of.

That's where we come in—the Guardsmen, that is…"

Germain smiled faintly in appreciation. "Correct deduction so far," he said. "Remember this. That Nrlanian sky city we blasted was smaller than the main one I contacted before. Friends, I have a hypothesis that, if true, calls for a supreme effort."

They waited for him to continue speaking, but instead he engaged them mentally. With the swiftness of thought, devoid of words, he implanted in their minds a concept. Relative densities. Earth, the crude, dense matter at the base of Nature's fractionating column. Then, higher levels of rarer matter. More attenuated planes where, all things being relative, life went on within the scope of its own reality. Lastly, there would be the rarest substance, composing the highest plane, which he referred to with a word—Etherea. In the latter plane were the great and ancient ones, and above and beyond them, the Unattainable. The spheres of influence of these latter were so tremendous, perhaps, that they could only take cognizance of the denser planes periodically, say once every three to five thousand years. In the meantime, the lesser planes, such as the one they had just visited, had to shift for themselves. Each planet would be surrounded with one of these secondary planes. Here Germain interposed another word—Atmospherea. These could be referred to as the "local" Heavens. Ergo, they had just visited the Martians' "local" Heaven. And Earth's secondary plane, deprived of its denser center, was falling apart.

Germain placed emphasis on one outstanding idea. Suppose that the Nrlani, seeking a positive hiding place from the Elder People while they prepared for invasion of the solar system over the period of several thousand years, had moved into these lower planes and conquered them without the knowledge of the Great Ones in outer Etherea? This would explain Earth's excessive tendency toward moral and social decadence, inasmuch as a Heaven in bondage would act as a barrier in the way of Man's awareness of higher purpose. It would dull Man's secondary or "spiritual" senses, leaving him the victim of animalism.

"In short," Germain concluded, verbally, "our mission seems to be an emancipation of the lower Heavens, both of Mars and of Earth."

Rocky shook his head to clear it. "If we're all batty," he said, "let's just keep it to ourselves. In the meantime, what about Central Control? If you could get into it, you might be able to call off the discs and all the robot fleets. With the rest of my fleet free, not to mention the Lunars and the Agarthians, we might be able to do something, even if the home of the Lunars is going to blazes."

In that moment, Germain's subconscious mind seemed to click, and the answer to all his troublesome deliberations popped up. As a result, he staggered, eyes wide, staring at nothingness, as segment after segment of his past observations fell into place, all focussed upon a tremendous conclusion.

"What's the matter, Stephen?" asked Janice, solicitously.

He groped, found Rocky's massive shoulder, sought support. "Let's get going on all these plans," he said. "Rocky and Janice, transfer to Turner's vessel. Start your Martian task force to converting their densifying equipment and send them on our trail as soon as each ship is ready. Then watch the *Nova* for signs of life, in case I get to Central Control. Once I do get there, I may be able to—to—"

"To what?" asked Borg.

"Never mind. Let's get going. Lillian is in Central Control, and she may be out of oxygen if Izdran's threat means anything..."

AFTER Rocky and Janice had been transferred to Turner's ship and Germain started the lab vessel through the process of attenuation again, Doctors Borg and Grange looked at each other and knew they were both thinking the same thing. Germain, sitting between them at the controls, knew what they were thinking, because it was a logical reaction.

"The most unusual part of all this," said Borg, "is that we

haven't taken time to consider what repercussions will ensue on Earth after it has been discovered that there is physical proof of human duality and continuation in the next plane of existence—that Man actually has a higher purpose to achieve."

Dr. Grange reflectively rubbed his nose. "The effects upon human thought and behavior resulting from the findings of such men as Kepler, Galileo, Darwin and Einstein pale into insignificance by comparison with this. This will be a moral-psychological earthquake. It will be the end of *Blind* Faith. The Passive part of mysticism will become Dynamic. It will be tantamount to a mass mutation. We will become, in effect, a new species of Man. Dynamic Spiritual Man."

"Perhaps," said Germain. "Just now we must concentrate on the emergency at hand. Look. We have arrived again."

They looked upon the Martian secondary plane once more, and the sight, which now met their eyes, caused them to fall silent for a long moment. Where there had been a city on the ground before there was a vast, deep crater, still smouldering from the effects of the blast created by the U.P. bomb. The Nrlanian sky city had not been vaporized entirely. Telltale shattered remnants of it lay across the landscape; giving them proof positive that it had been violently destroyed. Beyond, in the pale firmament of this plane, swung Deimos, apparently some ten thousand miles distant.

"That," said Germain, crisply, "is our immediate goal." His tightly compressed lips were an obvious signal to the two scientists that he did not wish to discuss the fact that to destroy the Nrlani innocent inhabitants of this second plane of existence had to be sacrificed. Whether or not the remaining people here would understand their motives or become their enemies there was no time to think about. Out there was Deimos, Central Control, Lillian Germain—and Eidelmann—not to mention the fact that this whole action was undoubtedly undergoing a jaundiced surveillance by Izdran, himself.

Thoughts of Izdran put Germain in mind of several interesting facts. The Martian secondary plane was removed from the primary planet's surface by some fourteen thousands of miles. Earth was larger than Mars. Germain calculated swiftly, taking volume and increased mass into consideration. Hypothetically, he could place Earth's secondary plane at about the fifty thousand mile level. It had been at that level that he had detected the main Nrlanian sky city immersed in secondary invisibility. Izdran was master of the solar systems secondary planes. That chainlike group of nebulous patches he could observe out there in space from his present position was all that was left of Earth's secondary plane. Perhaps even now Izdran was approaching him with the intentions of engaging him in direct, physical conflict.

"For some reason," said Borg, "it appears that while Central Control is in this plane the discs cannot be controlled. You will note that there are no discs here. Perhaps they cannot attenuate entirely into this plane. Nature has enabled them merely to utilize the intervening levels of attenuation as a means of self-protection."

"I hope you are right," said Germain. "That would enable Rocky to clean up the *Nova* and some of the other ships and get more of the fleet back into operation. Our task is not simple. We need all the help we can get not only in this plane but our own, as well. There is Mars to take care of, and there are rescue operations concerning the Lunar Interstellars living inside the moon, not to mention all the units of their fleet and of the Agarthian fleet. Time, fighting power, equipment and men are vital."

DEIMOS now loomed before them, cold, airless, dark. It was only dimly illuminated by the light of the sun. Strangely enough, they encountered no protective energy screens surrounding it.

"Don't let that fool you," admonished Germain. "I've tried out my ESP here and found a psychic screen. This has all the earmarks of a booby trap—designed especially for yours truly."

"Evidently Eidelmann doesn't suspect booby traps," said

Grange. "Look. He has already landed."

Far below them they could make out the circular Nrlanian type vessel, which contained the controls for the Zero Bomb. It rested on the surface of Deimos near another object, which became a great source of surprise to all observers on the lab ship. There on the arid, airless surface of Mars' outer moon was an ancient stone pyramid of unusual dimensions. It towered massively above Eidelmann's ship.

"That substantiates one of my suppositions," said Germain. "Ever since I examined one of those flying Martian gas pods I wondered if the ancient Martian priests of the moon gods hadn't discovered the real secret of the pods. Those pods are much heavier than air. They overcome gravitation through some sort of cross-polarization in their crystalline structure. The priests must have developed this principle and traveled to the satellites. Here, long ago, they set up their Holy of Holies. I daresay it was they who set up the original booby trap, right in that pyramid, making it impossible for any but a Martian to enter—which hints also at the historical probability of unpleasant visitations by the Nrlani in the old days when their planet was still intact. So Izdran had Martian drones or mental slaves set up Central Control for him, inside that ancient temple pyramid. He made sure that only the conditioned Martians ever got to Deimos. Intruders from any other planet would be snuffed out by the original booby trap, whatever it is."

"Interesting, if true," said Borg. "Let us hope that Eidelmann is not possessed of your powers of deduction."

"I suppose the Nrlanians could throw up defensive screens if they thought we were on a mission of destruction," remarked Germain, "but they evidently think I'm incapable of blasting the place because of the presence of my wife there. They expect me to walk into their trap—and maybe I shall."

Borg looked at Grange. Then they both stared at Germain. "What are you talking about?" asked Grange.

"Never mind. Look. There's Eidelmann out there in a space suit. He was almost to the pyramid when he spotted us. He's making it back toward his ship. We've got to get into that ship and take over the Zero Bomb controls."

"I see him," said Borg, watching the televiewer. "Now he has stopped. He knows he can't get there before us."

"He also knows he's exposed to our fire," said Grange. "Look at him run back toward the pyramid. Or rather, I should say he's hopping like a kangaroo in that light gravity."

Then all three of them saw the tiny, space-suited figure pause on a rise of ground before the temple doors and raise his dis-gun. He aimed it at his own ship.

Germain grimaced, then fired at Eidelmann. He was traveling too fast and maneuvering for a landing at the same time, so he missed him. A vacant area of the moon's surface two thousand feet from Eidelmann smouldered darkly and became a shallow lake of lava. In the same instant, Eidelmann's ship was blasted into wreckage. Eidelmann looked up at them briefly, then ducked into the temple.

"I follow his reasoning," said Germain. "He feels that once he gets control of what's inside he'll be master of the Solar System."

"But—the Zero Bomb," exclaimed Grange. "The controls have been destroyed..."

"That was a probability I have had to consider," replied Germain. "Now there is only one course left open."

"And that is?" queried Borg.

"Let's go see what happened to Eidelmann," Germain said, evading the question.

"And to your wife," put in Grange.

"My damned seventh sense is usually too late with too little," said Germain. "Now I suddenly have the feeling that Lillian is no longer there. I gather that Izdran has become impressed by the real danger of his position. What better defense against me than to hold my wife as hostage? I wouldn't be surprised if she were now a prisoner in his own sky city, nor would I be surprised to see that city any time now."

TEN minutes after the ship had landed, Germain, Borg, Grange and ten Agarthian spacemen stood at the entrance to the ancient pyramid. A gigantic archway led into somber gloom. Over that archway, Germain observed the meteor-scarred remains of ancient hieroglyphics that caused his blood to race.

He paused, still looking up at those markings, while all the tag ends of his past observations suddenly dove-tailed neatly together. An eager gleam was creeping into his deep-set, dark eyes when the others urged him onward, reminding him that Eidelmann was somewhere ahead of them. A faint smile played about his lips as he entered the ancient temple of the Martian moon worshippers.

Several ray men remained on the outside, ready to disintegrate any portal that might fall behind the others. Two other Agarthian spacemen led the way with powerful searchlights. There was also other equipment that probed the passage ahead with radar, tested the place for harmful radiations and photographed it in ranges of light above and below the physical spectrum.

"What about that psychic screen?" queried Dr. Grange. "Still blocking your extra-sensory perception?"

"It's there," replied Germain. "But it no longer recedes as I advance. My ESP takes me down three different passages ahead. In two passages there is no screen, but there is death in several primitive forms. One is a simple drop-off into the center of the satellite. Another contains an ancient trap constructed of two stone walls that will come together and crush any intruder. That passage leads to a dead end. But the third takes me to Eidelmann. Just beyond him is the psychic screen. I read in his mind that he is mystified by a wall of flame there. He is hurriedly making tests of it to see if it will harm him. I believe that there is a real trap and the real entrance to Central Control, where the temple's Holy of Holies used to be. Eidelmann is armed only with a dis-gun. Let's combine our portable generator outputs and I think we can take him without a struggle."

Germain was referring to protective energy screens, which their space outfits could produce. Under a combined output that protected them frontally they advanced down a curving passageway, which Germain indicated as the correct one.

"Why don't you paralyze Eidelmann?" asked Borg.

"Just as I was about to, back there a second ago, he stepped further into the passage. He is now beyond the psychic screen and I can't reach him. Whether or not he is in some way aware of that protection I don't know. I guess he is quite a clever and treacherous character. Let's watch him carefully. Take no chances. When he is within range, suffocate him with the heat ray, but don't burn him. I'd like to question him if he can be taken prisoner."

They rounded a corner abruptly and came within sight of Eidelmann, who fired at them instantly. When he failed to penetrate their screen he desisted, as though he had expected such resistance. But he laughed at them when they tried to ray him back. He, too, had a screen, more powerful than theirs. For the first time Germain became cognizant of the neat generator pack on his shoulders and the screen propagation antenna above his helmet.

He was vividly silhouetted against a curtain of cold flame that blocked any possible view of what lay beyond. Germain's sharp eyes detected a crystalline frame around the flame, and again he smiled faintly, remembering the hieroglyphics he had seen at the temple's entrance.

"What's holding you up, Eidelmann?" queried Germain. "Want us to rush you?"

"Just a little preparation," replied the latter. "That flame is a real death trap, as you have probably surmised. But I foresaw something of the kind and came prepared, whereas you did not. My screen is a block to all primary, energy except electro-magnetic propagations on the ten-meter band necessary for our present communication and light waves in the normal spectrum. This flame is primary. So it seems that only I may enter here. I thought it only fair to pause here long enough to warn you that to follow me will be suicide."

"Your concern for our safety is touching," replied Germain. "Furthermore, we are very much impressed. Why don't you enter Central Control, Eidelmann?"

The German scientist could be seen behind his faceplate, because his face glistened brightly with perspiration. He adjusted several controls at his waist, nervously.

"Go ahead, Eidelmann," urged Germain. "If your genius has prevailed against the science of the ancients, what have you to fear?"

"Ancients?" said Eidelmann. "What are you talking about? This is a camouflaged Nrlanian installation."

"On the contrary," countered Germain. "The ancient Martian priests overcame gravitation and were able to traverse space. They set this up on the basis of a science unknown to you. They set up this trap originally to keep the Nrlanians, themselves, out. Only Martians can pass through that trap. You'll never make it, Eidelmann."

Eidelmann hesitated. "What makes you think *you* can?" he said. Then a new thought struck him. He thought he knew what Germain might be thinking. Experimentally, he turned his dis-gun on the wall and fired, point-blank. A thin patina of age-old space dust disappeared instantly before the blast, revealing a wall of gleaming crystal.

"You will carve no path around the trap, my friend," said Germain. "The ancients sought every means possible to make this place proof against the Nrlani, or anyone else, for that matter."

Eidelmann stared incredulously at the unyielding crystal. "How is that possible?" he cried. "The dis-gun neutralizes proton cohesion."

"I believe you have before you a curious material blend of primary and secondary matter, the one pinch-hitting for the other, whichever is damaged first—and the stuff probably heals automatically. You can't disintegrate the walls."

"But—if the Nrlanians can't enter here, how did they—"

"They used post-suggestion. They had Martian slaves who were mentally conditioned to carry out their instructions. They controlled them also, no doubt, by means of augmented telepathy or some form of ESP. I repeat, Eidelmann, only a Martian can enter here. So give yourself up or we'll have to rush you. Which shall it be?"

Germain signaled to his companions and they began to close in on the German. The latter fired a dis-blast at them, futilely.

"Stop," he yelled. "Central Control is mine." Whereupon, he plunged into the cold curtain of flame.

As he did so, they saw him become a cloud of dust, which settled slowly to the floor of the passage.

"I must say," said Borg, apathetically, "that this trap presents a problem. How *are* we going to get through?"

Instead of an answer, he was met with silence. Everyone was still looking at the dust that but a moment before had been Gerhardt Eidelmann.

"Another question, please," persisted Borg. "After what we have observed here isn't it logical to conclude that Lillian never was here in the first place?"

"I believe that is true," said Germain. "There was no possible way for her to enter. She must have been with Izdran all along and he hid the knowledge from me."

"Then I repeat—how *are* we going to get through this trap?"

"Men," said Germain to all of them, "don't follow me, because you can't. You are not going through that barrier, but I think I am. If I don't succeed, you'd better prepare to defend yourselves against Izdran, I feel he is near."

Borg's gnarled hand, hard and bony even through his space mitt, detained Germain. "What are you thinking of?" he asked. "Is it autoportation? The psychic screen would prevent that, wouldn't it?"

"That's precisely why it's there," replied Germain. "The Nrlani foresaw that possibility. They no doubt deduced how I escaped from the *Nova*. No, I am going to walk through."

"Over my dead—" Borg started to say, but he stopped

talking when Germain's mind gripped his, momentarily paralyzing him.

Without further ceremony, Germain walked through the flame...

THERE was no time for exclamations on the part of those who remained behind the barrier, inasmuch as they all received an urgent call from the lab ship. A giant Nrlanian sky city had put in its appearance.

"*Izdran*," exclaimed Borg. "Just as Germain predicted. Well, he's on his own in there. There's nothing we can do but get back to the ship."

They left the temple, on the double. When they emerged, they saw the Nrlanian city approaching them cautiously from out of secondary space. Borg and Grange detected the telltale faint aurora above them, which indicated that the Agarthian operators had set up their defensive screens, both primary and secondary.

"Hold fire," ordered Borg to the ship. "Lillian Germain may be a hostage there."

"Too late," came the Agarthian's reply, as Borg and his men approached the airlock. "We've launched our U.P. bomb."

Even as this news reached Borg's ears, he and his companions were almost blinded by a tremendous flash that lighted all secondary space as far as they could see. The Nrlani had detonated the bomb in mid flight, but as it was separated from Deimos by hundreds of miles of vacuum they did not suffer from the effects of the blast.

"What are your orders?" came the Agarthian officer's voice from the bridge of the lab ship, as Borg and Grange and the rest reached the airlock.

"There may be nothing to do but surrender or run for it," said Borg, "unless—"

"Sir. The Guardsmen are here." The officer in charge lost the calm, which was required of Agarthian neophytes such as he. "They are emerging from primary space! I see three ships, five—ten! They are coming fast!"

Borg and Grange and some of the Agarthian spacemen with them all paused, before closing the airlock behind them, to peer outward into space in the direction of the Martian secondary plane far below Deimos, but they could see nothing at that distance.

"Do you think they see the Nrlanian city?" asked Borg.

"They are heading this way fast," was the reply.

"Then signal them not to attempt destruction of the enemy. Ask them if Janice Maine is among them. If so, she'll have to rig up heterodyners and project the paralysis beam on higher harmonics until she gets the Nrlanian mental frequency." Germain had discussed his psychic heterodyner briefly with Borg, and the idea came to him now as the only possible weapon to use. "Tell her Lillian Germain may be in the Nrlanian city. Nrlani will have to be taken without violence, if possible. In the meantime—all screens out on Universal Power. I think the U.P. generators can draw as much energy from secondary as they can from primary space, now that they have reached relative attenuation. Pool all energy transmission into a concentrated screen and go on defensive until the harmonic generators can be rigged. We'll join them now."

The lab ship had no sooner taken off from Deimos than the satellite was suddenly bathed in a greenish fire. That this phenomenon had its source in the approaching sky city was evidenced by a needle beam of greenish light emanating from the vast fortress. As a result, Deimos literally began to fall apart.

"Screen that," cried Borg, who had now reached the control room. "Intercept that beam!"

They did intercept it successfully, although their screens literally exploded with light and color at the impact. Deimos was only half a moon now, but they could still make out the pyramid that housed Central Control. Its outer patina of ages had been burned clean, and they observed that the whole structure was composed of the indestructible crystal substance discovered by the ancients.

The Nrlanian city moved swiftly, closer, dodging their screen, trying to get in another shot at Deimos. But just then Deimos, itself, began to densify, and as it did so it appeared to be surrounded by a luminous mist.

"Germain has succeeded," exclaimed Grange. "He's taking Deimos back into primary space."

"I'd still like to know how he got through that barrier curtain of cold fire—quick. Don't let the Nrlani follow him." Borg drew their attention to the fact that the huge sky city was also densifying.

By this time, ten Guardsman vessels swept into view and surrounded their objective with every screen they had, including the combined effects of their attenuators. All screens sparkled with color as the enemy sought to resist them, but the latter's attenuation ceased.

"Borg," came Steve Rockner's voice over the codawave speakers. "Janice is here but too busy to talk. What do you think we've been doing—star-gazing? Germain told us all about that heterodyning business and we've practically got it rigged up on the paralysis beams. I think we can hold this hot potato here, but it's a good thing we can all put out psychic screens. Otherwise those Nrlanian devils could get at us mentally. You'd better get back to Primary and give Germain a hand. The whole Solar System is falling apart. Earth has slipped another cog and now Mars looks like it's losing its orbit. Haven't you noticed an increase in rotation of this plane? No time, I guess. If you've got any miracles up your sleeve—"

"How many Guardsmen ships are coming through?" asked Borg, quickly.

"Just the Martian task force, all I could spare—about twenty-four ships. The rest have their hands full with Fortress Mars, although the surface natives are giving a hand now. We freed the *Nova* and it's making the rounds working on others, but those discs hang on like glue. Unless Germain can get hold of Central Control—"

"Germain is now the master of Central Control," replied

Borg.

"Thank God," said Rocky. "And I *do* mean that. It's our only hope and yet I don't see how even Germain can help now."

"Hold the Nrlani at bay if you can," said Borg. "We're going to follow Germain."

"We have only begun to fight!"

"Okay, Admiral Perry," cut in Stierman's voice from another Guardsman ship. "This isn't any fireman's picnic. What do we do now?"

"You asked for it," came Rocky's reply. "Have you got any suggestions?"

Just as Borg's ship began to fade out of Secondary, Borg and Grange and a few of the others observed a change in the Nrlanians' tactics. The sky city suddenly became the center of a glass-like bubble, miles in diameter, and as the bubble appeared, the Guardsman ships surrounding it were literally propelled away from it, as though they had been struck by a giant hand.

There was no time to wait and observe more. The watchers could only pray that ultimate victory would be theirs—that the remaining Guardsman units would join the embattled force that Rocky now headed. Swiftly, they densified and were soon surrounded by the interplanar mists...

CHAPTER EIGHTEEN

GERMAIN'S seventh sense told him that the time had arrived, which would be *the* focal point of modern history. It was the time of the Miracles—*his* miracle. If he did not succeed there was liable to be no further history, either in the primary or secondary planes of existence within the confines of the Solar System.

Central Control was a miniature Nrlanian city built into the great pyramid, which he had finally entered through airlocks. The latter had been easily workable inasmuch as the main lock on the whole place was the barrier flame. Beyond that, it had been the Nrlani's intention to give simple ingress to the Martian slaves who served them.

He found a few Martians on hand—mentally conditioned slave city Martians. Since he had penetrated the psychic screen by simply walking through it, he could use his mental powers at will, and this he proceeded to do so as the small Martian view attending the titanic machinery of Central Control turned upon him with various weapons. He promptly reconditioned their minds to serve him. He also read their minds and gained valuable information quickly. At once he learned that Lillian had never been here. Undoubtedly, then, Izdran still held her captive, if she was alive at all.

First of all, he made use of the fact that the installation was, among other things, a tremendously powerful space ship equipped with densifying and attenuating apparatus. It was fully capable of moving the entire satellite. This he proceeded to do. It was when the Nrlanian green fire struck that he turned on the densifiers. He noted that the temperature inside Central Control rose to almost one hundred and forty degrees Fahrenheit, in spite of its screens, and the Martians fainted.

After reaching primary space, however, they soon revived, to watch him in rapt silence as he proceeded. By means of giant visiscreens he was able to orientate himself and bring what remained of Deimos halfway between Earth and Mars. Then he turned his attention to Central Control, proper.

Its appearance was roughly that of a gigantic cybernetic machine, approximately four hundred feet on a side and ten stories deep. Small magnetic elevators gave physical access to all levels whereas multiple control panels gave electronic or wave-transmission access to every section. Utilizing his knowledge gained from the Martian's minds, in combination with his ESP and experience with Elder Race science, he quickly analyzed the general arrangement and purpose of the installation. That he had voluntary access to the prodigious powers of his own subconsciousness made his mutant mentality, in itself, a calculating machine, which equalled or surpassed the ability and complications of Central Control. By extra-sensory extension he could, in effect, engulf the entire installation within the scope of his mind to a point where, by considerable concentration, it acquired his faculties and simultaneously lent its own to his.

There were memory banks replete with knowledge sacred to the Nrlanian race—the history and science of thousands of years' accumulation. In mere minutes he was staggering, mentally, with the burden of a personality that was not individual, but ethnic. It was as though he were no longer a Terrestrial man, but a whole alien race.

Most important of all, there was a three-story section of control cells numbering some fifty million. Each of these controlled one of the flying discs. By virtue of his newly acquired knowledge he was aware of how the mysterious creatures of the void had been trapped, conditioned and tied, psychically, to Central Control in such a manner that the mere whim of any single member of the Nrlanian race would be magnified fifty million times and be acted upon over a territory that encompassed the entire Solar System. Thus by means of this system of extension any Nrlanian could become a godlike being and hold a great work of Creation in the palm of his hand—the sun and all its worlds, to a point far beyond the orbits of Pluto. As an incidental piece of information he gathered that there were two more planets beyond Pluto, small, frozen, lifeless. He noted that others were not so lifeless, but there was little time to concentrate on the torrent of knowledge that inundated his mind. Nor would he allow himself to be tempted by curiosity. Although Ganymede, being the source of *ca'ta*—

He willed himself to concentrate on the problem at hand. The discs and the tottering Solar System. The falling Moon, with its burden of life inside—the whole civilization of the Lunar Interstellars. Earth, caught in a warp of time, upsetting the balance of everything with its erratic actions. Mars, toppling off its orbit. Earth's secondary plane, torn to shreds, disintegrating.

After some deliberation, he conceived of a method of

blocking any possible mental contact by the Nrlanians, and then he learned how to take over the power of the discs, himself.

The first thing he did was to cause them to release all space vessels, which they had attacked. This, in itself, enabled some two hundred and fifty vessels to come to life again and take part in the struggle to set Creation back on its feet. Sixty-five incapacitated Golden Guardsman vessels were soon to join their fellows in action, both on Mars and in secondary space. Twenty-five Agarthian behemoths would soon be turning their attention Earthward and taking Pavlovich's robot-controlled forces to task, under cover of secondary screens. And a hundred and sixty Lunar Interstellars were freed to divide into a number of special units, not least among which would be a large force engaged in the rescue of their own race, waiting helplessly within the Moon.

Then—at long last—Germain prepared to try his miracle. He was aware that he was assuming powers not intended for Man, yet the urgency of the whole situation seemed to justify the experiment. It was dangerous, inasmuch as he would be tampering with Time, just as the Chronoperceptor did. Therefore, he had to utilize the full capacities of his prodigious mentality in calculating the probability factors involved in half a dozen different combinations of Cause and Effect. Desperately, he sought a common denominator, a key Cause, which would give the optimum desired effect with the minimum of undesirable new probabilities. And at last he thought of it—and hoped he was right...

For a moment, he reviewed the principle in his mind, which had made autoportation possible for him. He recalled a conversation he had had with Mandir in Agarthi just before Pavlovich's attack.

"You have delved into auto-synthesis of *faith* power, haven't you? Not the religious sense of blind faith, but the basic, metaphysical nature of faith. One of its manifestations is levitation."

"Yes," Mandir had replied. "Twice I achieved levitation.

The King did it easily. What are you getting at?"

"Faith power is based on the fact that any given set of results arises from a given set of causes and that, conversely, if the mind can perceive *as an absolute reality* a synthesized set of results for which there was no original cause, that *cause* will come into being in order to match the results..."

Then Germain recalled his encounter with a flying disc, alone, in his space suit, after escaping from the *Nova*. He carefully reviewed the results his subconscious mind had produced on that subject. The discs were pure mentality devoid of inhibiting fears of pre-conditionings. From there, where could his reasoning take him? The answer was: The discs were *perfect* media for the expression of faith. They would believe anything with a one hundred percent efficiency. In fact, what was implanted in them would be *reality*. Magnify that fifty million times and what did you have? A faith power to move worlds. In short, a miracle.

Through Central Control, Germain's mentality entered every disc in primary space, from the sun to Pluto and beyond. He drew the more distant ones inward and they came with the speed of light, gradually concentrating their powers.

He concentrated on one key thought, eliminating all other ideas from his mind, and that thought grew through those millions of racing discs and became a reality, a *faith fixation* that recognized a synthetic result that was *forced* to set up a set of causes in physical reality.

The key thought was: *The detonator on the Zero Bomb was a dud from the start.*

*   *   *

Cause: Faulty detonator. Result: No detonation. No possibility of an Earth destroying blast. No activation of the Chronoperceptor. No disruption of Earth's normal course along its orbit. No falling of the Moon or aberration of Mars. No disintegration of Earth's secondary plane. No earthquakes on Mars, no prominences on the sun, no shaking of other bodies of the Solar System.

But new probabilities precipitated set up of new conditions elsewhere...

*   *   *

WITH no disruption of Earth's secondary plane, Fortress Heaven remained intact. Thus Izdran operated along a new channel of probabilities. He did not, as a matter of fact, have a chance to intercept the Golden Guardsmen before they were upon him. In the old pattern of normal effect, the Guardsman ships had been violently engaged in struggle with the Nrlanian sky city above the Martian secondary plane. Suddenly, they were transplanted into a new pattern of probability without being aware of the change, because memory patterns were altered proportionately. Izdran, instead of coming to meet them, now remained in command back on Earth's secondary plane, which loomed in the firmament of secondary space as a silvery globe some hundred and eight thousand miles in diameter.

Stierman, impatient for the fight, put in a request for orders.

"What do you make of that globe?" Rocky asked him. He could not bring himself to call it either Earth, Heaven, or Atmosphere. He had the impression that neither he nor his companions nor any inhabitant of the primary plane of existence belonged here. He was aware of a subconscious urge to do his duty and get out. Caution and uncertainty in the face of the unknown struggled with a mounting tension within him, and he could see it in his companions. Definitely, it was not attributable to a fear of the Nrlania, but to something much greater, which they dared not describe.

"Well," came Stierman's reply, "from what I can see in the televiewers around here I'd say there's sixty million inhabitants there if there is one. I've never dreamed of such large cities. None of them industrialized to speak of—but they're big."

"And I'd say the Nrlani have had centuries to propagandize

them and condition them just as they did in the case of the Martians—on both planes. Try to spare the inhabitants when we move in, boys. Let's approach in wide deployment and concentrate gradually on the Nrlani once we find them. Use the psychic heterodyner. That's a strictly secondary energy weapon and seems to be the only thing that can touch them. Let's go."

More Guardsman ships had come through the "wall," as they called the interplanar mists, and soon over fifty of them were converging upon Earth's secondary plane. That they would meet with a bristling resistance on the part of the precondition-ed inhabitants, also, they had little doubt—

During the ensuing days, still more units from the primary plane crossed over and joined them in their mounting battle, including the tremendous *Nova*, piloted by Germain, himself. Atmospherea was definitely in the hands of the few Nrlani who ruled from their sky city and fought back with appalling power and efficiency.

However, as in any other occupied country, a useful underground offered its services in the form of sabotage and revolt. The psychic heterodyner finally won out over Izdran, after actual months of intensive struggle. Aided by newly con-ditioned Agarthian and Lunar Interstellar units, the Guardsmen finally caused the Nrlanian sky city to surrender, whereupon they promptly occupied it with forces representing Solar Government.

Those who were named in history as being present at the surrender and death of Izdran and his companions were Stephen Germain, Steven Rockner, Gregory Stierman and Samuel Turner. Weakened and paralyzed, mentally, by weeks of psychic battle, Izdran gave no struggle as the four men advanced under multiple-purpose screens and gazed upon the Nrlanian's true form under the dome of his tower in the sky city.

Rocky, for one, knew he would never be able to describe such a creature, for how does one describe a *mutant* robot?—a mechanico-synthetic form of life that has branched partially into a true life form. Some of Izdran's living organisms, tied in with his robot faculties, were installed in other parts of the building. The city, itself, was a common body to the remaining four Nrlanians there, and no human could tell whose set of multiple hearts, or dual brains, or other organisms belonged to whom. It was beyond analysis. Through mental awareness, alone, Germain was able to identify the personality that was Izdran.

"Before you die," said Germain, "you will tell me where you have hidden my wife." Through signals to a hovering control ship above the battered city he was able to have some of the paralysis eased, and Izdran was able to speak.

Feebly, he laughed. "You will never find her," he replied. "Or if you do you will regret it. She *lives*, Germain. But where? You will never know."

Germain's mind leaped out angrily and started again to probe deeply into Izdran, searching frantically through every recess of that multiple mind, but the recesses were many and the enemy's mental blocks required energy to break down while he remained conscious.

"Don't be naive," Izdran told him. "Now that defeat is upon us, ultimately and irrevocably, we die—before you can probe any further into any of us."

Germain took a step forward, futilely. Through transparent panels he saw several great hearts slow to a stop. And there was silence—even mental silence, which was the most convincing sign to Germain that Izdran and his inhuman companions had lived their last hour.

Taking no chances, however, he had all apparent parts of the Nrlani dis-rayed into nothingness and a fifty thousand year cycle of alien conquest ended. What the Elder People had started, the Solar Government, under Germain's leadership, finished.

STILL unable to shake off a bothersome sense of guilt in being present on the secondary plane, the rescuing crews in the Guardsman and Agarthian and Lunar fleets hastened to clean up the remaining remnants of resistance there and were at last relieved to discover those individuals who represented the old order of civilization in Atmospherea.

This titanic world, so broad that it seemed to have no horizons, was replete with low hills, rivers, forests and ancient cities of a charm and grandeur that tempted them to linger forever even as they hurried to finish their business and get out. There were many items to investigate and questions to be answered, but they dared not go into the subject even in the face of their insatiable curiosity.

In a palace that was older than they cared to calculate, Germain and his chiefs held a brief conference with several hundred leaders composing the nucleus of true government on the second plane. These latter, though appearing to be under a century old, were deceptive as far as their true age was concerned. Age was judged by the degree of wisdom to which each had attained. Gratitude was evident, but hurried anxiety was more characteristic of the general attitude on both sides.

"We, too, feel that although your presence here may be justified in the light of the unusual circumstances you should not prolong your stay," said one spokesman. He was a venerable, saintly looking patriarch with a beautiful, gray mane and eyes that appeared capable of seeing higher horizons than Tropospherean eyes could hope to see. "Although you have achieved attenuation you bring with you corporeal elements that are contagious and could defeat the whole purpose of our own existence here. We are inexpressibly grateful to you for this liberation from our most satanic oppressors, but we urge you to go. Furthermore, there should be no future traffic between us. There are reasons, which it would require many years of orientation to make you understand. Suffice it to say, what you have accomplished will work great new benefits in your own plane of existence. There will be proper contact and the parasitical spirits of the lower planes shall again be brought under control so that your own vision of the Infinite Goal will not be impaired—and there shall return to Earth a spiritual age advanced by new knowledge, in which Man will combine his talents to the benefit of the *Total Power* which he, himself, represents. Now go."

ALTHOUGH victorious Earth received its successful armadas with loud acclaim, the recipients came quietly and were reluctant to recount their experiences except in the form of a formal statement. The *Agarthian Report*, two hundred and thirty-five thousand words in length, concerning the physical existence of the Second Plane, formed the cornerstone of a new age.

But before the tumult and the shouting had died, Germain took a solo trip. He remembered that Central Control was filled with memory banks. Perhaps, he thought, somewhere in those banks he might find a clue to the whereabouts of his wife.

The shattered remnants of Deimos swung in a long, eccentric orbit about the sun. As he approached it he recognized the shining crystal pyramid, which contained the real object of his search. Severely shaken by his nervous anticipation and sleepless days and nights, he donned a space suit and entered the place once more, again walking through the barrier flame without mishap. When he opened the airlock, however, he paused and went no farther. It was as though a great voice spoke to him and said: *This is not for you—go back.*

Central Control was a mass of fused wreckage, as though it had been struck by a U.P. bomb. The cause might have been anyone of a dozen things—delayed reaction explosives, deliberate demolition on the part of the Martian slaves resulting from post-suggestion, which he had failed to erase from their minds, etc. But it was the positive awareness of another *Cause* behind this complete destruction, which made him turn about and leave the place in haste.

Just as he was about to enter his ship, he detected a faint aura about the satellite, or near it, as though someone had thrown up an energy screen out in space. For a moment he thought he detected the faint outlines of a titanic ship against the stars, transparent, vague, fading away into nothingness. A thought entered his mind, which he never expressed, to anyone: *They* have come, at last. This is their message to Man that such powers as were latent in Central Control are not for us, until, perhaps, we join them—*in Etherea...* Later he reported to

Agarthi that he, himself, had destroyed Central Control.

The flying discs were henceforth free agents, innocuous, even friendly. Future space voyagers were to regard them as the sailor regards the dolphin—a friend to navigation—because they always guided ships through the meteor swarms or through the asteroid belt or led the rescuer to the scene of disaster, sometimes even deflecting meteors from their courses to save an otherwise ill-fated vessel with a faulty meteor screen.

CHAPTER NINTEEN

GANYMEDE, some three thousand miles in diameter, presented an uninviting surface to Germain's bloodshot, sleepless eyes when, months later, he arrived to investigate a hunch. The Nrlani had gotten *ca'ta* from Ganymede, according to the memory banks of Central Control. Perhaps, if he searched carefully, using his ESP to the fullest extent—

There, in one of the deep natural caverns of the Jovian satellite, he found Lillian. The frail, translucent, humanoid unipeds who inhabited the caverns offered little resistance to his approach, but there were several telepathic robots to be eliminated. Beyond the airlock he found a large Nrlanian laboratory factory, deserted but illuminating. Here the native uniped slaves had not only processed *ca'ta* for Martian consumption, but their work in connection with *grabdal* made the secret of this latter substance apparent. These were incidental observations made in passing. What Germain was chiefly concerned with was his wife—and his infant son...

Lillian came running to him and swooned with relief when he took her in his arms. Later, when he revived her, he had a difficult time supporting her mind, mentally, to the point where she could find her own balance.

"In spite of my faith in your powers," she said, "I had actually given up hope of ever seeing you again. Darling, tell me it's over with at last."

Germain remembered Izdran's dying words: "You will never

find her. Or if you do, you will regret it." Why? he asked himself. *What* would he regret? Mentally, he probed her mind again and found it normal. With ESP he examined her internally. Again—normal.

Then, tensing, he suddenly looked at the child. A normal, healthy looking infant, considering the synthetic atmosphere and synthetic diet his mother lived on. Brown eyes—

"Those eyes!" he exclaimed.

Lillian sensed his alarm. "I think I know," she said. "He is a true mutant, darling. God has given us a little man to follow in the steps of his father."

The sparkling intelligence in the little eyes was apparent—a surface detail. But Germain refrained from mentioning what his ESP revealed. In the tiny chest—two hearts. And in that tiny, multiple mind—a seed of—of—

He saw Izdran's parting shot and tried to dodge it in his mind, but he knew that the future would not permit the possibility of avoiding it. His seventh sense gave him a picture of the years to come, but what that picture demanded of him in this tender moment not even he could accomplish.

For how could he kill his own son?—this erstwhile innocent spirit in whom an alien fiend and an alien science, by means of rays affecting genes and chromosomes, had implanted the seeds of malevolence so ingrained and backed by a mutant ability that it would one day rise to challenge Solar Civilization.

"Stephen," cried Lillian. "I see the trouble in your eyes. What is it?"

Instead of frowning, however, Germain suddenly smiled grimly and met the stare of his little son. Mentally he told him: *Never fear, little one. I accept the challenge of Izdran. You and I will have to come to terms—someday...*

WHILE Sergeyev Pavlovich languished, a prisoner patient, in Agarthi's psychiatric laboratories, a great celebration and banquet ensued above his head, in the palace where formerly the King of the World had ruled.

The personal occasion for the celebration was Sam Turner's marriage to Trinha Llih. The pair had made headlines throughout the world, as this was the first of its kind in history—an interplanetary mating. Trinha was popularly referred to as truly "out of this world." With her pale, red skin, dark eyes and modernly coiffured black hair, wearing a flowing bridal gown sprinkled with diamonds, which had been presented to her by the Terrestrial Government, as well as a priceless necklace from the secret treasure of Agarthi and brought to her from the Moon, she looked the part.

Germain, who had read her mind, had tipped Lillian off on a secret, as well as Janice and Ingaborg. Thus, Turner was mystified and Trinha was thrilled to read a cryptic message on the top of the wedding cake: *Long live Mrahl Sahn and Korla Na!* For Trinha, the old Martian fairy tale had come true, after all.

The official occasion for the celebration was the establishment of the new Solar Government under Stephen Germain. Terrestrial Government remained sovereign, but they accepted the Agarthian Charter and the Emergency Clause. There, present in the name of Terrestrial Government to give them this assurance, was none other than former Soviet T. G. Councilman Gormski. Before television cameras he rather sheepishly made his speech, concluding with an apology.

"Just as the young man, achieving maturity, wonders where his father learned so much in ten short years, we of the everyday world outside the walls of Agarthi have come to wonder where you learned so much in less than *one* year! But I believe the layman may be forgiven his inability to absorb a complete socio-historical mutation without at least a small degree of hesitation and doubt. Even now we find the Agarthian Report to be incredible, yet our eyes hold desperately to the indisputable facts and we seek a balance with you as we all enter together into Man's bright new era..."

In the midst of applause, he sat down beside Doctor Borg, who engaged him in conversation in their native tongue. The Russian scientist was explaining to him how Agarthi had managed to recondition the Nrlanian robots and make them useful. Even as he spoke, one of the three-eyed automatons politely offered the two men and Doctor Grange a tray of Agarthian grown fruit.

Michael Kent, seated between Lillian and Yvonne, his sister, suddenly rose to propose a toast. "To the Treasury of Solar Government," he said, lifting his glass. The toast was not strange to those who understood the curious financial problems of Agarthi, now that it had contacted the outside world and was launching into a system wide administration. "As Solar Government's newly appointed Minister of Finance I am happy to announce the establishment of a promising agreement we have made with both Mars and Terrestrial Government, whereby a substantial foundation for commercial relationships can be built up. Solar Government will retain sole rights to Martian *grabdal*, which, as you know, is the richest known source of Uranium. Although Universal Power eliminates the necessity for atomic energy in the larger projects of this world, the latter is still of vital importance to the myriad of smaller applications of power both here and on Mars and perhaps on other planets. The revenue from this one item should enable Solar Government to advance projects of exploitation on other planets and thus put our friend and Star Warden, Stephen Germain, on a sound financial footing. This and a five percent slice of Terrestrial Government taxes will make us solvent and launch us strongly into a true interplanetary economy. Long live the Treasury—and Germain!"

EVERYONE drank to this, including several giant Lunar Interstellars who had been invited to represent their own government at this historic celebration.

"One moment," said Dr. Borg, snarling affably and getting to his feet. "I have long been wanting to ask Germain a question. I think this is a time for confessions. Are you ready, Germain?"

Germain shrugged, while Lillian smiled, looking at Borg.

"How in Heaven's name did you pass through that barrier

flame and get into Central Control? It killed Eidelmann instantly."

All faces turned toward Germain. He raised his eyebrows and then grinned, sheepishly. "Oh, *that*."

"Yes, *that*," put in Rocky. "How did you do it?" Janice pinched him and he yelped.

"Well," said Germain, "I think you will find the answer quite interesting. My passing through that ancient Martian trap was the result of archaeological discovery and simple deduction. First of all, you will recall that Mars reveals evidence of an ancient civilization of moon worshippers and pyramid builders. Remember that those moon worshippers had *two* moons to worship. Now on Earth we have had pyramid builders and moon worshippers also, and I place particular emphasis on the Western Hemisphere pyramid builders, such as the Aztecs, the Mayans and the pre-Incans. The pre-Incans who built the great temple of Pachacamac in Peru were definitely moon worshippers. Now step from this point to the prevalent totem of the Twin Star. The Incans, themselves, represented this totem with two feathers in their royal headdress, whereas the Apaches represent the Twin Stars with two horns, accompanied by symbols that have been taken to represent mountains. I think those serrations under the horn head dress of the Apache medicine man really signify pyramids—the pyramids of Mars."

Exclamations went around the table, but Germain raised his hand for silence, while Trinha Llih, who had learned sufficient English to understand him, beamed at him comprehendingly.

"The ancient priests of Mars observed that the Martian djurnur pod overcame gravitation. They were able to develop that principle and traverse space, themselves, as was evidenced by the temple we saw on Deimos. That they also came to Earth I now have no remaining doubts. Many of the Western Hemisphere Indian races owe their origin to these facts. What cinched the argument in my mind was the entrance to the pyramid on Deimos. The hieroglyphics there were almost exact replicas of those I had examined among the ancient pre-Incan ruins of Tiahuanaco in Southern Peru, years ago. In that moment I realized that the totem of the Twin Star represented the *two moons* of Mars. I realized that as an almost full-blooded Indian I was probably Martian, as well. So I took the chance."

"Wait a minute," protested Rocky. "If you were at least Apache I might swallow that, but you said you were Sioux."

Again, Germain's smile was sheepish. "Well, great grandma always *claimed* she was Sioux, but I heard it differently from a grandpa of mine who was a black sheep of the family. She ran away from her Apache tribe with a Sioux brave, who was great grandpa. Later she always tried to claim she was Sioux, herself."

Lillian looked at him aghast. "Stephen! And you mean to say that you risked your life and all of us on the hunch that an old family anecdote had been twisted from the truth?"

"What would you have done?" he asked, and the question was put to the crowd, in general. The ensuing silence was an eloquent answer.

"Imagine," said Rocky, irrepressibly. "When the old European explorers started exploiting the great civilizations of the Western Hemisphere they were engaged in a real war of the worlds and didn't know it!"

IN THE meantime, an infant mutant found his father's great mind, groping instinctively for mental contact. Germain was quietly aware of the precocious power there, formless, weak of will, as yet, but a power that would grow. Its primal instinct was hate. He knew it would grow to hate the human race, but his own love for his flesh and blood was the only weapon he would ever be able to use.

For Germain, alone, this bright new dawn of Civilization was darkened by a growing cold on the horizon of his future—from which the dead hand of Izdran was to reach out and strike at him with thunders and lightnings that were yet to be felt in all the worlds he would govern...

THE END

If you've enjoyed this book, you will not want to miss these terrific titles…

ARMCHAIR SCI-FI & HORROR DOUBLE NOVELS, $12.95 each

D-91 **THE TIME TRAP** by Henry Kuttner
THE LUNAR LICHEN by Hal Clement

D-92 **SARGASSO OF LOST STARSHIPS** by Poul Anderson
THE ICE QUEEN by Don Wilcox

D-93 **THE PRINCE OF SPACE** by Jack Williamson
POWER by Harl Vincent

D-94 **PLANET OF NO RETURN** by Howard Browne
THE ANNIHILATOR COMES by Ed Earl Repp

D-95 **THE SINISTER INVASION** by Edmond Hamilton
OPERATION TERROR by Murray Leinster

D-96 **TRANSIENT** by Ward Moore
THE WORLD-MOVER by George O. Smith

D-97 **FORTY DAYS HAS SEPTEMBER** by Milton Lesser
THE DEVIL'S PLANET by David Wright O'Brien

D-98 **THE CYBERENE** by Rog Phillips
BADGE OF INFAMY by Lester del Rey

D-99 **THE JUSTICE OF MARTIN BRAND** by Raymond A. Palmer
BRING BACK MY BRAIN by Dwight V. Swain

D-100 **WIDE-OPEN PLANET** by L. Sprague de Camp
AND THEN THE TOWN TOOK OFF by Richard Wilson

ARMCHAIR SCIENCE FICTION CLASSICS, $12.95 each

C-31 **THE GOLDEN GUARDSMEN**
by S. J. Byrne

C-32 **ONE AGAINST THE MOON**
by Donald A. Wollheim

C-33 **HIDDEN CITY**
by Chester S. Geier

ARMCHAIR SCIENCE FICTION & HORROR GEMS SERIES, $12.95 each

G-9 **SCIENCE FICTION GEMS, Vol. Five**
Clifford D. Simak and others

G-10 **HORROR GEMS, Vol. Five**
E. Hoffman Price and others

www.ingramcontent.com/pod-product-compliance
Lightning Source LLC
Chambersburg PA
CBHW030325180626
46810CB00003B/1230